Hunter's Moon

Michael Jasper

UnWrecked Press

Chapter One

Tommy Roling stifled a growl the instant he caught the scent of the man who just walked through the front door of the tavern.

Picking up the smell of one man, even one as aromatic as this guy, was no easy task. He had to filter out the dozens of personal scents—from soaps to sweat to shampoo, not to mention the dreaded perfumes and colognes layered on top of them all. It took practice at first, but with focus and a willingness to let his inner canine take over, just the tiniest bit, he could now do it on demand. It was like pushing through different colored and textured clothes on a rack until he found just the right shirt.

Or in the case of this cigarette-and-beer-stained guy, the smelly undershirt he'd been hunting for all week.

No way am I letting this one slip away and ruin my streak, Tommy thought. *Bring 'em back alive, and without a—*

"Dude," a familiar voice whispered, pressing a set of bony knuckles into Tommy's upper arm. "Relax."

Tommy shrugged free of Burt's grip and forced himself not to lash out at his brother. He'd been staring through the mirror behind the bar, watching the skinny guy with the buzzed black hair and the ridiculous chin beard that came down to a point at the neck of his frayed gray T-shirt.

The guy stopped inside the entrance for just a few seconds, taking in the clientele. Then he shook himself like he'd been goosed and headed to an empty table near the back of the noisy bar.

"Alan Watts," Tommy said in a low voice. He lowered his gaze at last from the mirror, blinking down at his clenched fists on the scratched and water-stained bar. A stuffed red fox stared down at him with glazed marble eyes from its perch next to the dozens of liquor bottles on the other side of the bar.

"Who?" Burt said, and then he caught the look on Tommy's face. "Oh. One of your guys, huh?"

Tommy nodded, exhaling slowly.

Attix will flip when he hears how Watts just dropped onto my lap, he thought. *Guess I owe Burt for that.*

He checked his edgy-looking fugitive in the mirror again, catching another hint of the man's sour scent. One of the few people in the hot and muggy bar who was sitting all by himself, Watts downed a shot of something brown the waitress set before him. He followed it with half a mug of beer.

Bottles clinked, a man barked out a rough laugh, and a bar stool scraped against the wood floor. More human smells flowed in a wave across the bar as the front door opened and closed again.

Burt drained the last of his own beer while rolling his eyes at Tommy. His shaggy brown hair wafted around him in a cloud as his head kept the beat to a two-decades-old Pearl Jam song about being alive. Burt's latest obsession was grunge rock.

"*Excellent* song," Burt murmured, and then let out a long, rattling belch.

The voices all around them seemed to increase in volume as the guitars faded and the song ended. Tommy would've preferred a bar closer to campus, with people—mainly young *women*, though he'd never admit that to Nina—closer to his age, now that he was finally 21 and could drink legally.

But Burt had raved about the atmosphere and the general funkiness of the Fox Head Tavern, and Tommy needed a night off from studying and writing papers for his full load of classes at Kirkwood Community College. Not to mention trying to keep up with his feisty two-year-old daughter Corinne.

"Shh," Burt said, raising a hand as a new song cranked up from the ancient juke box, glowing blue at the far end of the crowded bar. He held his head cocked to the side, with a grin spreading across his bearded face.

"It's Temple of the Dog, man. Everyone always plays 'Hunger Strike' by them, but this one, 'Say Hello 2 Heaven,' is really their master work. Check out that fuzzy guitar intro, bro. I could listen to that all frickin' *day*. Killer."

Tommy let out a forced chuckle and checked Watts in the mirror one more time. Still there. He squirmed on the metal bar stool, which felt flimsy and delicate under his bulky, six-foot-two frame.

He'd memorized the guy's scent a week ago, in the dirty clothes and soiled bedsheets left in the basement room of a rental house the man recently abandoned. Watts was wanted for questioning in two different cases of assault and one murder investigation. A dangerous guy, on the loose, who'd evaded the police for over two weeks now. Attix was convinced he'd taken off for California or Canada, but Tommy had his doubts. Watts was a local, with family here and other deep ties to the area.

Which was why the strongest thing Tommy was drinking tonight was Sprite on the rocks, with a lime. Even if it was supposed to be guys' night out, with Aunt Melanie watching Corinne for him, and Burt off work tomorrow. Burt *always* seemed to be off work lately.

On the bar stool next to him, Burt swayed his skinny body in time to the music. He grinned as he caught the eyes of two young women, obviously University of Iowa students, hovering nervously with their bottles of light beer at Tommy's end of the crowded bar. The brown-haired girl gave Burt a half-smile before pointing out the stuffed fox behind the bar to her blond friend.

The girls were definitely in the minority tonight. The Fox Head was filled mostly with older men from town in work boots, jeans, and well-worn T-shirts similar to those worn by Alan Watts. Tommy also saw some hipster-looking grad-school types near the pool table, out slumming and ironically drinking Pabst.

He also saw an intense young woman with curly brown hair perched at the bar next to the jukebox, furiously scribbling into a hardback journal, oblivious to the people, music, and chaos all around her. Tommy was impressed by her intense focus.

He elbowed his brother to make him stop his air-guitar solo at the bar.

Burt dropped his arms and his imaginary guitar with an exasperated sigh. The early-'90s grunge ballad rolled on through the tavern without him.

"*You* need another drink," he said, rubbing the thick, reddish-brown beard he'd been cultivating all year. His chick magnet, Burt called it.

The girls at the end of the bar, Tommy noticed, had turned their backs on Burt.

Some magnet, Tommy thought with a laugh.

Meanwhile, Burt ordered his third draft beer of the night. They'd been at the tavern for less than an hour, and his big brother was well on his way towards getting snockered. Again.

In the mirror, Alan Watts no longer sat alone at his remote table. Tommy stiffened and forgot to breathe.

A slim woman now sat with her back to Tommy, blocking half of Watt's face. The newcomer had short black hair cut almost like a man, at least from the back. As Tommy watched, the other person leaned close to Watts, demanding all of his nervous attention. Tommy saw Watts nod multiple times, his dark eyes widening and his grin shrinking with each nod.

And then a waitress weaved through the crowd, blocking Tommy's reflected view of the duo. By the time the waitress moved out of his way, the visitor at Watts' table had disappeared.

Here we go, Tommy thought as he elbowed Burt.

"You got money for all those beers, bro?"

"Hmm?" Burt said, turning away from the old guy he'd been chatting with at the bar stool next to him. "Money?"

"I'm gonna have to bail."

Burt frowned. "Some guys' night out, Tommy. I mean, you're not gonna jump this guy Watts right here in the bar, are you?"

"No."

"Okay. So can we just enjoy our drinks, then? Let me introduce you to my good friend Buddy here. That's *really* his name. Your fugitive from justice don't look like he's going anywhere—"

Burt snapped his mouth shut as he and Tommy watched skinny Watts get up and stagger toward the bathrooms.

"Well..." Burt began, but Tommy ignored him.

In the mirror, he'd noticed something odd. Watts' lips were moving as he worked his way around tables, past booths, and through clumps of people. Like he was having some sort of argument with himself.

Within seconds Watts crossed the bar and pushed out through the side exit.

"Okay, gotta go." Tommy thumped Burt on the chest. "You might want to hang out here another half hour or so, just to be safe. And don't be afraid to call a cab to bring you home."

Burt began to complain about the cost of a cab, but Tommy hurried off toward the side exit, all concerns about his brother shoved to the back of his mind.

By the time he'd left the bar and its barrage of overlapping smells and ear-battering sounds, he was already in full-blown hunter mode.

In the semi-darkness of the side streets, breathing fast through his mouth, Tommy followed the man's whispering voice.

Usually his quarry made it harder on him than this, but tonight Tommy's luck had finally turned. After half a month of not finding a single one of the never-ending flow of bail-jumpers, probation-skippers, and criminally accused that

Attix paid him to track down, he had a wanted man in his sights. Tommy wouldn't let him get away.

On foot, the muttering Watts moved with an unsteady, beer-induced gait past a row of apartment complexes and split-level houses that had been converted into apartments or rented rooms. Since it was early August, most of the college kids hadn't returned yet from summer break, though a handful of yellow lights burned at the various residences on this quiet and late Thursday night.

Tommy stayed a block behind Watts, walking soundlessly in his size fifteen shoes, doing his best to look like a somewhat-buzzed summer school dude heading home for the evening.

But even at that distance he could still hear the soft hiss of Watts' voice. He couldn't make out any words other than the occasional curse or a repeated "No."

Tommy couldn't see a phone in the guy's hand, so Watts was either arguing with himself or drunk, possibly both.

Five grand, Tommy reminded himself.

That was his half of the reward money offered for Watts' recovery. The other half went to John Attix, an Iowa City cop in his mid-forties. Tommy had been working with Attix for over a year now, ever since he'd been assigned to the cop as a shadowing exercise for a criminal justice class he'd been taking at Kirkwood CC.

Since that meeting, he'd found every single one of their fugitives, twenty-one total, even if some of them had taken him a few weeks to track down. And Attix was looking at his second promotion in six months.

When Watts paused two hundred yards ahead to take a leak next to an old pickup, Tommy slipped into the shadow of a big oak whose roots were tearing up the nearby sidewalk. The skinny man's whispering never let up even as he watered the street and the side of the truck. To Tommy's hyper-sensitive nose, the man's urine smelled like beer, whiskey, and sickness.

He fisted his hands involuntarily. He usually didn't need to resort to violence when he took in a fugitive—most of them pretty much gave up when they saw how tall and thick he was—but there had been a few dudes who'd wanted to try their luck. A couple months ago he'd split three knuckles on one guy's head before the guy decided to come along to the cop shop.

And he always had that one last trick up his sleeve. One he had yet to resort to using. But just knowing it was there was a confidence-booster.

This guy has been peeing for two minutes, for crap's sake, Tommy thought. *What's he doing, marking his territory?*

He calmed his impatience by thinking of Corinne, safe at a sleepover at Aunt Melanie's place. He missed the carefree days of living at Mel's with her two young boys, Trey and Tyler. Tensions grew to a fever pitch a few months ago, when Corinne started kicking and biting and scratching her older cousins—even though she wasn't even two years old and barely twenty-five pounds.

The last straw had been Burt, who'd also been living at Aunt Mel's after the drama in their hometown last year. Melanie admitted she could handle Corinne's growing wildness, but she couldn't forgive Burt and his nearly constant drinking. Not after all that had happened with their drunk Uncle—*druncle*—Carl.

So Burt and Tommy and Corinne moved out right, before Corinne's second birthday last month.

Imagining his little strawberry-blond-haired daughter snuggled into the bed next to Melanie, Tommy smiled and unclenched his hands.

Corinne's in good hands tonight, he reminded himself. *No need to worry about her.*

In his peripheral vision, Watts trotted off ahead of him at last, muttering that something was too loud, followed by a half dozen hissed "shit"s.

Three blocks later, the houses thinned out, along with the working streetlights. At the same time, Tommy's head began to ache, followed by a weird buzzing in his fillings that left his mouth tasting like metal.

He held his breath when he realized he couldn't hear any footsteps or whispering. He leaned against a dead tree, and listened. His eyes widened, taking in as much sparse street light and moonlight as he could. He sniffed once, twice, searching for Watts and his smelly shirt.

There.

About a hundred yards ahead of him, a gray and wiry shape shambled around a car, crossed a street, and stumbled over the curb. Tommy trotted after him as the man started climbing a ten-foot-high chain-link fence that surrounded an electrical substation.

That, Tommy thought, *explains the weird vibrations in my head and teeth.*

His skin prickled, and all the hair on his body stood out straight as spikes. He was glad he kept his blond hair clipped short, so it wasn't standing up like a pin cushion.

Walking fast, he held tight to the waist of his jeans to keep them up. Like his baggy Van Halen t-shirt, the pants used to be tight six months ago. But he'd lost almost thirty pounds in the year he'd been working for Attix. Now his old clothes were perfect for jobs like this, in case he needed to make a quick change.

Which seemed doubtful tonight. He watched Watts struggling to pull himself up the fence and shook his head.

In the dim light, the chain links were invisible, and the skinny man looked for a second like he was suspended in the air, a fly in a spider web.

You're making it too easy, Watts, Tommy thought, breaking into a soundless jog. *Too many cigarettes and cans of cheap beer.*

Before Tommy could reach him, however, Watts suddenly shot straight up and over the fence with a raspy grunt that almost sounded like a growl. He cleared the top of the fence by a good three feet and then landed with a graceless belly flop.

Muttering louder now, Watts crawled on all fours toward the buzzing metal structure that looked like a lethal jungle gym with its wires and wicked-looking silver and black appendages. Watts ducked under the various metal cages, fans, and cables and disappeared.

Tommy started to run, pressing his lips together to keep from laughing. Watts had trapped himself in there.

In the past few week of idleness, he'd forgotten about the thrill of the hunt. Even with the stink of stored electricity in his nostrils, he missed getting down and dirty, like back in his football days—chasing the quarterback out of the pocket and making him scramble for dear life. He lived for this, switching over to his animal side. Losing just that little bit of control.

He made it to the chain link fence in ten seconds, and clawed his way over it in three seconds more.

He hit the ground with a growl of his own.

The violent Mr. Watts is in for the encounter of his life, he thought, baring his white teeth in a wide, wicked grin. *And I dare him to try to fight his way out of it.*

Tommy's bravado lasted about five steps inside the shadow of the substation.

The buzzing of all that stored power quickly became a dull weight that filled his ears and made his temples throb. He had trouble seeing through the shadows. Usually his vision grew sharper on a hunt, but the darkness seemed to cling to this area. And Watts was hiding somewhere inside it.

Tommy paused before ducking under the main structure that stretched a good forty feet above his head. He listened for Watts' whispering voice, but the buzzing drowned it out. He had no desire to electrocute himself in here, so he stepped back. Keeping the chain link fence on his left, he tiptoed around the interior to the back, where the door to a small metal shed stood cracked open a few inches.

Tommy crept closer, head aching and mouth dry. His grin was long gone. Watts was inside the shed, whispering

"Never shoulda 'greed to this," a whiny voice muttered from inside the shed, the words running together. "And now they're doin' it to me 'gain. *Makin'* me do this."

Listening to the anguish in Watts' voice, Tommy felt a twinge of sympathy. Then he remembered the man's record, and the woman whose life Watts was accused of taking.

He paused outside the door to the shed, matching up the scent of the man inside with the man he'd spotted at the tavern. A reek of sweat and cheap alcohol and cigarettes. Same guy.

Tommy took a deep breath, looked up for just a moment at the half moon, and felt a calmness wash over him despite the maddening buzz still filling his head.

Strength flowed into his arms, back, and legs, but only so much. He cut off the rest of it, picking and choosing what he needed most right now without giving in to it completely.

Here we go, he thought for the second time that night.

Tommy ripped open the shed door. He didn't realize it right away, but he'd yanked the door off two of its three hinges.

At that moment, he was focused solely on Watts. The man sat hunched under a bare light bulb, sharpening an eight-inch-long hunting knife. Next to him was a metal box filled with many more knives.

"Put down the knife, Alan Watts," Tommy said. Attix always told him to use the fugitive's full name right away. It not only let them know they were busted, but it also unnerved the perps. "I need you to come with me, *now*."

"What the *hell*?" Watts said in a high, surprised voice, that was different from the low, whispering voice Tommy heard the past fifteen minutes. "You scared the shit outta me, man!"

"Put the knife down and come on, Alan."

Tommy's muscles quivered, waiting for any sudden movement. *Hoping* for it.

Watts looked down at the knife in his right hand and the whetstone in his left, as if he'd forgotten they were there.

"No," Tommy said. "Don't even try. Just put it in the box with the rest of 'em, and close the box."

The knife lifted the tiniest bit. Tommy rushed into the shed and brought his foot down hard on the man's right wrist. The knife flew into the shed wall, and Watts cried out hoarsely.

"*Damn* it," Tommy said, stepping back from the man down on the floor. "I *told* you not to do that."

Tommy kicked the box of knives shut and went to one knee with his back against the side of the shed.

"You broke my wrist," Watts said, his voice dull. "This is really gonna hurt when I sober up."

Tommy wasn't quite ready to pull out one of the heavy-duty plastic zip ties he always carried with him. He needed the adrenaline in his blood to recede first. He'd gotten a little out of control when he saw that big knife move.

"Tell me," he said instead, bothered by what Watts was whispering, "about *them*. Who are they, and what are they making you do?"

Watts blinked and looked closely at Tommy for the first time.

"You *know* what I did. I mean, she sent you after me, didn't she? Had to be her."

Tommy worked to keep his face blank. He shrugged.

Attix told him not to talk to the fugitives any more than he had to, but sometimes he couldn't help himself.

"Man," Watts said, leaning back against the shed wall as well, still cradling his injured wrist. "I don't know how she found me in the first place a couple weeks ago. I just wanted to get myself straight, but they all kept hounding me, wantin' me to do a job for 'em."

He laughed at that, a short, barking sound that was almost like a cough.

"And then that job led to another one. Never satisfied, these folks. But the money was good."

Tommy nodded, slowly, but said nothing.

Watts paused, eyes going wide as he looked Tommy over, up and down.

"Hey. You didn't know that guy in Mount Vernon, did you? I swear, it was nothing personal."

Tommy had heard enough. He felt like he was back in control of himself again, and now he just felt tired and hungry.

But Watts wasn't done talking.

"The guy had this *voice*, man," he said. "Most amazing voice I'd ever heard. I wasn't supposed to take the ear plugs out, she told me not to do that, but I *had* to. It was like, like..."

Despite the ache of electricity filling his bones and the stink of this other man up so close, Tommy leaned forward.

"It was like *music*," Watts said, looking right at Tommy with rapturous eyes that were seeing something else altogether. "The best song you ever heard. Your favorite song, when you heard it for the first time."

Tommy thought of his skinny older brother back in the Fox Head, jamming to his grunge music with his eyes squeezed shut. And here was this strung-out guy with his box full of knives.

"Let's go, Alan Watts."

Watts shook his head.

"I killed that guy," he said, "with that knife there. I made the music stop. Even though he tried to tell me to stop, it was too late—"

"Alan..."

Watts lifted both hands, injured wrist and all, to cover his ears. His face tightened into a mask of agony.

"But I can *still* hear his voice. He won't shut up! It keeps telling me to stop, ordering me to, but I disobeyed. I put the ear plugs in just in time and silenced his voice. Killed him."

Instead of coming closer to his prey, Tommy pulled back in surprise. He forgot about the hum of electricity radiating all over his body for a moment. He once knew a guy with a

18

voice like that, back home in Dyersburg, over a year ago. And he'd met another person like that right here in Iowa City.

When he spoke, he could barely maintain the confidence in his voice.

"It was hard to not listen to that guy's voice, wasn't it? To not do what he said?"

Watts nodded with a quick jerk of his head.

"They *made* me do it. And now they're makin' me do it again. But he *still* won't shut up..."

Tommy wished now that he'd called Attix. It was going to be a long walk back to his car at the Fox Head, dragging Watts along with him each step of the way.

And Attix would want to kill him for missing this confession.

This noisy substation made him feel like puking. Maybe the buzzing helped Watts keep away the sound of the murdered man's voice.

"I know a place where it's quiet," Tommy said in his calmest voice. "No voices."

Watts shook his head. "I'm not going back to jail again."

Tommy glanced around the shed, looking for any other potential weapons, but the place was empty except for the box of knives, the hunting knife next to it, and Watts.

"Relax," Tommy said, "You'll be safe there. You won't need to do any more bad things for those people. Is that what that person at the bar told you to do? Kill someone tonight?"

Watts didn't answer. He just closed his eyes tight and shook his head from side to side.

"Well, it's not gonna happen," Tommy said. "Your bosses aren't getting their way tonight."

"Wait," Watts said, opening his eyes and lowering his hands from his ears with a grimace. The pain from his injured wrist seemed to clear the fog of alcohol and confusion from his dark eyes. "You're not *from* Mount Vernon, are you? And if *she* didn't send you, then..."

"Let's just get this around your hands," Tommy said, holding up a thick white zip tie from his pocket. "It'll make things easier for us both."

Watts let out a sudden growling sound, and Tommy's entire body tightened, ready to fight.

But before he could jump towards Watts again, he caught a scent from outside the shed. It was such a familiar smell that it didn't make sense at first here, out of context. On his next, shallow breath, he recognized it.

No, he thought. His dry mouth fell open as he inhaled the smell again. *It can't be.*

He heard the scuffle of tiny feet outside the shed door, and a flash of fear went through him as he thought of the huge wires and transformers all around them. Electrocution and death.

With Watts just a few feet away, backed into a corner and growling, Tommy risked a look at the open door to the shed.

Just outside the crooked door, ears flattened and tiny white teeth bared, stood a wild animal with reddish-blond fur. It was growling at Tommy and Watts.

To anyone else, the animal would've looked like a wild dog or maybe even a young coyote, but Tommy Roling knew better.

"Corinne!" he yelled, his heart in his throat. "I told you to stay *home*, girl!"

This was a wolf cub, and the wolf cub was Tommy's two-year-old daughter.

Chapter Two

Burt Roling glanced up at the faded Miller Lite clock perched next to yet another stuffed fox behind the bar. The tavern had at least a dozen of them scattered around, all in different frozen poses. They were all creepy and more than a little bit smelly.

I don't wait around for nobody, he thought with as much bravado as his three beers could muster. *I'm not scared, not here in my new city.*

He sighed and ordered another beer, knowing he would wait half an hour before leaving anyway, just as his little brother had ordered. At least that long, if not longer. This place *was* a tavern, after all. The best kind of place to waste time.

The music switched over to '80s hair band garbage, and the noise level in the bar increased in time to the tired tunes. He rubbed his bony chest where Tommy had thumped him for no good reason before rushing off. Even if the guy had lost some weight this past year, he was still a big dude.

Burt breathed through his mouth to avoid the worst of the smells, from the various sweaty people as well as the long-dead stuffed foxes. He wished he would've brought some smokes with him. But like always, he didn't have much cash, and Tommy the boy scout refused to buy him a pack.

Sipping his fresh beer now instead of gulping it the way he wanted to, Burt turned to say something to his new best friend, the seventy-something Buddy, but the older man had slipped away while Burt was calculating the passing time.

He hated leaving a conversation with a new drinking buddy—*Buddy!*—unfinished. He'd been explaining to Buddy all the problems with his new job at the movie theater, and he hadn't even gotten to the part about how the idiot manager cut his hours and put him on the crappy shifts. Kids' movie time on Saturday mornings? Unbelievable.

It's only a matter of time, he could hear Tommy saying, *and you'll be filling out more job applications.*

Burt winced through another lame Bon Jovi guitar solo and wished the absent Buddy a good life. He tried to locate the two cute girls at the end of the bar who'd been checking him out earlier. But in their place now stood a trio of chunky women in their forties, drinking Bud Lites and scowling at anyone who came close to them.

Just great, he thought, rubbing his cheek through his beard. *Nobody here worth a damn.*

And then he noticed the intense girl at the other end of the bar.

Even though she sat right in front of the ancient jukebox as it blared out a power ballad by Whitesnake or Warrant or Cinderella (Burt could never tell them apart), she was still writing away just as fast as she did an hour ago when he first glanced her way.

Wow, he thought, impressed. *How much could one person have to say?*

He took a big gulp of his beer to fortify his courage, and then he pushed away from his stool to go find out.

When he stood up to walk towards the girl, he felt a looseness in his joints from all his beers, and the crappy music grew louder with each step he took down the bar. These things usually worked best if he didn't think too much, but just did and said what came naturally to him, in the moment.

The girl was a lefty, Burt noticed, and that hand covered most of the words she was scribbling in her tiny handwriting. Before he could read any of it, she snapped the book closed and dropped the pen. A pair of intense hazel eyes now stared up at him. She smelled of jasmine and bourbon.

Burt smiled, surprised, still thinking about what he'd seen on the page for just an instant. He could've sworn those words were in another language. They seemed more like Chinese or maybe even hieroglyphics instead of English. Gazing into the owner of those eyes, he felt a shiver of unreality run through him.

And then he dropped himself as gracefully as possible into the bar stool next to her.

"Sorry to interrupt," he said over the music. "Just wondering if I could buy you a beer so you can take a break." He let out a goofy, nerve-induced chuckle that he regretted instantly. "All that writing looks like thirsty work."

The girl peered at him, her right eyebrow slightly raised, for a good five seconds. Burt tried not to squirm in the silence that followed the end of another song.

Then she said, "Excellent idea."

Burt hoped his exhale of relief wasn't too loud.

The girl held up an index finger with a black-painted fingernail.

"Just hold on for a second and let me finish up this thought first."

She reached for her trusty pen and journal again.

"*Stay*," she added with a devilish grin.

Burt couldn't have left if he'd tried. He felt glued to his seat as he watched her delicate hand put the black pen through its paces across the pages of her hardbound journal. Her pretty face, flushed red in the cheeks from the warmth in the bar, focused only on her words.

And again Burt couldn't make out what she was writing. It made his eyes want to cross, just looking at the tiny, unreadable words.

So weird, he thought. *I love it.*

She wrote for what must've been another minute, but Burt found he didn't mind. He used the time to take a look at her long legs in her black jeans, ending in no-nonsense chunky black boots. His gaze moved up to her short-sleeved white blouse with a nicely open neckline, then to her wrists wrapped in a series of thin black bracelets. Her fingers were decorated by rings with an array of gems on them: ruby, emerald, topaz.

The girl had stopped writing and was now staring back at Burt.

"Busted," he said before he could stop himself.

"O-*kay*," she said with a laugh. "Awkward."

Burt felt himself relax. He hadn't realized how tensely he'd been holding himself as he waited for her to finish writing or coding, or whatever it was. Like she was testing him to see if he had the guts to wait her out.

As she slid her journal into a brown leather satchel, Burt caught a glimpse of two other identical journals, along with at least two dozen pens lined up inside the bag like unspent ammo. Then she rapped a knuckle on the bar.

"I'll take that drink now," she said and waved at the bartender.

"*Wait*," Burt said, desperate to regain control of the situation. It didn't help that the jukebox was now blasting out Huey Lewis and the News and totally killing his buzz.

"Let's start over," he said, holding out his hand. "My name's Burt."

"I'm Lilly. Nice to meet you."

They shook. She had a surprisingly strong grip. Burt liked that, though it made a part of him feel a little less confident, somehow.

He waved at the bartender, and then he nodded at Lilly's satchel. It rested next to her feet, the strap hooked protectively on the toe of one boot.

"That's some serious work you're doing here. Most people just come to a bar to relax, not get in some overtime. What're you working on, if you don't mind me asking?"

"I *do* mind," Lilly said, and then made Burt squirm a bit longer before she laughed.

Burt drained the last of his beer, savoring the sound of her laugh.

A beautiful sound, he thought.

"I just get lots of ideas, sitting in a bar. I can never keep up with them or write them all down fast enough. I keep thinking I will one day, and when that happens, I won't have to do it anymore."

Burt nodded, as if this happened to him all the time. He much preferred meeting new people and just *talking* to them rather than writing anything down. His few experiences with writing consisted of some painful term papers back in high school. He liked to live in the moment instead of being all thoughtful and putting things into written form.

"Oh wait, I've heard of people like you," he said, forging ahead without letting his brain slow him down. "Are you part of that writing program at the University?"

Lilly gave him an *As if* look, and then shook her head.

"Nah, not my style. Not much of a joiner. I don't need a workshop to find inspiration. If you wanna call it that."

The bartender set a glass tumbler filled with some ice and what appeared to be a large amount of liquor in front of Lilly. Burt tried not to wince at how much that drink was going to cost him.

"In any case," he added, rolling with it now, "I felt like you would appreciate my company. I'm incredibly witty, and according to many ladies in the Iowa City area, I'm not too hard on the eyes. You may have noticed my beard."

"I did," Lilly said with a half-smile that leaned towards a smirk. "Impressive."

Burt rubbed his chin and cheeks as if deep in thought.

"What can I say?" he said with a shrug. "It's a gift."

They spent the next half hour drinking and discussing music and where they were from. Burt left out most of the gory details about his abrupt departure from Dyersburg that had brought him to Iowa City last year. Some things didn't need rehashing, especially when talking with such a pretty and sharp and funny young lady as Lilly.

He kept trying to steer the conversation back to whatever it was she was writing in her journal, but she danced around that issue easily.

Before Burt knew it, the bartender rang the bell for last call, and they finished up their final set of drinks. Then the jukebox wound down for good, and it was just the two of them at the suddenly quiet bar.

"Walk me home?" she said.

Burt started nodding vigorously even before she finished her sentence. He slid the bartender his worn credit card and said a silent prayer he hadn't yet hit his spending limit. The prayer worked—this time—and he walked out of the tavern with an amazing woman on his arm and a swagger in his step.

He risked a look at the side street where Tommy had parked his gray Grand Am. Still there. He stifled a shudder and let Lilly pull him down the road.

Be careful out there, bro, he thought to Tommy, somewhere out there in the darkness.

"My place is just two blocks away," she said. "And my roommate's out of town until the fall semester starts. Also, I've got wine."

"Huh," Burt said, scarcely able to believe how this night had turned around for him. It made him speechless, if only for a moment or two, which for Burt was saying quite a bit. "That's... *nice.*"

"You bet your ass it's nice, Burt!" Lilly said with a sharp laugh.

Burt let out a laugh as well. This girl was a bit odd, and he liked that. He saw his opening and took it, unable to let go of those weird words and shapes in her journal.

"So be honest here. What makes you write like that? I mean, you must've filled a couple books already with that—"

He was going to say "stuff" but didn't want to push his luck. He just let his cut-off sentence hang there in the dark as they walked. At some point she'd taken his hand, and now she squeezed it, hard.

"Is it like some other language?"

They crossed a road and stepped onto an uneven sidewalk that led to a split-level house broken up into apartments. The streetlight in front of the place had burned out, and the screen door hung crookedly on its hinges.

"I have a lot of catching up to do," Lilly said. "I may never get it all down."

"What do you mean? Get all of what down?"

"All the facts of the situation. Someone has to record them all. It's gotten worse lately."

They stopped right in front of the beat-up screen door, which was swaying the tiniest bit in the cool breeze. The door made an irregular squeaking sound that made Burt want to stick fingers in his ears.

Lilly looked up at him—she was a foot shorter than him, though she'd seemed taller back on her stool at the bar—and shook the brown curls on her head.

"That's some seriously boring stuff to talk about at this point in the evening. It's just my work. We all have a job to do, you know?"

Burt nodded at that, a slightly confused half-smile on his face. He could listen to her talk all night long. But it appeared they had better things than that in store for them this evening.

"I'd better go inside," Lilly said. She touched the side of Burt's mouth, and he felt an electrical current run through his body. "It's pretty late..."

"Yeah," he said. He was already backing away on his traitorous legs before he caught himself.

What the hell am I doing? he thought in a panic. *I can't let this night end!*

Lilly let out a laugh as she pulled open the crooked screen door and unlocked the wooden door behind it.

"Oh, I'm just messing with you, dude," she said, and then her voice lowered the tiniest bit. "Get your ass in here."

Burt nearly ran her over in his eagerness to do exactly as she'd ordered.

Chapter Three

Tommy left Watts growling in the shed and reached for his little girl standing outside in her wolf form. She promptly bit him in the hand.

The shock was both immediate and familiar—she had sunk her teeth into him at least a dozen times before in the past few months. He barely even registered the pain as he tried to push her back out of the way. But her wiry little body was too quick for him, and she sprang past him into the shed.

"Corinne!" he cried, reaching for her with a bloodied hand that was already stretching and shifting into something less than human. He needed to hold off the change in front of Watts, but after one look inside the shed, he knew he didn't need to worry.

Watts was now down on all fours, no longer a strung-out-looking man with buzzed black hair.

He'd made the change into his own wolf form—an emaciated-looking black beast with yellow and red eyes—and he was now squaring off and growling at tiny Corinne. The man's clothes lay in a shredded pile on the concrete floor, and the long fur on the chin of Watts the wolf quivered, looking just like his pointed little human beard.

Tommy leapt into the shed after his daughter, changing in mid-air from a tall, stocky human into a huge wolf with thick, dark-blond fur and paws twice the size of Watts'. He landed on the concrete floor on all fours just as Corinne attacked.

Watts was lightning-fast. He lashed out with a high-pitched whimper—not unlike his fevered whispering from earlier—and struck Corinne hard on her furry shoulder. She flew across the shed in front of Tommy and hit the metal wall with a surprised bark.

Tommy saw red. With a growling bark of his own, Tommy fell on the other werewolf.

Somewhere in the deep recesses of his consciousness, he heard Attix whispering "Always bring 'em back alive."

And then Tommy heard nothing else but the harsh snapping of bones.

Half a minute later, Tommy stood in his human form, naked and breathless in front of the bloody, broken body of Alan Watts, while his daughter whimpered at him from a few feet away.

He wiped the blood from his hands on Watts' ruined clothes, and then he called to his daughter while he pulled his own clothes back on.

"Corinne," he said. "Come here."

He didn't try covering up the body of the dead man for her sake. Watts had changed back to his human form as soon as the life had been crushed from his wolf body. Corinne had seen worse in her two short years of life. Tommy couldn't help that, though the thought haunted him. No wonder she was getting so wild.

Unlike Tommy and Watts next to him, Corinne didn't change back into her human form. She seemed to prefer her stronger, four-legged self, and he'd find her "wolfing it up"— as Burt called it—more often than not.

Tommy, on the other hand, had grown up stifling his werewolf genes, convinced by Mom he could only use it once or maybe twice a month, only when the moon was full. Mom had never been one for honesty.

He rubbed Corinne's furry head and checked out her left shoulder where Watts had hit her. She seemed fine, and her werewolf abilities would heal any damage from the blow faster than her human body would.

"You are in *big* trouble, little girl," Tommy said, earning yet another nip from her. This time she didn't break the skin.

He let out a shaky breath.

"And so am I," he added, smelling the coppery blood that had spilled from Watts behind him. "Shit."

Corinne curled up into his lap, rubbing her snout against his chest. Tommy petted her from the top of her head down her back to her tail, feeling each sharp ridge of her spine, every taut muscle of her wolf body.

Somehow she'd made it here all the way from Aunt Mel's house, which was a good three miles away, and across the Iowa River.

"How in the world did you *find* me, girl? Did you catch my scent all the way from home? Were you worried about your old man?"

Tommy knew better than to expect an answer from Corinne in her wolf form. She only talked when she shed her wolf skin, and while Tommy understood her perfectly most of the time, other people had trouble figuring out what she was trying to say. They just didn't know how to listen, Tommy figured.

The smell of blood and death, along with the insistent buzz of the electrical substation around him, pulled Tommy back to reality. Corinne's dark eyes had closed while she was curled up in his lap, no doubt exhausted from her wild run tonight. Tommy shuddered, picturing his little girl sprinting through town on all fours, dodging cars and trucks and people to get to him.

"We've got to go, little one," he murmured to Corinne. "Aunt Melanie's never gonna agree to watch you again, you *know* that, right?"

Tommy lifted Corinne off his lap and set her unsteadily back on her four clawed feet. Thinking of Mel, he pulled out his silenced phone and there they were: five texts and three missed calls from his aunt. He tapped out a quick "I've got her, be home soon" text and sent it. He silenced the phone again and pocketed it without waiting for her angry response.

At last he turned and looked down at the wrecked body of Watts. He stared at the man for a long time, thinking about all he'd told him tonight, calculating how much to tell Attix.

He knew someone who might have been the next person on Watts' list. A friend of his, actually.

There had been a guy like that back in Dyersburg, too— that guy Lance, who had suggested Tommy kill his ex-girlfriend and baby mama Suzanne, and Tommy had wanted to do it as soon as Lance said it—but Lance had died on Tommy's chaotic last night in his hometown.

He could at least warn his new friend here in Iowa City, though he knew it would sound totally crazy.

Hey Dennis, he imagined himself saying to the skinny guy with the ponytail, *watch your back, because there's this shadowy group looking to off people with voices like yours, and they've been using werewolf assassins to get the job done. Just a quick heads-up for ya, pal.*

Shaking his head and wishing he could laugh about it all, Tommy instead pulled out his phone again and called Attix.

N ow *this* is something else," officer John Attix said fifteen minutes later, standing over the body of Alan Watts. "What happened to his clothes?"

Attix was an intense black man in his early forties, a head shorter and a hundred pounds lighter than Tommy, but with so much presence he seemed much, much bigger. Tommy had been working with him for over a year now, and even in black sweat pants and a gray University of Iowa Field House T-shirt, the guy still intimidated him.

"Well," Tommy said, swallowing hard. "He was naked when I found him. Messing around with his knives. His clothes are over there, and I didn't touch 'em."

"Ugh," Attix said. As if that explained everything. Tommy had learned that the less he said, the better. Attix filled in the rest on his own, intuitively.

Tommy glanced outside to make sure Corinne was still in the thick bushes on the other side of the fence. He didn't have time to try to run her back to his car at the Fox Head, so he'd taken her there before Attix had arrived and ordered her to stay. As usual, Burt wasn't answering his phone, and Tommy couldn't bring himself to call his aunt. And how would it look to walk into the tavern to find Burt with a small red wolf—or worse, a naked little girl—in his arms?

"Tom," Attix said, irritation in his voice. "Stay with me here. Relax. What's out there that's got you so distracted?"

"Just looking out for cops and stuff."

"Hey, we *are* the cops and stuff. You did the right thing, calling me. Some jokers would've tried to cover this up, or tried to hide the body. Or worse, bury him. That *never* frickin' works."

Tommy let out a soft, nervous laugh. He'd considered all of those things before calling Attix. But then he remembered the other man's advice: *We take care of our own, so don't try going off on your own.*

He also needed his half of the reward money, which he still planned on getting even though their fugitive was no longer breathing.

"So," Tommy said, "we make it look like an accident?"

Attix gave a cynical laugh.

"Nah, man. The more you try to cover something up, the more problems you create. I'm just gonna call this one in myself, tell them I got an anonymous tip about a body in here. What I *won't* tell them is that you were here. So you need to get gone."

Tommy wanted to check on Corinne in the bushes again, but forced himself to look only at Attix.

"Okay."

He dropped his eyes and felt glad that the shed had a concrete floor instead of dirt, which would've shown all kinds of tracks, human and otherwise.

"You didn't try to move him or do anything else to the body, did you?"

Tommy shook his head, squirming a bit from Attix's sharp voice and intense gaze.

"Good," Attix said. He rubbed his chin as he looked down at what was left of Watts. "You really did a number on this guy, Tom. He must've put up some kind of fight. You sure you didn't use a baseball bat on him? Or a sledgehammer?"

Tommy just shook his head. He knew anything he might say at this point would give him away.

"Fine," Attix said after an uncomfortable pause. He turned back to Watts and sighed.

Tommy had been running on adrenaline and nerves for the past hour or two, and now his energy suddenly left him. His shoulders slumped forward, and he nervously pulled at his too-loose jeans.

Attix sniffed and cleared his throat. "So he didn't talk, did he? Tell you anything?"

Tommy shrugged. "He just said something about how *they* made him do it. I told him to save it, and then when I tried to secure his wrists, he lost it."

While Tommy spoke, Attix checked out Watts' hands without touching the body.

"Speaking of wrists," he said, "his right one got crushed. You do that?"

Feeling nauseated all over again, Tommy nodded. "First thing he did was go for one of his knives. I stepped on his wrist to get it free. Maybe a bit too hard."

Attix straightened up and directed his high-beam gaze right at Tommy. He had a look on his face like he wanted to ask more questions, or maybe throw a theory or two Tommy's way. Tommy had never told Attix about his werewolf abilities, and he definitely didn't want to confess to that now. He had a feeling that Attix suspected something about him, but knew better than to ask. The promotions and his share of the reward money this past year had been way too good for him.

"I know all I need to know, here, my friend," Attix said with one last clearing of his throat. "One less scumbag to deal with here in our fine city. I'm calling this in now, so you need to hit the road."

"All right," Tommy said, already backing out of the shed. "Thanks," he added.

"No problem," Attix said, already distracted by his phone. "You did good, getting this guy off the street. Just try not to kill the next fugitive you track down, okay?"

Tommy slipped away without another word, wishing he could block the memory of Watts' broken body from his mind forever.

I did that, he reminded himself. *Because I let myself lose control.*

He climbed over the fence and hurried around the other side into the darkness surrounding the bushes. With sharp jolts of panic hitting him with each step he took toward the bushes hiding Corinne, he convinced himself that his daughter wouldn't be there when he got there.

He'd have to track her like he'd tracked Watts tonight, but it wouldn't be nearly as easy as following a drunk and whispering man reeking of cigarettes and beer. He'd have to change, no doubt, and chase her through Iowa City in his wolf form until he found her.

But when he pushed through the bushes, he found his little strawberry-blond two-year-old snoring softly on a pile of pine needles inside. She still hadn't made the switch back to her human form, most likely due to the warmth her fur coat gave her as the summer night turned cool. Or maybe she just preferred her four-legged self these days.

Tommy had a sudden urge to curl up next to her and sleep the night away in there. But this place would be full of cops soon, and they needed to get back home.

He scooped up his little wolf daughter and carried her out of the bushes. Keeping to the shadows, he hurried back to his car near the Fox Head and secured the four-legged Corinne somewhat awkwardly into her car seat in the back.

On the way to their rented house on its three acres just outside Iowa City, Tommy fought to keep his own eyelids open as the events of the past few hours caught up to him.

Burt better be home, Tommy thought, *and not out drinking up the last of his paycheck. He owes me for his half of rent from last month.*

They'd only been living here for two months, and his big brother was already dropping the ball with his share of the bills. That was one of the things he'd wanted to discuss with Burt tonight at guys' night out, along with a possible visit to see Mom and Dad back in Dyersburg for the first time in over a year. Corinne needed to see her grandparents, as much as a trip back home would suck for Tommy.

But then Watts had shown up to change those plans.

Tommy hit the brakes hard to avoid a doe and two half-grown fawns darting across the lane to their rental house. He'd seen these three deer countless times since moving here this summer.

Dumber than dirt, Burt would say every time they showed up, usually to leap right in front of their moving car. *Too dumb to live.*

Waiting for his heart to stop hammering, Tommy looked down the lane at their little three-bedroom ranch. It was a great place, with a wide, fenced-in yard for Corinne that Tommy thought would help to keep her contained. The light blue paint needed a fresh coat, and the porch had some rotted-out places, but that didn't bother him. It was private but still close to town, and it was theirs. So long as they made rent each month.

The lights were out, so either Burt had gotten a cab home and crashed for the night already, or he was still out partying despite Tommy's request for him to head home earlier. Tommy was betting on the partying, always a safe bet with Burt.

He knew he should call Aunt Melanie with an update, but he couldn't deal with her anger and disappointment with both him and his little girl right now. He'd make it up to her later. Somehow.

Before starting down the lane, he took a look up at the stars and thought for a guilt-ridden moment about Watts.

He never should've hit her, Tommy thought. *I could've held it together if he hadn't done that.*

Tommy's thoughts shifted from Watts to his new friend Dennis, who worked with some of the women's sports teams at the university. The first time he met him, Tommy had just dropped off a pile of pizzas for Dennis and at least a dozen college-aged girls playing video games inside his apartment, and those girls had devoured the pizza as soon as Dennis yelled "Go!"

Tommy dropped his gaze back to his windshield and the now-empty lane in front of him.

No, Tommy recalled. *Dennis hadn't yelled "Go!" He'd yelled, "Feedin' time!" And the girls had* attacked *that pizza like wild animals.*

Looking back at that time now, Tommy knew that all the girls must've had the werewolf gene, but he could tell that Dennis did not have it in him.

He remembered feeling unnerved to be around so many other weres all in one place. He'd wanted to dive into the fray and risk life and limb for a slice of Pizza Pit pie. Pack mentality was hard to overcome, even in his human form.

In the past six months, Tommy had become friends with Dennis, and they'd hung out quite a bit since that time, playing video games and tap-dancing around each guy's more-than-human skills. Tommy appreciated the fact that Dennis had never used his voice on him, except for possibly one time when Dennis had wanted to win that Call of Duty mission and Tommy's guy had taken a dozen bullets for Dennis' guy.

Surely that hadn't been Dennis in the nearby town of Mount Vernon who Watts had killed.

He wanted to call or text his new friend to warn him somehow that he might be in danger. But it was late, and he didn't know how to warn him without sounding crazy.

Watts is dead, and Dennis is safe, he told himself silently. *Go home already.*

With that Tommy drove down the lane, his daughter still breathing deep and slow in the back seat, her furry hind legs feet twitching as she ran in her dreams. He vowed to call Dennis first thing in the morning, and hoped he wouldn't regret waiting until then.

Chapter Four

Burt woke with a jolt as a ray of sunlight jabbed him in the eye through the cheap blinds above him. The blanket covering him was coated in what felt like thick fur. His head ached, his limbs felt heavy, and a naked young woman was curled up next to him in a lumpy single bed.

Opening both eyes wide in the early morning light, Burt bit back a whine when he realized that what was covering him was not a blanket.

He'd *changed* at some point last night, and he was still in his wolf form, his skin hidden under reddish-brown fur. Full-on canine, with the doggy breath to prove it.

He was afraid to move an inch for fear he'd wake the girl beside him.

What was her name? he thought as he lay there, immobile, trying not to let his panic blind him. *Ellen? No.* Lilly. *No way I told her about my special gene. Right? I wasn't that drunk, was I?*

All the details about last night, starting right after Tommy left and Burt walked down the bar to Lilly's spot, were a complete blank.

Burt closed his eyes and forced himself to relax despite the annoying shaft of light still poking him in the eyes, the uncomfortable bed, and the closeness of Lilly.

Unlike his brother, who'd learned about his wolf side when he was barely six or seven, Burt was a late bloomer. He'd just learned how to shift into his wolf skin last year, pretty much by accident, during all the craziness back in Dyersburg. He only had a year of were-experience compared to Tommy's decade and a half.

And his attempts to relax and change back weren't working.

How'd I let my guard down like this? he thought. *First I let myself change around someone else, and then I stay changed while I was sleeping?*

Making it happen was never an easy task, and it always hurt. Coming back to his human form had always been a relief, and he kept a constant watch on himself and his emotions to prevent such things like this from ever happening by accident.

But he'd also had a lot to drink last night, and as he lay motionless on the narrow and crowded bed, trying to keep his tail from wagging, he started to make out a fuzzy memory of multiple glasses of red wine in Lilly's living room.

He opened his eyes and swallowed with a clicking sensation. When he lifted his head, something tightened around his neck. Burt felt a stab of fear stronger than the early-morning rays of light slipping into the room.

Slowly, shakily, he lifted his right paw—the one not wrapped around Lilly's naked shoulders—and felt a leather collar encircling his thick wolf neck.

He bit down a shriek of pain as what felt like dozens of needles punctured his paw from the collar.

Panicked and in pain, he needed to get away from the girl in bed with him, but he was terrified of waking her and allowing her to see his wolf side. He swung his big head gingerly to the left to scan the room for something to help him make sense of last night, but the room was empty except for a long black table covered in papers, pens, journals, and one large leatherbound book.

The walls, Burt realized with disbelief, weren't covered in peeling wallpaper as he'd assumed at first that morning. They were actually decorated with blank pieces of paper torn from a square journal like the one Lilly had been slapping words into last night at the Fox Head.

Who was *this girl?* he wondered with a chill of fear filling his gut.

With that thought he kicked the sheets down off himself so he could leap off the bed and get away from her.

He never made it off the lumpy mattress.

The collar was attached to a three-foot length of black leather that had been secured somewhere behind him.

A leash.

Burt wanted to howl as he clawed at his neck, cutting up his paws even more with each attempt to get free of the spiked collar.

Paws seared with pain and slick with blood, he tried to force himself back to his human form once more so he could use fingers instead of claws to pry off the collar. But the more he pushed to make himself human, the more his head hurt, and the more the collar tightened.

Rearing up on shaky hind legs on the bed, he pulled as hard as he could on the leash, which was attached to a metal bolt in the wall. His shock turned to panic-fueled anger, and he felt something give, just the tiniest bit, in the leash. Burt yanked harder.

As he struggled to pull the leash off the bolt in the wall, or pull the bolt out of the wall, whichever came first, he knocked Lilly off the bed.

She dropped onto the floor with a dull, lifeless thump. He didn't dare look down at her as his throat began to tighten and close from his efforts. Collar, leash, and bolt were all connected seamlessly. As if they'd been designed for such entrapments.

Burt smelled his own fear, along with a bounty of other scents. He inhaled Lilly's jasmine-tinted perfume and sweat, along with a disturbingly unhealthy odor coming from her mouth. It wasn't just morning breath.

Panting, he lowered himself down to all fours from where he'd been standing on the mattress. He had just enough slack in the leash to slip off the bed and reach for her on the floor.

He could also smell the mildew of this basement bedroom, along with the acidic stink of vomit and something darker. Earthy.

Before he could identify the strange scent, he pushed his furry snout closer to Lilly, collar tightening. He wanted to cover her nakedness—he had his own *fur*, at least—because she looked so small and vulnerable there on the floor. All she wore was her thin black bracelets, her rings, and a grimace.

Burt's sense of doom intensified as he realized she was barely breathing.

"Lilly," he said through his mouthful of teeth. It sounded horrible to his own ears. "Lilly, wake up!"

She felt cold. He tried not to get the blood from his injured paws on her face and neck as he tried to revive her, but it couldn't be avoided. Up close, her breath reeked like the most potent bug killer he'd ever smelled.

Somebody else *did this*, he realized. *Not Lilly, the girl with the pen who was always trying to get caught up with... something. Somebody wanted to hurt us both.*

Straining against the leash and collar, Burt lifted Lilly closer to him and pressed his wolf lips hard against her blue-tinged lips, as if he was some sort of furry, four-legged Prince Charming. This kiss felt so different from their kisses last night that he wanted to scream with frustration.

Instead, Lilly did the screaming. Her eyes snapped open as she pulled away from his rough snout. She gulped in a huge, ragged breath and let an ear-piercing shriek.

Burt's wolf ears ached from the sound, but his relief overwhelmed his discomfort. She was *alive*. She'd woken to a man-sized wolf inches from her face, so he didn't blame her for freaking out.

"It's okay," he said, knowing his voice was too rough to comprehend at first. He kept talking. "It's me, Burt. I have this, um, condition. I usually keep it hidden, but something's wrong. I can't change *back*. We're in trouble, Lilly. Someone's trying to hurt us."

As he talked, Lilly had grabbed a sheet with trembling hands and wrapped it around herself, though it seemed more from coldness and fear than embarrassment. She blinked fast and widened her eyes while she looked at him, as if trying to get her hazel eyes adjusted to Burt's voice coming from that long and narrow face. The intensity had quickly returned to her gaze.

"I know," she said in a raspy voice. Her grimace returned as she swallowed.

Burt had left her side so he could work on the collar and leash again. They weren't budging. He must've imagined something loosening earlier.

"Which part do you know?" he said, dropping back down to all fours again with a wince. The collar was tighter than ever.

"*Every* part. It's this thing I have," she said, her left hand twitching as if it needed a pen. "I can figure things out pretty fast. Almost immediately, really. Not like telepathy. I just sort of pick up people's stories out of the air around them, I guess. Sometimes it gets to be too much, so I try to write 'em all down. That's what I was doing last night, then you walked up. *Your* story was all about the problems in your family, and how you caused most of them. Or how you *think* you caused them all."

Burt swallowed with another painful click.

"That's gotta be a handy skill," he said, thumping the wall with his tail. He didn't know what else to say.

An odd feeling came over him, something he didn't recognize at first due to the other emotions swirling around him right now.

It felt like... *relief.*

A sense that he wasn't the only one with some strange-ass curse haunting his every move. That he wasn't the only freak.

"Handy," she said, "and totally annoying. My mom and my older brother had it, too, and it drove them crazy. Literally. You don't want to know."

Burt wanted to reach over to her, bloody paw and all, but the leash wouldn't let him. She sat down on the floor with her back to the bed, just out of his reach.

"I *do* wanna know," he said, sniffing the air for that other, darker scent he'd picked up earlier. "But first we have to get out of here. Whoever did this will be coming back."

Lilly nodded, and her eyelids fluttered. All this talking seemed to be draining her.

"I have to ask you a big favor," Burt said, and her head drooped forward. "*Lilly.* Are you okay?"

She jumped and sat up straighter. The sheet fell down off her left shoulder, exposing a black-inked tattoo barely three inches wide that he hadn't noticed before. It looked like an abstract, almost geometric design. Sort of like some of the ancient-looking words Lilly had used to fill the pages of her journal.

"I'm fine. Just a bit dizzy, and my head's killing me. But other than that, just fine." She swiped at the blood Burt had left on her cheek, smearing it. "What's the favor?"

Burt tried not to smile at her resilience; he knew how horrific all his teeth would look to her right now.

"Try to find your thickest sweater, or maybe a pair of jeans," he said, struggling to enunciate with his wolf mouth. "And use it to protect your hands. We've got to get this collar off me."

"That thing's covered in tiny *needles*, Burt. You felt them, didn't you?"

Something shifted in the house above them. It could've been a footstep. Burt felt the collar tighten again as all his muscles clenched.

Control, Burt thought. *Tommy's always talking about it. We have to control it. Control ourselves.*

As Lilly walked unsteadily over to a beat-up dresser, Burt took deep breaths and pictured himself at a bar with a fresh beer in front of him, the radio playing the opening chords to a Temple of the Dog song.

Calm down, he told himself. *Control it. Say hello to heaven.*

When Lilly came back, she wore a pair of thick, black, leather gloves.

"They're my roommate's, so don't ask," she said, wiggling her fingers inside the gloves, and then she grabbed the collar with both hands. "Ready?"

He leaned back to get more slack in the leash, and then he forced himself to start the change back into his default human form.

"*Pull*," he said to Lilly.

The next ten seconds were the most painful seconds Burt had ever known. The collar crushed his windpipe and cut off his air as Lilly tugged it up higher on his neck, inch by inch. Meanwhile, his body fought the transformation from wolf to man, all of his cells battling with one another for dominance. It felt like he was churning himself up from the inside out.

He focused all of his energy on his neck and head, needing to make his jaw and skull smaller so Lilly could get the collar up and off him.

Desperate, he grabbed at the collar as well, ignoring the needles entering his paws—*fingers*—and helped push the collar up.

Say hello to heaven...

When the collar reached his chin, something shifted in him.

With a sudden popping sensation, he and Lilly shoved the collar past his chin, over his face, and off his head at last.

Lilly fell forward, and he caught her cold body in his hot, sticky, bloody arms. His *human* arms.

They dropped to the floor in a heap, and in that moment, holding Lilly as they both laughed hysterically with relief, Burt knew that he had fallen hopelessly and helplessly in love with her.

After a while they figured out how to stop laughing, and Burt touched Lilly's bare left shoulder. He traced the black squares and whirls of the tattoo there with his claw-less, delicate-looking human finger.

"Tell me what this means," he said.

Lilly turned to him and touched his sore neck. The pain receded almost completely under her fingertips.

"Someday," she whispered. "It's a long story."

"Bet you've got a lot of those," he whispered. His normal voice felt strange to him, and it sounded too high and clear compared to the voice he'd just been using a few seconds ago. "Stories, that is."

Lilly kissed his neck, and Burt felt a thrill run through him so big he really wished he had some clothes on at that moment.

"Too *many* stories," she said, and then paused. "It means victory, if that helps."

"Cool."

The house shifted again above them, and Burt tensed.

"We've got to get out of here," he said. "I think someone's here to pick up the pieces after last night."

They dressed quickly, and Lilly shoved the big leatherbound book into her satchel, along with a few more pens and another journal.

"Just in case," she said with a slightly sheepish grin, latching the bag to protect its valuable contents.

Burt nodded at that and tiptoed over to the door. He opened it as quietly as he could and sniffed the air. Without his wolf nose, he couldn't pick up smells as strongly, but he did get a whiff of that dark, earthy scent once more.

He closed the bedroom door, locked it, and considered moving Lilly's big dresser in front of it. Too noisy, and not enough time.

"We're going out the window," he said.

Lilly had slipped back to her desk again, fiddling with something in a drawer. Burt caught a whiff of something sharp, like gasoline or lighter fluid, just for a second.

Without waiting any longer for her response, he stepped onto the bed, slid open the window, and punched out the screen.

It felt good to be moving like this after being trapped on the end of that leash. He'd have to ask Lilly later why her bedroom had that bolt in the wall. It didn't make sense.

Nothing made sense, other than keeping Lilly and himself safe.

The house shifted again while he helped Lilly, her full satchel held tight to her chest, up and out of the basement window. He pulled himself out after her, glad that his hands had stopped bleeding at last.

Lilly waited outside for him, fear and anger battling on her tired face. She grabbed his sore left hand, and they ran together down the street, away from her apartment and the stranger—or strangers—creeping towards them from above. Burt could've run with her for miles, forever.

Chapter Five

At half past six, Tommy slipped out of bed and tiptoed through his house, avoiding the creaky spots in the floor, so he could check on the kids.

Corinne was still snoring softly in her pink princess bed with its half-sized mattress. The brightly colored birds soaring above her head on her mobile swung gently back and forth in tiny flight patterns. She'd finally reverted back to her human form in her exhaustion, and Tommy covered her to the chin with her frilly comforter.

Burt's bedroom door remained open, his unmade bed still vacant. Usually Burt kept the door shut until nearly noon so he could sleep in and not be bothered. Last night the guy hadn't even bothered to come home. Tommy tried not to think the worst of that turn of events.

And then there were those five seconds of rage with Watts. Tommy had woken up every hour or so last night, thinking his phone was vibrating with a call from Attix. That the cops needed him to come in and talk. After each sudden waking, it took a good fifteen or twenty minutes for him to relax and fall back to sleep. As it turned out, nobody had tried calling him.

He stepped out onto the front porch and sucked in a clean, cool breath of country air. He forced Watts out of his head so he could focus on the people that really mattered.

Corinne and Burt, and now Dennis.

I'm so damn tired of taking care of everyone, he thought. *When do I get to cut loose and be carefree for a while?*

He froze, listening. He thought he'd heard Corinne waking. Sometimes she'd roll out of bed a few seconds after he checked on her, and she was good at creeping up on him, despite his heightened senses.

He held still for a good ten seconds, and then continued toward the steps with his phone in hand. False alarm.

In sixteen more years, when she's off to college, he figured. *That's when I get my chance to go wild and be a party animal once more.*

With a grim, mirthless laugh, Tommy sat down on the front steps in a patch of morning light. He inhaled the smells of manure, cut grass, hay, and a hint of exhaust coming over from I-40 on the morning breeze. In a field half a mile away, he saw the mother doe and her two fawns nibbling at stray weeds.

Convinced that Corinne was still asleep and Burt wasn't returning any time soon, Tommy exhaled the mingled scents of his new home and called his friend Dennis to make sure he was okay as well.

Dennis answered on the second ring, which surprised Tommy. He figured he'd still be asleep.

"Hey Tom," Dennis said, cheerful and relaxed as ever. "You're up early, man."

"Yeah, hope it's not too early for you."

"Been up since five, man. Had to get the girls started on their five-mile run, make sure they were all there, then I grabbed a latte and came back home. The exciting life of an athletics manager."

Dennis worked with female student athletes at the U of I, and he never seemed intimidated by any of the strong, beautiful, and very intense young women who surrounded him every day. Tommy always went all tongue-tied whenever he went over to his apartment and "the girls" were around.

The fact that most of the girls had the werewolf gene, and Dennis had a voice that could yank them into line at any time, probably helped in the confidence area.

"Glad I didn't wake you," Tommy said, allowing himself to relax and feel some relief after last night's events. He swallowed. "Everything going all right?"

"Busy, but good. You? Ready to go back to slinging pizzas?"

"No thanks, dude. I got a good gig working with Attix, you know."

There was a somewhat awkward pause, as if Dennis had gotten distracted, or possibly he was choosing his words carefully.

"I bet that is a good gig," Dennis said, and paused again. Tommy felt his face go hot. That pause spoke volumes about the secret that Dennis knew about Tommy, which was the same secret the girls on Dennis' sports team had. "Does your lady friend Nina miss you at the pizza place?"

Tommy flinched at that. He hadn't thought about Nina since last night. He tried not to think about her at all lately. The discomfort—he couldn't really call it *pain*—from their separation returned as he pictured her brown eyes and her smile.

I really talked too much when Dennis and I were playing video games together, he thought. *The guy has a memory like a steel fricking trap.*

"She's spending the summer in Chicago with her family," Tommy said, rubbing his face. He got up and walked down the front steps to the edge of the lawn. "She's not sure if she's coming back for the fall semester. Or if she's coming back at all..."

"Ah, man. That sucks. She sounded pretty cool. Let me know if you ever want to start seeing anyone else. There's this sophomore soccer player who's pretty amazing, and smart, and funny, and ho-o-ot—"

"Okay, okay," Tommy said. "I *will* let you know. Damn. You're worse than an online dating site."

Dennis brayed laughter into the phone, and Tommy finally gave in and chuckled along with him. Dennis loved giving him a hard time about women.

Dennis went quiet as Tommy heard a faint knocking sound on the other end of the line.

"Hold on," Dennis said. "Someone's at the door."

Tommy had no choice but to wait. Dennis had *told* him to hold on, and his voice was that powerful, even over the phone. He couldn't figure out what it was about Dennis' voice that did this to him, and he couldn't say another word.

Careful, he wanted to call to his buddy, but couldn't. *Don't let anyone in you don't know.*

The sun had burned through the haze of early morning, bright in his tired eyes and warm on his skin. A pickup rattled past on the road perpendicular to his lane. The deer had stopped eating in the field, and all three were looking right at him, still as statues.

Tommy stood, his whole body tense. He held his breath and focused all his energy on listening to what was going on. He could tell that Dennis still had his cell phone in his hand as he went to the door.

Check the peephole. It's seven in the morning. Don't just open—

Tommy grimaced as he heard the clatter of a doorknob and the squeak of a door opening.

"Hey there," Dennis began, and then the phone dropped with a clatter.

"Shit," Tommy hissed, finally able to speak again now that Dennis had spoken to someone else; that was how this voice thing seemed to work.

"Dennis!" Tommy shouted into his phone, but nobody answered him.

For a painful half-minute, Tommy paced through the wet, too-long grass of his front lawn as he listened to faint shuffling and thumping sounds on his phone.

Something hit the floor of Dennis' apartment, hard. Followed by the sounds of struggle, panicked footsteps and things breaking.

Tommy's breathing sped up, and his instincts turned wolfish. All sounds and smells sharpened, and he nearly coughed from the poisonous stink of exhaust filling his nose from the interstate.

He didn't dare shout his friend's name again for fear the intruders would hear it. The sounds stopped for a few seconds, and he froze in the middle of the grass, looking at the twisted path he'd made in the dew behind him.

Then he heard more footsteps, followed by a clattering sound. Someone had picked up Dennis' phone.

"Your friend's going away for now," a low voice murmured into Tommy's ear through the phone. Even with his canine senses on high, he couldn't tell if the voice was male or female. "He's been recruited."

"Leave him alone!" Tommy shouted, but the connection went dead.

He shouted again until his vocal cords hurt, feeling strangely pleased by the mad scrambling of the three deer out in the field as they bolted from his yelling.

With a shaking hand, he shoved his phone into his pocket, though he was tempted to launch it at the old barn at the edge of their front yard. He was fumbling in his other pocket for his car keys when a tiny yawn from the front porch stopped him cold.

"Daddy?" Corinne called. She rubbed her eyes and then touched her left shoulder as if it were still sore. "You walkin' 'roun', Daddy?"

Why are you walking around, Daddy?

Tommy hurried across the yard and scooped up his daughter. He rubbed her back and held her close enough to feel her delicate heartbeat against his chest.

No way am I letting her out of my sight again, he vowed. *Not after last night. Watts could've killed her there in that shed.*

He tried to clear the image of Watts swiping his daughter out of the way last night, followed by the sight of the other were's broken body on the floor of the shed.

"Come on, little girl," he said in a shaky voice as he stepped down off the porch and toward his car. "We're going for a ride. Right now."

"Righ'," Corinne said, already squirming in his arms with excitement. "Righ' righ' *now*, Daddy."

Ride. Ride right now, *Daddy.*

"That's my girl," Tommy said as he maneuvered her wriggling body into her car seat. "We need to go see our friend Dennis."

Corinne just cackled in the back seat, as if she knew a secret that she wasn't telling her Daddy.

Tommy fired up his dusty Grand Am and gunned it up the gravel lane. He should've gone over to Dennis' place this morning instead of just calling him. He wasn't going to screw this up again.

"Dennie talk an' talk an' talk," Corinne said in a sing-song voice from the back.

Dennis likes to talk and talk and talk.

"That's right," Tommy said as they flew down the road toward town.

Corinne had never, for some strange reason, been affected by the voice of Dennis. He could tell her to sit down or roll over and she'd just laugh at him. She'd been that way with other people like that, including that smooth talker Lance working with Gwen back in Dyersburg, and it had saved both of their lives.

"We're gonna go listen to Dennie talk real soon, baby. He can talk all he wants, too."

Chapter Six

Burt really wished he'd left his Camaro at the tavern instead of letting Tommy drive last night. Now they were stuck on foot, and his feet *hurt*. Every part of him hurt, for that matter.

Neither of them spoke a word after escaping Lilly's basement bedroom. They were too busy running for the last three blocks in their untied shoes and boots. When they reached the empty parking lot of the Fox Head, they both slowed to a fast walk without a word.

Burt found himself strangely disappointed that his brother Tommy's car was gone, as if he'd half-expected the big guy to be sitting behind the wheel of his Grand Am with the engine running, waiting for them. Having Tommy at his side would've eased Burt's mind, big-time.

The tavern itself looked small and lifeless in the harsh light of early morning. With the exception of a jogger or two off in the distance, the streets remained deserted. Nobody was chasing them from Lilly's house. The world remained asleep and unaware.

Burt stopped walking and pulled Lilly to a stop as well, which took most of his strength. She was a sturdy girl.

"Who the hell was *back* there?"

At first he thought she didn't hear him, because she tried to keep plowing forward even with his arms on her shoulders. She seemed to want to head toward downtown and the university beyond that, but Burt didn't know what her actual destination was, or why.

He tried a trick that Tommy taught him and channeled some of his wolf strength into his arms. He felt a surge of *something*, but mostly it felt like gas, mixed with heart palpitations. It definitely wasn't wolf strength.

Damn, he thought, embarrassed. *I got a lot of learning to do.*

When Lilly finally stopped and looked at him, her eyes were bloodshot and strangely dilated, with big black half-moons like bruises under her eyes. She was panting, and he could once more smell the foulness of her breath. It was more than just the typical stale morning breath that came after a late night of drinking.

"I'm gonna assume," Burt said when she refused to answer, "that it wasn't your roommate back there, coming home early from summer break. I mean, there *was* someone else in the house with us, right?" He rubbed at his beard, trying to recall those shifting noises above them. "Now I'm starting to doubt myself."

Lilly shook her head, then nodded. She looked utterly lost.

"All my writing's back in there," she said, talking more to herself than to Burt. "How'd they find me this time?"

She was looking back in the direction of her apartment, absently rubbing her writing hand.

"*This* time?" Burt whispered, but she didn't seem to hear him. "*They?*"

His breathing and heartbeat had returned to normal, but the pain in his throat intensified. He couldn't imagine what it must be like to hear all those stories of people around you, especially the stories you didn't want to hear.

She should really be using a computer, he thought out of the blue, *with a humongous hard drive for her work, instead of those journals. Then she could back them up to the cloud. However* that *worked...*

Feeling even more unnerved by her vacant gaze, Burt reached out and grabbed her hands. They were cold and trembling, but she gripped him tightly.

"What happens if someone else gets those journals of yours? I mean, can anyone else even *read* them?"

She glanced once more over her shoulder, and then she pulled him over to the wooden stairs at the side entrance to the Fox Head. They sat on the top step, surrounded by trees that hid them from the street, still locked together at their hands.

"So you saw my cipher," she said. "You're pretty quick. Most people don't look that close."

Her eyes were more focused now, and she seemed to be looking right at him instead of some nightmare vision inside her head.

"*Girl*," Burt said, inching closer to her in his enthusiasm, "I couldn't look away. You were writing so fast, which was what got me interested in the first place, and then I saw *what* you writing, and I had to know more."

"You weren't just trying to hook up?"

Lilly gave him a small smile, which encouraged Burt. She was recovering a bit from this insane morning. He still felt all shaky and weak inside, so he just rolled with it, which was always his approach in any intense situation like this one.

"Well, *yeah*, of course I was trying to hook up with you. I mean, you're hot and all. But I also happen to like interesting people who write code—um, I mean *cipher*—into hardback journals while sitting in a noisy and smelly bar on a Thursday night in the big city. Call me crazy."

"Not crazy," Lilly said immediately. She rubbed the back of his hand with her thumb softly, and he hoped she would never stop. "You're sweet. Even if you are half wolf."

Burt wanted to squirm away, but Lilly held him tightly with her hands in his.

"I guess you probably knew all that as soon as I sat down next to you, huh?" he said, his face hot. "When you plucked my story out of the air, or whatever it is you do."

"Actually, no. You managed to *hide* that part of yourself from me, which is impressive. All I picked up about you was your issues with your family. Your *pack*, I guess I should call it. I didn't know about your, um, animal side until you woke me this morning with your puppy kisses."

"Well I wasn't trying to hide anything," Burt blurted out before he could stop himself. He cleared his throat nervously and immediately regretted it. That collar had done a number on him, and the fact that it kept him from changing out of his wolf body totally unnerved him.

Out of control, he thought. *Trapped in my animal body.*

"Can we please change the subject?" he said, rubbing his aching throat. "And shouldn't we get moving?"

"Relax," Lilly said with a smile. "Let's just be still for a little bit longer."

The whites of her eyes were less bloodshot now, but the dark skin under those hazel eyes remained bruised-looking.

Burt wondered again about the wine they'd drank last night. In his full-on panic mode from earlier, he was positive someone had tried to poison them both. Maybe *that* was what had triggered his change—his body, desperate to cleanse itself of the poison, went into panic mode and made the change for him. His wolf self was much better at healing quickly.

But maybe he'd overreacted. Maybe they both had, and they were running from nothing.

No, he thought. *No overreaction, damn it. Somebody had knocked us both out, and then came into her bedroom last night to slap that collar on me, and put me on a frickin' leash. Like they were saving us for later.*

Lilly was watching him, that small smile back on her face. Burt's heart did a wonderful flip-flop as he met her gaze and returned her smile.

Oh, I'm in deep, he thought. *After just one night.*

"Want to know the story about my tattoo?" Lilly said.

"Oh yeah."

She let go of his hands and pulled her shirt down off her left shoulder.

"It's actually not a tattoo at all," she whispered. "It's a brand. Touch it."

Once again, Burt couldn't disobey her order. Barely two inches high and two inches wide, the geometric design on her shoulder wasn't black ink after all, but scar tissue. He ran his shaking fingers over its ruler-straight raised edges as delicately as he could, and then he couldn't help himself. He bent close and kissed each right angle of the brand, like a secret combination to a lock.

"That had to hurt," he said as he sat back, face flushed from his impulsive gesture.

Lilly didn't seem to mind.

"It wasn't that bad, 'cause the branding iron was really small, and *hot*. But yeah, it was a brand, because this was the kind of thing you do *not* want to get wrong. My mom gave it to me when I was old enough to write, when she taught me the cipher. It's pretty easy to learn when you're a kid. It's like a big game, and only you and a few other people even know the game exists, much less understand the rules."

Burt thought back to last night, through the fog in his memory, and remembered Lilly saying something about her mother being crazy.

Literally, Lilly had said.

That might explain the branding. Poor little young Lilly and her shoulder.

Lilly paused and took a deep breath.

"It means victory," she said, tipping her head toward her brand.

"Hmm," Burt said, still unable to prevent himself from talking. "Victory over who, or what? Illiteracy? Dead trees and ink?"

Before Lilly answered, Burt flinched as something high-pitched hit his ears. It was far off, but coming closer.

"Victory over the darkness," Lilly said.

She was watching him closely now, and Burt made sure he met her gaze without blinking or flinching, even as the distant whine grew louder in his ears. His skin had grown cold, prickling into goosebumps.

"Darkness," he repeated in a soft, cracking voice. "Always a good opponent to be victorious over, I guess."

Lilly nodded and waited, as if choosing her next words very carefully.

Just let 'em fly, Burt wanted to tell her, *the way you'd write 'em in your journals.*

The whining became the howl of sirens assaulting his ears. Fire engines. The first one roared past them, heading away from downtown. Burt had been smelling smoke for the past few minutes, but he'd been too caught up in Lilly to realize it.

"My family and I moved a lot when I was young, because we had to." Lilly began as soon as the second fire truck had blasted by them, siren wailing. "The people who brought the darkness always found us. Luckily Mom always saw them coming."

Burt caught himself thinking about full moons and bloodlines and transformations.

No judging, he told himself. *How would my history and my family's curse sound if I described it out loud to her?*

"What did they want?" he asked, his throat suddenly dry.

"Us."

"Your whole family? What about your dad? You mentioned your mom and your brother..."

"Never knew him," Lilly said in a cool voice. "He bailed before I was born. My older brother doesn't—didn't—remember him either."

Burt noted the use of past tense, but didn't want to ask about that. Not right now. He was rolling with it.

The sirens had stopped, he realized, but his ears continued to hurt. He forced himself to stop shaking.

"What did these, um, bringers of darkness want with you?"

"We'd have to join them, of course. And we'd be their secret weapons for spreading the darkness. One mind at a time."

"Not cool."

Lilly laughed at that, hard. Burt thought about how they'd laughed back on the floor of her bedroom, right after she'd helped get him free, both of them naked and scared out of their minds.

He felt almost nostalgic for that time, before he knew all this about her. Because now he was convinced that Lilly was mentally unbalanced, and that made him desperately sad.

"Definitely not cool. Which is why I can't let anyone get my books," she said, lifting up her satchel. It bulged to the point of breaking. "All that knowledge would be used for their nasty plans."

Burt had no response for that, so he pointed at her satchel instead.

"Holy crap, that thing must be heavy as hell. Let me carry it."

Lilly shook her head and watched a red Chevy Blazer with an Iowa City Fire logo on it rush past them.

"It's my burden to carry. But thanks."

Burt rubbed his ears, which still rang from the sirens. He took a sudden breath, inhaling more smoke and the scent of burning plastic.

Burning...

"Lilly," he said. "You didn't."

"What?" she said, innocently.

"You set fire to your apartment! That's what you were doing right before we snuck out!"

She pushed herself up and away from the steps with surprising agility, though she'd left her precious satchel behind.

"Who," she said, turning back to him with a laugh that had a slightly hysterical edge to it, "*me?*"

Burt was floored.

Who was *this girl?*

"But what about your books and papers and everything in your place?"

"Better to be burnt up than in someone else's dirty hands. And the rest of it—my clothes and computer and bed and stuff—it's just stuff."

She pulled him close, eyes wide, a mischievous grin on her face.

"Want to go watch it burn?"

"No," Burt said immediately, and then he stopped.

He laughed, rubbing the reddish stubble on his chin.

"Actually, *yeah*. Let's go watch that sucker go up in smoke."

Maybe we'll see whoever was in there, he thought, *come running out like a rat abandoning a sinking ship. And he and I can have some words.*

He stood up with a rush of blood to his head, a painful reminder of his hangover, and he staggered after Lilly as if he was drunk all over again. She jogged ahead of him, toting her full satchel on one shoulder as if it didn't weigh a thing.

He shook his head and rubbed his throat again, admiring Lilly's curves from behind.

Why not go watch her place burn up? Burt thought with a sudden thrill. *This day could only get more frickin' weird.*

Chapter Seven

Tommy nearly had a head-on collision two blocks from Dennis' apartment. Some idiot in a blue pickup with a white horizontal stripe down the side had turned the wrong way down the one-way street and barreled right at his car. The pickup had Illinois plates and a hood the size of a city block.

Tommy's reflexes heightened just in time, allowing him to not only swerve out of the idiot's way, but to also get a good look at the driver: a red-faced white dude with messy bleach-blond hair and arms covered in tattoos.

The two cars passed inches from each other, and Tommy swung back to the right-hand lane of the one-way street.

Stupid out-of-towners, he thought.

Dennis' apartment complex on Lynn Road was quiet when he drove up and parked on the street in front of it. He carried Corinne on his hip up the front walk and then up the steps to his friend's apartment.

Whoever had been here hadn't bothered closing the door. Holding his breath, Tommy pushed it the rest of the way open. He kept a close grip on Corinne in case she got any ideas. The door let out a painfully loud creak as it opened, and they stepped carefully inside.

Dennis' place looked like he'd had one of his post-game parties. A couple chairs in the kitchen had been knocked over, and someone had overturned the coffee table and broken one of the wooden legs off of it. The leg was nowhere to be found. Two of the four white Bose speakers had been pulled from the walls and smashed underfoot.

Tommy winced and pushed the front door mostly shut behind him.

Dennis wasn't—isn't—that burly of a guy, he thought. *He always seems frail to me, but there's a toughness to him that everybody sensed. Even if they weren't werewolves.*

He checked the rest of the apartment to make sure that nobody else was there. The kitchen, bathroom, and bedroom were empty, and the bed was more or less made. Tommy couldn't find any signs of struggle in here.

"Stay close," he told Corinne as he set her down back in the living room, which opened onto the cramped kitchen area.

He tried to recreate what had happened based on the positions of the overturned kitchen chairs and coffee table, along with the sounds he'd heard on his call with Dennis earlier.

"He's been *recruited*," Tommy whispered.

He thought about the bleach-blond guy in the pickup, wondering if he was somehow involved. But the pickup had been empty, as far as Tommy could see, and it was almost 8 now, half an hour since his interrupted call with Dennis.

Corinne bounced on the couch cushions next to him, kicking up dust and more mixed scents with each bounce.

Tommy drew a deep breath and relived the events of the phone call as he examined every square inch of the trashed living room.

At least two people had come in here. The person who'd picked up the phone, and the other one who'd done the subduing. Dennis had put up a bit of fight, enough to knock over the chairs and smash up his beloved surround-sound speakers. The missing leg of the coffee table, though, filled Tommy with dread.

He sank into the couch, inhaling the faded scent of pizza, pepperoni, and stale chips.

How many video game marathons slash pizza feedings had this couch seen? he wondered. *Too many to count. But that's all in the past now if they killed him.*

"Wait," he said, more to himself than Corinne, who had slipped off the couch and was now tiptoeing toward the bedroom. "They didn't just off him right here, Corinne. They *took* him somewhere. Recruited him. This wasn't an assassination like Watts was talking about last night. He's still alive. Gotta be."

Corinne stopped in the doorway to the bedroom and gave him a curious look, her strawberry-blond head tilted and her nostrils flaring.

"Don't wander off," he said, not wanting her to leave his sight again. Not after last night.

Staring at the amputated leg of the coffee table and the hole it had left in the overturned table, Tommy pulled out his phone. He knew he should call the cops. They would know how to deal with this situation and get the right people on the case to help Dennis.

But ever since Dyersburg and the corrupt way Smith the town cop there had dealt with that situation—covering everything up until the whole works blew up on everyone—Tommy had been having trouble trusting the police. Even if the police had been his employer for the past couple of months.

So instead of dialing 911, he hit Attix's number. The only cop he could trust, and he was pretty sure Attix trusted him.

He'd taken care of the Watts situation for me, Tommy thought as he waited for Attix to pick up. *Hadn't he?*

"John Attix." The older man's voice sounded a bit tired, but alert as always. "That you, Tom?"

"Yep," Tommy said, swallowing back a sudden flood of fear as he remembered Watts and the mess from last night. He inhaled Dennis' scent and couldn't say another word.

"Tom? You okay?"

Tommy pushed himself up off the couch to check on Corinne. "Yeah, I just. Well. Wanted to check on how things went last night."

The line was silent for a few seconds, long enough for Tommy to find his daughter bouncing on Dennis' unmade bed. He beckoned for her to come to him, but she just bared her teeth at him and bounced some more.

"You don't need to worry 'bout that," Attix said, his voice a few degrees cooler now. "Is that really why you called so early and woke my ass?"

Tommy exhaled, thinking, *Trust him.*

"No," he said. "I got another incident on my hands."

"Damn, son. What's gotten into you lately? *Now* what?"

"It's a friend of mine. I was on the phone with him this morning when someone came to his door and attacked him. I'm at his place right now, and the place is torn up, and he's *freakin'* gone."

"All right," Attix said, all business now. "These things happen like that sometimes, back-to-back and all that. Usually in threes, but hey, the day's not over yet, right? Anyway, you hang tight there, and I'll send a couple of uniforms over there. I'd come myself, but I gotta meet with my boss about that incident last night."

Tommy forced himself to relax. Help was on the way.

"Thanks."

"You know the routine. Don't touch anything, and don't try to cover anything up. We'll find your friend."

"Got it. I'm sorry about this."

"Nope," Attix cut him off. "Don't wanna hear it. Talk to you soon."

With that he hung up, and Tommy tucked his phone into his pants pocket with a shaky hand. A part of him wondered if calling Attix had been a good idea. Something about the way that Attix had said *Now what?*—with a hint of disappointment—had reminded Tommy of Mom all over again.

"Come *here*," he called to Corinne, who was still rolling around on the bed.

This time she listened, and they both went back into the living room.

Time's wasting, he thought. Each second he spent here, Dennis' recruiters took him farther away. He couldn't stop thinking about the guy last year with the voice. They guy had been working with the alpha-female Gwen back in Dyersburg. Gwen and Lance, just like in the King Arthur story.

Had she come back to Iowa, Tommy thought with a sudden chill, *not for me, but for* Dennis? *Did she need a new voice for her pack? A new wolf whisperer to replace Lance?*

"I frickin' hope not," he muttered.

Corinne tottered over to him, giggling all the way. Tommy held out a hand and caught her as she tripped on the overturned coffee table. He'd seen that one coming a mile off.

She wriggled out of his grasp by turning into her wolf form. And that gave him an idea. He wouldn't even have to touch anything, so this time at least he'd be following Attix's orders.

He didn't bring the change on all the way like his little wolf girl had, but just enough to make him get down on all fours. It just felt more comfortable this way as he put his nose (*snout? half-snout?*) to the carpet right next to where the coffee table was missing its leg.

"Dennie!" Corinne growled through her mouthful of sharp white teeth, and then she pushed her snout into the carpet like her daddy. She said his name again and bounced up and down, claws digging tiny gouges into the carpeting.

I smell Dennis!

Still down on the floor, Tommy reached out to pat her furry head absently. He'd also picked up his buddy's scent, but the trick now was to back-burner that smell so he could focus on any new, unfamiliar smells. Unfortunately, Dennis invited so many athletes and friends over on a daily basis that the carpet was saturated with multiple, overlapping scents.

Tommy's head wanted to swim with all the possibilities, but he refused to let it. Instead, he inhaled the scents, categorizing them, sifting them and sorting them by degrees of freshness—the newer ones had a kind of redness to them he could detect with his wolf nostrils, while the older ones were more green, like mold.

Within five minutes he had two new, very fresh, very *red* scents that he'd never smelled here before. They had to belong to the intruders who'd taken Dennis.

He locked those scents in his nose and wolf-brain and was about to push up from the carpet when he saw the blond fur covering his hands and arms. His fingernails had lengthened and curved into claws.

The change had come over him almost all the way, against his will. He hadn't even realized until that moment how tight his clothes and his shoes had become—especially his shoes, as his feet would expand to almost twice their usual size fifteens when the change came full-on. His mouth felt too full of teeth, and a low growl filled his wide chest.

"No," Tommy said, forcing himself to stop the change, but it was no use. A whimper slipped out his mouth, and he thrashed like a drowning man from where he'd hunkered down on the carpeting.

His arm flailed out, and he knocked another leg off the upside-down coffee table. It broke with a sharp snap, like a dried twig.

Tommy caught the broken leg in his claws before it hit the ground.

Gotta turn back, he thought with a low growl. *Before the cops show up and see me like this.*

As his shoes and jeans started to tear, Tommy looked around the room for Corinne.

"Can you turn back, girl?" he called out to her, voice husky and deep.

She shook her wolf head at him and bounded away. He couldn't tell if she understood his question, or if she thought he was just playing with her. Two-year-olds were *so* much fun.

Ignoring the change for the moment and instead keying in on those two new scents, Tommy padded through the apartment on all fours, sniffing every nook and cranny to try to find where the two people had been. Corinne followed him, barking with laughter as Tommy left a trail of his own tattered clothes in his wolfish state.

She beat him to the small black rectangular object under the couch that the scents had been pointing him toward.

"Careful!" Tommy said. He thought it might be a tiny bomb, or a nasty little bladed weapon. With the way the past twelve hours had been, he was ready for anything.

But all it turned out to be was a simple on/off switch that was half the size of a light switch. It had no wires, and didn't seem to be connected to anything. Before he could stop her, Corinne flicked the switch with one paw.

With a breath-taking rush—and an achingly familiar surge of disappointment he felt every time the change ended— Tommy shrank back into his regular body. His fur receded and his bones and sinews popped back into their default human size.

His little wolf-daughter, however, didn't change at all. She was still wolfing it up.

"What *is* that thing?" he whispered, reaching out a shaky hand for it. Corinne growled at him at first, and then grudgingly handed it over.

He fought the urge to flick the switch the other way again and shuddered. The thought of not being able to change out of his wolf form, *ever*, was something that had haunted his nightmares from the moment Mom took him out under his first full moon as a kid. And this switch somehow controlled that.

As soon as I got close enough, he thought, *it triggered my change. And wouldn't let me change back.*

He looked over at his daughter and let out a nervous chuckle.

"Good thing we didn't bring anyone else along who didn't know about our were side. That would've been awkward."

Corinne scampered away as he spoke, bouncing from the couch to the overturned coffee table and into the kitchen, suddenly full of wild energy.

Tommy ignored her for a moment so he could examine the little black gadget. He couldn't see any markings on the switch itself, no ON or OFF imprinted into the hard gray plastic.

But on the back of it was a tiny sticker, barely a centimeter wide. Despite its size, he could make out the logo on the sticker as clearly as if the sticker was a foot wide. There were no words. Just a sickly-looking wolf face, not unlike that of Wiley Coyote from the Road Runner cartoons, trapped in a red circle. A red line cut the wolf's face in half, diagonally.

He'd seen this before, on a website that should've gone away for good a year ago.

It was the logo for Antiwolf.com.

"*Shit*," Tommy said. Corinne stopped running circles through the apartment and skidded to a stop at the sound of his voice.

She was at his side in an instant, pawing at the switch in his hand. He knew she wanted to get it in her mouth and bite it in two.

"No, girl," Tommy said, carefully sliding the switch into the pocket of his torn-up jeans. He stood up with a growing rage filling him. "We're going to take this back to the sick fu—I mean, *fella* who made it. Maybe our buddy Dennis will be there. But Uncle Carl is going to wish he'd *never* created his nasty website to sell stuff like this."

Chapter Eight

The burning apartment was half gone by the time Burt and Lilly made it back. Orange flames ate at the blackened portions of the walls that were still standing, and the wooden front door was holding on by just one hinge. The basement apartment that had belonged to Lilly and her absent roommate was hidden in fire, rubble, and soot.

A crowd had gathered on the street, which had been blocked off by fire trucks and the red Blazer with the Fire Department logo. Burt and Lilly tried to lose themselves in the crowd as the fire heated up the morning air until it was hard to breathe.

All those books, Burt thought. *All those papers. Even if she did just think of it all as* stuff, *it was her stuff.*

Burt moved closer to Lilly and took her fisted hand, unable to think of anything to say to her about her losses. She'd just let it all burn.

He *hated* feeling sad. It was such a worthless emotion, never helping him whenever he felt it. But standing next to Lilly in a growing crowd of rubberneckers as they all watched the firefighters try to put out her burning apartment, a sense of melancholy filled him.

This was not how his day was supposed to turn out after last night's amazing turn of events, starting with meeting Lilly. He was fascinated by her, even if she was a bit on the crazy side. Burt could handle crazy.

The last remaining rafter holding up the roof gave way with a sharp crack, and the burning apartment collapsed in on itself. The firefighters yelled at the crowd to get back, and then they charged at the fire one more time with their hoses, like soldiers sensing weakness in the enemy. It was almost enough heroism to make Burt want to be a fireman. Almost.

He looked over at Lilly next to him. He'd expected to see some tears, maybe a dull look of shock on her face. But she wasn't even looking at the fire. Her gaze darted all over the crowd around them, examining each face as if searching for a familiar face. Unlike Burt, she'd remained on high alert the moment they'd come in sight of her burning apartment.

Her eyes blinked fast, like she was trying to get soot out of them from the fire, and her mouth moved, just barely. Like she was talking to herself.

Her hand clenched even tighter under Burt's fingers.

"There he is," she whispered, nodding her head a fraction of an inch. "The guy in the Iowa State Cyclones T-shirt over there, with the black hair. He's one of *them*."

Burt tracked through the crowd, which had grown to nearly four dozen people now, all of them gathered like sheep around the dying fire. Closest to the fire, with one hand gripping the yellow Do Not Cross tape stretched in front of him like a lifeline, stood a dark-haired guy about his age, maybe a couple years older.

The guy pretended to study the fire. But Burt could feel the guy's eyes on him, somehow. Like he had *two* sets of eyes, and one set was invisible and way stronger.

"That takes some guts," Burt muttered in a joking tone, hoping he could cover up the fear in his voice, "wearing a Cyclones T-shirt in Hawkeye country."

"Or maybe he just doesn't care," Lilly said. She slid her satchel around her body until it was behind her, keeping her body between its precious contents and the dude in the red State T-shirt.

"What did you, um, *hear?*" Burt said. Goosebumps filled his arms despite the heat from the fire. "What's his story?"

Lilly slipped her hand out of Burt's grasp and looked at him like she'd forgotten he was still at her side. She rubbed her face and shook her head.

"He keeps it all pretty tight inside him. But I can feel his confidence, and his anger. We messed up his plan this morning."

And what was his plan? Burt thought, afraid to ask. *To come back and gut us? But he could've done that last night, while we were passed out, possibly poisoned.*

Caught up in his own personal conspiracy theories, Burt didn't realize for a few seconds that he was now standing by himself. Lilly was off, pushing through the crowd toward the guy. Burt reached out to stop her, but she didn't even slow down when he pulled on her arm.

"Damn," he muttered, rubbing his aching throat. The smoke made it hurt worse, and it clogged his nose and made his sore eyes water.

This better not end up with me on a leash and wearing a collar again.

But by the time he'd pushed past the dumbstruck neighbors in their pajamas, T-shirts, and sweat pants, and caught up to Lilly, the guy in the red T-shirt was gone.

Lilly paced in a big half-circle behind the crowd, nearly getting run over by a couple firemen lugging four-foot long axes. Her lips moved fast this time as she searched the crowd and the rest of the street around her. She shook her head and gave him a hollow-eyed look.

"He was just here," she said as Burt approached her.

He stopped to look up the street at the houses surrounding Lilly's ruined apartment. No red T-shirt anywhere.

Lilly stepped closer and rested a hand on his chest.

"Can't you smell him," she said, "and track him down by that?"

Burt recoiled, embarrassed and ashamed of his weak wolf skills. His only defense was a good offense. Or, in this case, a mediocre offense.

"Can't *you* snag his thoughts out of the air," he said, irritation slipping into his voice out of nowhere, "and find him by that?"

Lilly gave him a long, disgusted look and then turned her back on him.

Our first fight! Burt thought with a giddy mix of excitement and dread. *Hope it's not our last.*

He took another look at the crowd, and he noticed that more than a few people were looking at him and Lilly curiously. They were attracting the wrong kind of attention here.

Burt left Lilly by the first fire truck and walked toward the second, pretending to watch the fire with what he hoped was a dazed look on his face. All while he searched the crowd for anyone suspicious.

He tried to pick out that dark, earthy smell he'd first scented back in the apartment, but his nose was nowhere as sophisticated as his brother's. He was like a blind man hunting for a light switch.

I could just keep walking, Burt thought. *Leave this whole crazy scene and never have to deal with those so-called "bringers of darkness" from Lilly's delusions again.*

His dark thoughts made him slow to a stop at the other side of the blocked-off street. The sidewalk that headed off toward downtown away from here seemed to beckon to him. It was a straight and smooth hike from here. No bumps, no detours, no side tracks.

And no Lilly.

Burt took one last deep breath of smoke and charred apartment, and then he nearly jumped out of his skin.

He'd singled out two unique scents in that long inhalation. One was Lilly's smell of jasmine, mixed with bad wine and nervous sweat. The other was that dark, earthy scent. The one from Lilly's apartment, right before they'd escaped.

Burt nearly laughed out loud at his unexpected success. He'd never done this sort of thing before, despite all of the training Tommy and Aunt Mel had tried to give him in the past year.

Now that he had the smells separated in his head, he could follow each one, like two trails splitting off in the woods. He tracked Lilly's back to her, and he wrapped an arm around her waist and squeezed. He felt a sudden urge to apologize for thinking her delusional.

"Follow me," he whispered into her ear instead. The words came out almost like a growl. Lilly complied immediately, letting out a tiny gasp at his sudden appearance.

Or maybe it's my renewed confidence, Burt thought. *Or possibly my beard, which always takes the ladies' breath away.*

They left the crowd and the fire behind. Giddy with his newfound powers, Burt charged after the earthy smell. He tracked it past the front bumper of the fire truck and across the front yard of Lilly's next-door neighbor. The trail grew a bit unstable for a moment, probably due to the water thrown up from the fire, washing out the smells. Burt wanted to panic, but instead he drew Lilly close and found the scent trail again.

They hurried through the neighboring back yards, with Lilly's satchel back at her side and bouncing into Burt's hip every few steps. They spread out a bit so they could move faster. A few seconds later they were both jogging, and then, as the trail grew even stronger in Burt's nostrils—his nose had grown cold with condensation at some point—they started running.

"Crap," he said a block later, out of breath and slowing to a fast walk.

The trail led right to the bank of the twenty-foot-wide Iowa River. And at the water, the trail simply stopped.

Burt ran toward the river, as if moving faster would keep the scent from washing away. His legs burned, and his injured throat felt like it was bleeding on the inside, leaving a hot trail of destruction down into his belly.

We let him get away, he thought. *The dude who tried to poison us both. And tied me up like a dog.*

Lilly walked to the edge of the river, staring at the muddy water rolling past. She hugged herself as if she were freezing, but the summer day had grown warm already, with little humidity at all. Another perfect August day, with arson and bondage and wild goose chases and more on the agenda.

Burt was too out of breath to speak, and too ashamed to meet her gaze.

Tommy would've caught this guy. Caught him and beat him to a pulp.

There were no tracks on either bank that he could see, but he knew the guy had come this way. He must have jumped into the nasty water and what—swam downstream? Crossed to the other side? Flown away?

"So," Lilly said. "Looks like the bringers of darkness won this round."

She shook her head sadly, and then she suddenly clapped her hands together and looked over at Burt with a slightly manic grin.

"Wanna go get some breakfast?"

Chapter Nine

Tommy wished he could just take Corinne to Aunt Melanie's and have his aunt watch her for the next few days. He had a feeling he wasn't going to be attending any classes at the community college for a while, and Attix's other fugitives were going to have to remain missing for a little bit longer. He didn't want to think about what he might do to any runaway law-breaker if he caught up to one of them now, anyway. In his current state, it would be Watts all over again.

But going to Aunt Mel's would require a ton of explaining and apologizing after Corinne's run-off last night. And then there was the whole issue of the return of Druncle Carl's werewolf-bashing business, which Carl was most likely running through his website now that his store was closed for good.

Dammit, Uncle Carl. Why couldn't you just stay away?

Waiting for the light to turn green on their way out of Iowa City, Tommy checked on Corinne in the back seat. She watched him carefully in the rearview mirror, her big blue eyes laser-focused on his reflected gaze.

"Hey baby," Tommy said with a catch in his voice. "It's okay. I'm not mad at you. It's just that da—I mean, uh, that *poopy* Uncle Carl who's got me all ticked off."

Corinne let out a laugh at that.

"Poopy Unka Carlo!"

Tommy grinned and hit the gas as the light finally changed.

"You are *so* right, little girl."

He remembered how upset Melanie had been near the end of her marriage to Carl last year, after he'd moved out. She'd been fielding drunken texts from him every day and fearing for the safety of her two boys every night. Carl hadn't been able to wrap his brain around the fact that the woman he'd been married to for over a decade was actually a part-time wolf.

It had all come to a head on that bad, bad night in that fancy house outside Iowa City. The same night that Corinne showed that she had it in her for the first time, to the family that had wanted to adopt her, illegally.

He shuddered at the memory. Blood and fur everywhere, on those expensive tile floors. And Melanie—in her wolf form—had been the one to pull Tommy and his little baby girl out of there, permanently screwing up Carl's drunkenly laid plans for the adoption.

The bright sun cut through the windshield as they passed the last few University-owned buildings and entered the strip-malled section of the small city next door to Iowa City. The smells of gasoline, hot asphalt, and fried food quickly filled the air. Tommy had never been a big fan of Coralville, so of course that was where Uncle Carl had ended up.

"I'm hoping he's closed up his little computer shop and moved on," Tommy continued. Talking to Corinne helped to settle his nerves, and she always seemed to be listening intently.

Maybe my voice has the same effect on her that Dennis' has on me, he thought. *You never know. That'll come in handy when she's a rowdy teenager.*

He felt a sharp twinge of guilt and fear for his missing friend, and he tried to stifle it by talking more to his little girl.

"He was supposed to shut his website down a year ago, remember? Right after he caused all that trouble with his sneaky lists of people he knew or suspected might be werewolves, like you and me." Tommy paused and swallowed, feeling a sudden tightness in his chest. "He even had *Nina's* name and address on his list, out there on the web for anyone—"

"Nina! Nina Nina Nina!" Corinne called out, clapping her hands wildly at the mention of her daddy's friend.

Friend? Tommy wondered. *Or was it girlfriend? Ex-girlfriend?*

He wasn't sure anymore. They hadn't talked or texted or anything in over two weeks. He could feel Nina slipping away. Just like everyone he used to be close to, except for Corinne and Burt.

Tommy sighed and tried to put her out of his mind once more. It wasn't an easy task.

The road here ran parallel to the brown expanse of the Iowa River on their right. The river was at its widest here, separating the two cities like a protective moat. Tommy caught a glimpse of the dome to the Old Capitol up on its ridge, and then chain restaurants and pawn shops blocked his view of the campus.

Tommy took a couple turns off the main drag and ended up at the empty shell of Carl's old store.

He knew he was supposed to stay at the apartment to wait for the cops to show up and help start the search for Dennis. But that anti-wolf logo on that nasty little switch had filled Tommy with a need to move, to act, that he couldn't ignore. Somehow his uncle had gotten involved in this, which made it family. And that made it personal. The cops would just have to play a little catch-up, for now.

The sign for Hi-Tech Computers up on the red-bricked wall had been painted over, but a handful of yellowed signs and posters still covered the square plate-glass window. The round window set into the heavy-duty door was cracked in a dozen different places, and the door itself had a big black gouge in it right next to the doorknob.

Tommy parked in one of the three empty parking spots in front of the store and slipped out of the car for a closer look. He kept the engine running and reminded Corinne to stay where she was.

With a sinking sensation in his gut, he caught sight of two tiny anti-wolf logos on the various papers and posters taped to the inside of the big window. Tommy fought the urge to punch the thick glass. Part of him had been hoping that the logo he'd seen at Dennis' place had been a fluke, no connection to Carl. But this cinched it. Carl *was* involved. At least it gave him a lead on Dennis, slender as it was.

Who needed the cops, he thought, *when you're as good of a detective as me?*

He scanned the rest of the faded ads and signs in the window, but there was no information about what had happened to the store, no mention of where it had moved or if it had closed permanently. Just dusty advertisements for out-of-date sales on phones, tablets, and laptops, along with a poster for a tech conference that was now six months in the past.

He peeked around the ads on the dirty window, but it was too dark to see anything inside. He moved back to the front door.

Someone had tried to force their way into the store here, most likely with a crowbar. Tommy glanced up and down the street around him, checked on Corinne back in the car—she was leaning forward as far as she could while strapped into her car seat, watching him intently—and then tried the doorknob.

When it refused to turn, he focused all his strength on his right hand and arm.

With a hot flush of blood that shot through him like electricity, his hand widened and grew thick with fur, just long enough for him to twist the knob hard, once. The door popped open with a creaking sound, and then a rank smell of mildew hit him.

Turning back to his car with a triumphant grin, he shook out his right arm as if it had fallen asleep on him. It returned to its normal, less-hairy state immediately.

A year and a half ago, he thought, *I never would've been able to even think about doing something like that.*

He went back to shut off the engine to his car and unstrap Corinne from her seat.

"In we go," he said to her, holding tight to her hand. He felt a mix of excitement and dread at what they might find in there. "Let's see what your not-so-Great Uncle was up to before his latest plan backfired on his drunk butt."

Tommy had never been inside Hi-Tech Computers before, and he could tell that even when it had been open for business, the place hadn't been too impressive. The store itself was barely four hundred square feet, with room for just two aisles of merchandise and a register set up on a metal countertop to Tommy's right.

The shelves that had made up the pair of aisles were overturned on the ruined, greenish carpeting. The carpet gave off a mildewy stench, clogging Tommy's nose. It looked like a pipe had burst at some point and soaked the floor, and nobody had ever cleaned it up. Water dripped through the cracked tiles in the ceiling in the exact center of the store.

If there had ever been any hi-tech computers or gadgets in this place, there was no trace of them now. The shelves now held only rust and green splotches of mildew. Tommy picked up a squirming Corinne and walked carefully inside, wincing as his ruined shoes squelched in the wet carpeting.

Maybe Uncle Carl got his stuff out of here, Tommy thought, *before anyone broke in to clean him out. Maybe, but I hope not.*

He checked the register, but it refused to open, and it looked water-damaged and rusted beyond repair. He couldn't find any relevant papers or other traces of Carl's business in the main area of the store at all.

He crunched through the debris to the little room marked Not an Exit in the back of the store, and he once again wolf-handed the locked door open.

As soon as he stepped into the five-by-five office, Tommy's vision went black, and Corinne screeched in his arms.

He didn't feel any sort of pain other than Corinne's claws digging into his arm and his side. Just a total lack of vision. Blackness.

He staggered back into the store, nearly slipping and falling on the slick, slimy carpeting. His vision returned as he regained his balance and pried Corinne's claws out of his side.

She'd changed into her wolf form the instant they'd tried to pass through the door to the cramped office. Tommy checked himself for fur and claws as well, but he knew from the dulled smells in his unstretched-out nose that he was still human. Corinne's reflexes were just that much faster than his own when it came to leaping into her wolf skin.

He wanted to set her down to get some distance between those razor claws of hers and his bare skin, but he didn't dare risk it. Not with whatever was in that office.

Carl must've left a little parting gift for us, he thought, *just like the people who'd taken Dennis away from his apartment. A gift for any weres who might visit this shithole. Nasty.*

He crept closer to the office, looking carefully at the doorframe and the door itself. Whatever Carl had put in there, it had affected Corinne and him both, at the same time. He wondered if her vision had gone blank on her too, but there was no way to ask her that and have her understand the question.

"Hush," he whispered to Corinne, who was whining and wriggling in his arms. "And don't nip your father. We're not going back in there. Not yet."

The doorframe was cheap wood that had been painted white to match the rest of the décor of the place, though everything now was tinged with green from the water leakage and the humidity. In both corners of the doorframe, two small black buttons had been installed on the inside.

Bingo, Tommy thought with a sneer. *More anti-wolf tech, no doubt.*

Tommy set down Corinne and picked up a piece of metal shelving. He used the metal to pop the first button off the frame. He caught it before it fell into the office. The only markings on the button, which was no wider than a quarter but twice as thick, was a red antiwolf logo on the back.

With a growl—and using more force than was really needed—Tommy pried off the second button and caught it. He dropped them both to the floor and stomped on them like bugs.

What kind of messed-up tech was this? he thought, staring at the broken bits of buttons under his shoe. *Who'd ever make something like this?*

Imagining electrical fields and underground dog fences, Tommy motioned for Corinne to stay back. He inched through the doorway again.

Nothing.

No blacked-out vision this time. He'd guessed right—the buttons had been the culprits for that little trick with the doorway.

He took another step inside, waiting for another mental blast that never came.

The tiny office wasn't carpeted, and it had stayed protected from the burst-pipe flood thanks to the closed door. It held just a cheap metal desk on the right, a black table on the left, and a pair of filing cabinets straight ahead of him. The tops of the desk and the table were completely empty except for layers of undisturbed dust.

Tommy searched the sides and bottom of the desk before he picked up the metal folding chair that had been knocked to the floor behind it. The desk didn't seem to be booby-trapped like the door had been. He sat down and allowed himself to exhale. Corinne jumped onto the desk, landed on all fours, and slid halfway across the smooth top with a squeal. She left a trail behind her in the dust.

"Shh," Tommy said, and then let out a laugh as Corinne came back to lick his face.

The desk drawers were all empty, just as he'd expected, and the file cabinets behind him were locked. For the third time that morning, he used a burst of wolf strength to force open the locks. In the bottom drawer of the second file cabinet he was rewarded with a small treasure trove from his uncle.

He pulled out a pile of receipts and invoices, a pair of dented hard drives, a small stack of twenty-dollar bills that smelled like fish, and a cheap black flip phone. He set all of it on the empty, dusty desk and began going through it.

The paperwork focused on Carl's failed business, and the papers were dated no later than the end of last year. Tommy drummed his fingers on the two hard drives on the desk next to Corinne. He thought about stuffing the smelly cash into his pocket, but realized he didn't want any money that Carl might have touched.

That left the cell phone. Tommy doubted it even had any charge left in it, so he and Corinne both let out an exclamation of surprise when the phone beeped happily the moment Tommy unfolded it.

He hit the voicemail button, just for kicks, and got only one message: thirty seconds of hissing static, with occasional bumping sounds, as if someone had dialed this number by accident while driving down the road and never realized it.

Something about the lack of a voice on the other end, though, unnerved Tommy. He noticed that Corinne's fur was now standing straight up, but she was looking out through the office door and into the ruined store.

We need to go, Tommy thought suddenly.

He killed the voicemail playback and folded up the phone. He was just about to shove the flimsy phone into the pocket of his jeans when it started buzzing in his hand.

He looked from the phone over at his daughter. Her canine eyes were as big as his must've been at that moment.

"No way," he whispered as the phone buzzed again. It seemed to get louder with each insistent buzz.

Corinne nudged the hand that was holding the phone closer to his face. Her nose was wet and cold.

"This better be Uncle Carl," he muttered, opening the phone to take the call.

"You haven't been using this phone in a long time, Heying," the voice on the other end said before Tommy could say a word.

It wasn't Uncle Carl.

The voice was low, deeper than the voice he'd heard on his interrupted call with Dennis earlier that morning, but this time it was obvious the speaker was male.

"I haven't needed to," Tommy said, the first thing that popped into his head. He couldn't stand the silence on the other end of the line.

"Huh," the other person said, sounding the tiniest bit amused. "You must be the *nephew* Heying told me about. Checking up on your uncle's *store*, are you?"

Tommy's mouth was suddenly too dry to speak.

How did he know we were here? he thought.

He needed to kill this call, scoop up Corinne and those hard drives, and get the hell out of here. But his legs felt like tree trunks, rooted to the office floor. He looked at the walls and ceiling, but couldn't see any kind of cameras aimed at the office. Just cobwebs and water stains.

"I'll send someone by to assist... *Tommy*, isn't it? Tommy Roling. A beast since you were what, three or four? You must be *fairly* strong now. We could *use* a fellow like you. And is your little *girl* at the store, too? We'd *love* to meet her as well."

At the mention of Corinne, Tommy broke his paralysis. He stepped closer to the desk to grab her, and he pressed the phone tight to his ear.

"Any friend of my uncle's," he hissed, "is nobody I want to meet, today or ever. Screw you."

He killed the call and stared at the tiny phone, which was dancing on his quivering palm.

We could use a fellow like you.

Tommy didn't even have to summon any of his wolf strength to crush the cheaply made phone in his fist. It broke into tiny pieces with a satisfying crunching sound.

We'd love to meet her as well.

"We've got to get out of here," he whispered to her as he dropped the pieces of the phones to the floor. "And we've got to get out of *town*, too."

With a flurry of sudden movements, he grabbed Corinne and the two hard drives and left everything else spread out on the desk in the office. His shoes slapped across the wet carpeting of the store as he maneuvered past the fallen shelves. He kicked open the door leading outside, glad to breathe in the fresh air from outside. He didn't even bother closing the door behind him.

They'd be looking for him now. And Corinne, too. He'd just put a target on both of their backs with this little visit.

Half a minute later, with Corinne secure in her car seat and the hard drives next to him, Tommy was charging out of town toward the interstate and their rented farm house. He couldn't get out of Coralville fast enough.

Chapter Ten

Burt refused to let this Lilly situation spiral out of hand. He hadn't felt this excited about something in his life in a *long* time. Not since the big move to Iowa City from his hometown. In the past year, he'd had a blast exploring his new city, jumping from one job to the next, knowing that nothing was permanent and all that really mattered was having fun and staying ahead of the bill collectors. He met some cool folks here, added a ton of numbers and contacts to his phone, and memorized the streets and roads that crisscrossed the city.

I was so naïve and ignorant back then, Burt thought as he bit through the half-inch layer of cream cheese coating his everything bagel.

He had to restrain himself from shoving the whole thing into his mouth and then going up to the counter of the bagel shop to order half a dozen more.

He swallowed, wiped his mouth, and looked over at Lilly at last. With her bagel and large coffee sitting next to her, untouched and growing cold, she was back in the world of her coded writing. She'd pulled out her journal the moment she'd sat down in the bagel shop, and followed it with her trusty black pen.

They hadn't spoken a word since their walk here from the river.

Burt took a deep breath.

"You want to explain why you just gave up back there?" he said as calmly as he could.

Lilly kept right on writing.

He fought the urge to grab the pen out of her hand and toss it across the room. Luckily, she looked up at him right before he could make a move for it.

"Gave up?" Lilly asked, blinking quickly as if to get back to reality from whatever it was she was scribbling down.

Probably gibberish, Burt thought.

He took a big gulp of hot coffee. He exhaled, tongue burning. It made the pain in his throat seem to fade a bit, which was worth it.

"You didn't even try to chase that guy down back at the river," he said. "I could've caught him. I had his scent nailed down. I was in it, man. So close. We could've caught the guy who messed with us last night."

Lilly set down her pen and closed her book.

"I know," she murmured, reaching out a hand for him, but stopping a few inches from his fingers. "I just got scared. You were brave, though. I'm glad I was there when you made your breakthrough. You were really excited to be able to tap into your wolf skills like that for the first time. I could tell."

Burt squirmed a bit at that. She'd plucked his story out of his head like pulling an apple from a tree.

Thanks, he thought, *for reminding me I'm a werewolf newbie.*

"So that guy. What was his story? What did you learn about him? Was he part of that army of darkness or whatever?"

"*Bringers* of darkness," Lilly said, and then shrugged. "Like I said before, he kept things pretty tight inside himself."

"But... there was something you got from him, wasn't there?"

Lilly glanced around the café at the stay-at-home moms and their little ones, along with a few serious-looking folks with their laptops or tablets, typing and tapping away.

Her lips moved softly, as if she couldn't quite keep up with all the stories she was hearing. All the voices in her head. Then her mouth became a straight line.

"He wanted to *kill* me, Burt," she said.

Burt swallowed with a grimace as a chill ran through him. Her eyes looked so tired and so scared that he didn't know what to do or say. He touched her hand with his, but it felt too little, too late.

"I pushed hard," she said, "back at the fire, while you were trying to get through the crowd to grab the guy. Maybe a little too hard. I think I spooked him, poking around in his head, and he ran."

Burt squeezed her hand.

"What'd you see?"

"It was the strangest thing," she said. "I got just pieces of his story from last night and this morning. He was definitely inside my apartment before we got there, and he injected something nasty into the bottle of wine we drank—he had these syringes with tiny, tiny needles, and he shot poison or whatever it was into all three bottles of wine we drank last night."

"*Three* bottles? Did we *really* down three, just between the two of us?"

Burt wanted to give Lilly a high five, or at least a fist bump, but fought the urge. That was some hard-core drinking.

"As if the wine alone wasn't enough to knock us flat," she said, rubbing her face. "Anyway. He was in my roommate's room the whole time, hiding and waiting. That was him creeping around this morning, too. With a big-ass knife. For *us*, Burt."

Burt nodded almost absently at that. Knives didn't worry him too much, not when he could overpower the wielder of that knife with his wolf self. But a knife had to be pretty terrifying to a non-were like Lilly. He could relate.

"So why wait? He could've slit our throats at any point last night. What was he waiting for?"

Lilly just stared at him.

"Listen to you. You make it sound so matter-of-fact, that he could've killed us both while we slept."

Burt thought of all that had happened back home in Dyersburg last year. Things had gotten pretty ugly his final night there, with the multiple werewolf attacks and the ugly scene at the bar. He felt that same dizzying, drunken sense of being out of control again right now. It was a feeling he both loved and hated.

Realizing she was waiting for him to respond, he just shrugged. The movement made his sore throat twinge again.

"What about the other stuff from this morning?" he asked her. "The leash and the collar? And how about that bolt on your bedroom wall?"

Her eyes clouded over, and her pale face suddenly flushed pink.

"You're not going to believe me."

Burt reached out with his other hand so he could lift her chin. His hand shook, the tiniest bit.

"Just tell me," he said, and then let out a soft laugh. "I know it's been a helluva morning. But when you start your day waking up naked next to a huge wolf—well, things can only get *better*, right?"

Lilly shook her head incredulously at that, and when she grinned, Burt felt his world shift back into place. She was going to be okay. As okay as she could be, given the circumstances.

"That bolt," she said, giving his hand a quick squeeze of her own, "has been there ever since I moved in."

"What?"

"Told you. I know it's weird and messed-up. After a while you'll get used to the crazy."

"You never wondered why your bedroom had that?"

"My roommate's bedroom has one, too. They said it was a special feature when we toured the place. You could use it to hang stuff, super-heavy stuff. We all made lame bondage jokes, and then... we kinda forgot about it. Weird, the things you get used to, isn't it?"

"Yeah," Burt said, feeling suddenly tired. The coffee wasn't having any impact, and something about the way Lilly kept avoiding the issues was wearing him out. It was like she *wanted* to be a victim.

"Was the guy working with someone else, or was he there on his own with his special leash and collar? Are we dealing with a lone loonie here, a murderous stalker maybe, or something bigger? Did someone find out about your books and your skills?"

Or, he thought, *did they find out about* my *skills?*

Burt snapped his mouth shut before asking that question. He'd hidden it so well, buried all thoughts of his werewolf life so deep he didn't think anything would be able to uproot any of it.

Lilly didn't answer. She just sat there, rubbing her ink-stained hand, looking down at the table.

Burt thought about the weird sense of double vision he'd gotten from the time he'd met the gaze of the Cyclones guy. How the guy hadn't looked directly at him, but he could still feel the guy watching him intently. Somehow. It didn't make sense, and he didn't have the words to ask Lilly about it at that point in their breakfast date.

"So," he asked instead, "what do you suggest we do?"

"Run," Lilly said, without hesitating.

"Where?" Burt said just as quickly. "Where is any place safe?"

"Far from here. Like where my mom is, maybe?"

"I thought you said she went crazy?"

"An institution is pretty safe, once you get inside."

Burt fought the urge to put his face in his hands.

"We can't go there," he said, softly. "We can't just *run.*"

He leaned back to take a look around him. The other people in the café were starting to feel different to him as the morning stretched towards noon. The mothers seemed to be hovering over their little kids, unsmiling and waiting for the first sign of misbehavior. The college kids didn't seem to be studying, but pretending to be poring over their books only so they could eavesdrop on what Lilly and Burt were discussing. His skin prickled with paranoia and fear.

"It's all I know how to do," Lilly whispered.

Burt let go of her hands and pushed away his half-eaten bagel and cold coffee. All the other folks in the place seemed to hold their collective breath and lean in closer. Even the barista stopped steaming milk and grinding beans.

"Fine," Burt said as he got to his feet. He leaned in close over Lilly so she was the only one in the shop who could hear his voice. "I'm taking you to see my brother. He'll talk some sense into you. He'll show you that *staying* here is the best thing to do."

W e've got to *go*," Tommy said as soon as he'd closed the door to Corinne's room so she could take her nap in peace.

Burt was still stinging from the $20 for cab fare he'd just spent to get back home. Tommy hadn't answered his phone all morning, and he didn't dare call up and ask Aunt Mel for a ride, not after their big falling-out this past summer. That woman was touchy when it came to drinking and partying. So it was a yellow cab from the bagel place to the farm house, and Burt's wallet was officially empty. Lilly took care of the two-dollar tip.

"*No*," Burt said, hating the whine that crept into his voice. He drummed his knuckles on the kitchen table where he sat next to Lilly. "I want to *stay*. Right here, Tommy. This is my home now, bro."

Tommy sat down in the squeaky chair across from them and looked at Burt as if he'd grown a second head.

"Why?" Tommy said. "Everything's going to hell here. Uncle Carl's been stirring up the pot against us werewolves—" he sucked in a breath and looked over at Lilly "—hope I didn't spoil anything there, Lilly."

When she shook her head with a distracted grin, Tommy continued.

"And bringing in all this gadgetry to mess with us weres, like these switches. It's almost like he's trying to start some sort of revolt against us. The guy's not right, I tell you. And he's gotten hooked up with some other folks who sound even worse than him. I think they're watching him, or looking for him. We need to get away for a while, wait for things to cool off."

Burt picked up the small switch from Dennis' apartment that had been sitting in the middle of the table. It gave him something to do other than to look at the fear on his brother's face. He thought about all that Tommy had told them about his own set of adventures this morning, first at Dennis' place, and then at Carl's abandoned computer store.

Something had gotten to Tommy this morning. Something, or some*one*.

"But what about Dennis?" Burt asked, turning the switch over and over in his hand like a coin, but never flipping the switch from its OFF position. "How can you sit there knowing someone took him away?"

"*Recruited* him," Tommy corrected, almost automatically. The sound of his voice made Burt and Lilly both look up at him, but his eyes were distant as he stared in the direction of Corinne's room.

"But he's gone," Burt said in what he hoped was a calm, soothing voice. "Most likely kidnapped, man. Let's call your buddy Attix, for starters."

"Already did," Tommy said, dropping both big hands onto the table with a pair of hits. "I just don't know how much he and the rest of the cops can help."

Burt shot a quick look at Lilly, but her face was expressionless as she tapped her pen on her lips. Burt tried to shrug off the awkward silence. He lifted the tiny black switch higher in his hand.

"Who the hell would make these things?" he muttered, turning the gadget over and over with his forefinger and thumb.

"People who hate wolves," Lilly said, drawing bits of her cipher on a paper napkin while they talked.

"It's nothing new," Tommy said. "Just think about your whistle you got last year that can jerk anyone out of their wolf skin. They just found a way to mass-produce stuff like that, with batteries and electrical fields and who knows what else. Carl's probably working on an anti-wolf phone app right now."

Burt let out a shaky laugh.

"Listen to you, talking tech. Aren't you the same guy who never learned how to work the remote for the TV?"

"It's just a theory. I don't understand *how* they work at all. But after the phone call I got this morning at Carl's old store, it all seems more and more plausible. They were monitoring Carl's cell phone for any activity. They called me *right* after I tried to listen to his voicemail. Freaky."

Lilly set down her pen at that. She crumpled up the napkin and snapped the cap onto her pen.

"Think they followed you from your uncle's store?" she said in a low, emotionless voice.

Tommy's face tightened the tiniest bit at that. He hadn't thought about that, Burt could tell.

"I doubt it," Tommy said, rubbing the blond stubble on his chin. "But there was this blue pickup. I nearly had a head-on with him on my way to Dennis' place. And then I could've sworn I saw the same truck in Coralville, behind me. Twice."

"Oh hell," Burt said. "Do you know how many blue pickups there are in this city? Especially in Coralville, where all the hicks live? It's a coincidence. And you two are ridiculous. Are you really planning on leaving?"

Tommy nodded.

"It's not safe here. Uncle Carl and his people are trying to get to us, get revenge or something. They left a trail of those damn gadgets all over the place."

Burt let out all his frustration in one loud exhale.

I've worked hard to get here, he thought. *I'm not bailing now, just when things get a little weird. We need to stay and figure all this out. But nobody will listen to me, damn it.*

"And how can you help Dennis if you leave town?"

"He's not here anymore," Tommy said quietly. "He's gone, too."

"How do you know?"

"I just do."

"Where you gonna go?"

"I've got a couple places picked out."

Burt realized he'd been holding tight to the seat of his chair in his irritation. He loosened his grip and lifted his hands, only to see fur covering them again. He put them under the table again, fast.

"You okay, Burt?" Tommy asked. He'd seen the fur, no doubt about it.

Burt let out a wordless growl.

"Burt?" Lilly said from the other side of the table, her voice tight with fear.

"Throw that thing out," Burt said, his voice low. He couldn't stop the change coming over him, and the little black switch on the table seemed to be causing it. "If you don't break it, I will."

He didn't dare look at Lilly right now, as he fought to keep his wolf side down for the second time that day. He felt embarrassed of his true nature, his cursed wolf side. If she saw him turn, and heard his agonized screams from the process, he'd never be able to meet her eyes again. It was humiliating.

Tommy snatched up the gadget and hid it inside the palm of his big hand. Burt saw the dark blond fur on his brother's hand and arm thicken, just for an instant.

Burt's bones began to stretch, fur covering his arms and legs and face, his nose dripping from the explosion of smells filling it. A groan started to slip out his tightly clenched teeth—which had elongated as well—when it all stopped with a small crunching sound.

He looked up and saw Tommy drop the pieces of the ruined switch onto the table from his big hand.

"Thanks, bro," Burt whispered in his regular voice, his body fully human again.

And then he promptly fell over backwards in his chair.

"Are we in agreement, then?" Tommy said as his face hovered into view above Burt, a grim smile on his face. He reached a hand down to help Burt up from the floor. "That it's time to hit the road?"

Burt would've preferred to stay on his back and close his eyes so he could sleep off the past half-day and write it all off as a bad dream. But Tommy wasn't going to let any of that happen, the pain in the ass.

"*Crap*," Burt said. He stood up with a rush of blood to his brain, nodded at Lilly, and let go of Tommy's crushing hand. "I fricking hate it when you're right, man."

Chapter Eleven

They were on the road to Chicago no later than two o'clock that same afternoon.

Tommy could barely grasp how fast everything had just changed, for him and Burt and Burt's odd friend Lilly. And Corinne—poor Corinne—was back in her car seat once more, fidgeting and growling at Burt next to her with every bump they hit in the road. At any moment, Tommy expected her to flip over to wolf mode.

"Can we please put some music on?" Burt said from the back seat, in an *are-we-there-yet* tone of voice. "There's gotta be a '90s rock station somewhere."

Tommy ignored his brother. He'd killed the ringer on his cell phone, and he'd been tempted to turn the thing off altogether, for fear that whoever had called him back at Carl's old shop would track him down again.

How long would it have taken someone to get to Carl's shop? he wondered as he goosed the accelerator. *Five minutes? Ten? Or had it all been a big bluff, just someone with a grudge against Carl messing with me?*

Tommy hadn't felt so out of his league since his teenage years, when they'd played a big-city school for a football scrimmage, and he'd gotten his bell rung by a guy fifty pounds and half a foot bigger than him. That same guy was supposedly getting ready to go in the first or second round of the NFL draft, he'd heard.

He didn't like feeling small like that. So it was time to put some distance between this place and him and Corinne.

And as for Dennis...

Sorry, man, Tommy thought. *You'll have to be on your own for now. Hopefully wherever they take you, you'll be surrounded by gullible werewolves who love the sound of your voice. Because for right now, I've got to protect my little girl. My pack.*

"I think someone's following us," Lilly said just ten minutes after they'd hit Interstate 80 heading east out of Iowa City. She sat in the shotgun seat as Tommy drove, and she'd been silently watching the city recede through her side-view mirror.

"Hush," Burt said from the seat directly behind her, an edge of exasperation in his voice. "You're just imagining it, Lilly."

Tommy checked the rear-view mirror and saw that Burt was in the middle of what looked like a potentially dangerous game of patty-cake with Corinne in the back seat. Every now and then, Corinne's fingers would curve, the nails stretching into claws, and Burt would pull away as fast as he could. Corinne cackled with glee at this violent game.

"I don't *see* anyone," Tommy said to Lilly, careful not to sound too judgmental. "And I've been keeping an eye on things back there since we left home."

"Hmm," Lilly said, shaking her head and going back to watching the road behind them in her mirror. She didn't sound convinced.

Tommy could only shrug. He didn't know why Burt had decided to hit on this pretty—but obviously unstable—girl last night at the bar, though they'd both noticed her intense writing without commenting on it.

Maybe he just got lonely after I left, he thought. *The guy didn't like to be alone, ever.*

Back in their kitchen this morning, Lilly had gotten more and more agitated as time passed and they hadn't yet got on the road. At that point they hadn't even decided where they were going to go.

Tommy had been itching to know what Lilly's story was, but he hadn't been able to ask Burt about it. Not while she was sitting at their kitchen table, spouting off her weird tales about the creatures of darkness and her far-from-sane family. He didn't dare look at Burt while she was talking, though his skin had prickled with discomfort and no small dose of fear from Lilly's stories.

And then there were the hard drives.

When Burt had started to dig in his heels again about leaving town, even after Tommy had gone over everything that had happened in Carl's store twice, Tommy had pulled the beat-up old drives from his car. He just hoped that his laptop's antivirus software was up to the task of dealing with any crud they might encounter on Carl's hardware.

"I don't wanna see Uncle Carl's porn stash," Burt had said, pacing back and forth behind the kitchen table. Meanwhile, Tommy and Lilly leaned in close to the laptop's cracked screen.

She'd picked up her hardbound journal and pen again, Tommy noticed, scribbling away without even looking at her writing hand. He'd already gotten used to her behavior, and he knew better than to look too closely at her coded text. It made his eyes want to cross.

"I *hope* that's all we find," Tommy muttered absently, using his mouse to click through the mess of folders and files littering the first drive he'd hooked up to his laptop. "But I doubt it. Here. Look at these invoices he scanned in, all for his store. Fifteen, no, sixteen payments here for Hi-Tech Computers back in January, February, and March. Each of them for seven grand even, every week, all from some company in Chicago called Great Plains Tactical. Carl had some good business going there for a while, and then it looks like it all went away. Probably about the same time his business went belly-up."

"Seven grand every *week*," Burt said. He'd stopped pacing and was squinting down at the screen, one hand on Ellen's back and the other on Tommy's left shoulder. Tommy could feel Burt quivering with excitement, and possibly fear. "Not bad, Uncle Carl. I could go for that sort of income stream."

"But just like everything else with him, he couldn't make it last. I wonder who he pissed off back in March at Great Plains Tactical."

"I don't like that name," Lilly said softly. She scribbled her unreadable letters and shapes even faster with her left hand.

"I hear you," Tommy said. "Sounds like a company for gun nuts or something. Tactical what?"

"Let's not get caught up in the details, kids," Burt said. He reached for the mouse, but Tommy slapped his hand away.

"Can you write down this address?" Tommy asked Lilly, pointing at the last invoice, dated March 21st.

She looked over at him, blinking quickly as if she was just waking up, and lifted her pen from her journal for a second.

"Lilly?"

"Sure," she said, scribbling it down in tiny block letters— readable letters, in English—on a fresh page of her journal.

Tommy glanced back at Burt as Lilly carefully tore out the sheet with the address, a pained look on her face. Burt's face was carefully blank, and he avoided Tommy's gaze, pretending to be examining the laptop's screen.

They ended up collecting half a dozen different addresses, all from the Chicago area, before the first hard drive made a loud whirring sound and died on them. The second drive refused to be read at all, but by that time all three of them were too agitated to try more Tech Support on it.

"So is this where we're going, then?" Burt said. "We can't just Google them from here?"

He used his finger to pin the piece of journal paper containing all the addresses to the kitchen table. The fingernail of that hand was starting to stretch into a claw, Tommy noticed.

"Chicago?" Lilly said, a hint of hope in her voice.

"Damn," Tommy said. He grabbed the piece of paper from under Burt's claw, thinking of the miles between here and there, and all the potential trouble waiting for them at the end of it. And his friend—possibly his girlfriend—Nina as well.

"Chicago," he said.

* * * * *

The tires hummed loudly down the interstate as they approached the Iowa border. Tommy felt oddly nervous about leaving his home state for Illinois, and he kept wanting to tap the brake pedal to knock out the cruise control so they'd slow down. He'd only been to Chicago twice in his life, and both times he'd been overwhelmed by the traffic, all the people, and the sheer immensity of the sprawling city.

A sharp cry from the back seat made him jump, and the car rocked as he involuntarily jiggled the steering wheel.

"Shit!"

Tommy could tell by the gravel in Burt's voice that his big brother had changed. When he did manage to risk a look into his mirror, two wolf faces—one small and grinning and the other much bigger and growling—looked back at him.

"She frickin' *bit* me," Burt growled.

"Torry Unka Burt!" Corinne said. *Sorry Uncle Burt!*

And then she burst into tears.

"Okay," Tommy said in his best dad voice. "Everyone calm down. I really don't want to have to pull over, but you guys have to stop fighting while we're on the interstate."

He checked the rearview to make sure no fur was flying. Burt had already changed back—Tommy caught a wince of pain on the guy's skinny face, just for a second—but Corinne was still wolfing it up. It usually took her a while to go back to her human self, especially if she was upset. She snuffled and whimpered a bit longer before settling down, but she kept her fur on.

"Oh my God."

Lilly had turned in her seat to take in all the action in the back. Tommy struggled to keep his gaze on the road as he watched Lilly's hazel eyes widen and her mouth drop open. She stared at Corinne in shock.

"She's got it in *her*, too," he began. "I thought you knew."

But Lilly was already shaking her head, never taking her eyes off Corinne's furry face and red-rimmed eyes.

"No," she whispered. "It's not that. I've already come to terms with all that, thanks to Burt this morning."

Tommy caught his brother's gaze in the rearview, just for a second, and raised his eyebrows suggestively.

Burt answered with a raised middle finger.

"It's just," Lilly said, "I can't *hear* her. Her story. It's like she's muted to me."

Tommy touched the brake without even thinking about it. The car rocked and began to slow.

"What do you mean?"

Lilly dropped back into the passenger seat, exhaling a long breath that smelled like rat poison to Tommy's hypersensitive nostrils. She patted his forearm gently.

"There's nothing wrong with her," she said. "I've just never had that happen before. She's a complete blank slate to me. I got nothing on her."

Good, Tommy almost said, but bit back the word.

"What do you do with all these stories?" he said instead. "I mean, I know you write them down and all, in your code, but... then what?"

Tommy felt the car begin to descend slightly as they approached the Mississippi River bridge north of the Quad Cities. They were going to have to deal with city traffic for a while, so he needed to hear her story quickly, before he got distracted.

"We put it all together," Lilly said.

"Who's 'we'?" Burt interrupted from the back seat, where he'd been using baby wipes to clean blood off the hand where Corinne had sunk her razor-sharp wolf teeth.

"Well, we're *supposed* to do that," Lilly said. "Bind them all up into books and seal them. But Mom never showed us how to, before she, well. You know. Before she lost it. So I just write them all down as fast as I can. It helps me stay sane. I guess she and my brother never figured that out."

"Or maybe they just didn't write fast enough," Burt added from the back seat.

Lilly turned and gave him a sharp look at that, and Tommy focused his attention on the cars starting to build up around them as they approached the northern edges of Davenport and Moline and the start of late-afternoon commuter traffic.

Wonder what she wrote down in her journal about me, Tommy thought. *And Corinne, too.*

Tommy stifled a shudder at that thought. But the idea that Corinne was able to somehow keep Lilly out of her head was fascinating. The kid never failed to amaze him. He thought back to that night in the bar in Dyersburg, right before all hell broke loose with the other werewolf pack.

She'd saved my butt that night. My sweet little girl, who'd been barely a year old at the time.

Corinne had been able to ignore the commands of Lance, the guy that Gwen had brought with her to convince Tommy's pack to do her bidding. Lance had that same kind of command in his voice that his friend Dennis had.

Has, Tommy added. *Present tense.*

He thought again about how he was running from Iowa City instead of trying to find Dennis. But the sight of that Antiwolf logo on the gadget—which had messed with his and Burt's ability to control the change—had made Tommy so determined to track down Uncle Carl that he'd nearly forgotten about his friend who'd been abducted that morning.

He inhaled through his nose, easily recalling the two distinct scents he'd uncovered this morning in Dennis' apartment. He'd find them, and he'd find Dennis, too. But he had a little girl to protect, and he had a feeling the person he'd spoken to on Carl's cheap plastic phone had an antiwolf agenda of his own.

When given the options of fight or flight, it was easy to stop and fight when it was just you. But when you had someone small and defenseless in your care, flight made a whole lot more sense in most cases.

But that didn't take away the sharp sting of betrayal he felt about his missing friend. He just hoped Dennis wasn't caught up in the same drama as Watts and his puppetmasters.

I should've left Corinne with Aunt Mel and gone off after Dennis, he thought. *Instead, I let some bogeyman on the phone chase me off, to Chicago of all places. I should turn around right now...*

But instead of pulling a U-turn, he pressed down on the accelerator and weaved around a pair of tractor trailers.

Tommy glanced in his rearview. The silence in the car had grown awkward. Even Corinne had gone quiet in the back seat. Tommy tapped the brakes as traffic thickened, and he glimpsed the gray length of the four-lane bridge stretching out over the dark brown waters of the Mississippi ahead of them.

The next time he checked his rearview, a blue pickup shot out behind the tractor trailers as well, gaining on them. Tommy stared hard at the pickup, needing to see if the driver was the tattooed guy with the bleached-blond hair from Iowa City, even though he knew that was impossible as well as utterly paranoid. No way that guy could've been the same guy he'd nearly crashed into on his way to see Dennis this morning.

He stared a second too long, just long enough to see that there were two white guys in the cab of the truck. One dark-haired in the shotgun seat, one light-haired in the driver's seat.

When he looked back through the windshield he saw that traffic just ahead of him had slowed to a crawl for road construction at this end of the bridge.

"Hang on!" he yelled, braking hard.

The Grand Am's back tires squealed, and the car slid to the right, giving off acrid black smoke. But Tommy managed to avoid rear-ending the red Festiva in front of him, which was creeping along with the clogged traffic at twenty miles an hour.

"Dude!" Burt shouted from the back seat. "Excellent stunt driving! But really, not necessary, bro."

"Tunt diving, Daddy!" Corinne cackled from the back seat.

While waiting for his pounding heart to go back to normal, Tommy let the car slowly roll forward along with traffic. He risked a quick glance over at Lilly in the passenger seat.

She wasn't smiling. She leaned forward to stare into the side-view mirror, her lower lip trembling, her pen and journal forgotten on the floor of the car.

"It's him," she whispered in a voice that made Tommy want to shift fast into his wolf body. Rubbing the strange black tattoo on her left shoulder, she added, "One of the bringers of darkness. And he's *right* behind us."

Tommy didn't even hesitate. He cranked the wheel hard to the left and punched the accelerator.

No way are any of Uncle Carl's cronies catching us today, he thought, just as his car obliterated its first orange-and-white construction barrel.

Chapter Twelve

I should be the one behind the wheel, Burt thought as he held on for dear life next to his niece in her wolf skin.

Corinne was about to claw her way out of her car seat in her excitement, but Burt had no intentions of reaching over to try and hold her down. Not after she'd taken that bite out of his hand earlier.

He yelled as Tommy's Grand Am plowed into another orange construction barrel on the left-hand shoulder and sent it flying. By the third collision he'd gotten used to it enough to look back through the rear window to see who it was they were running from.

At first he didn't notice anything strange behind them other than all the cars backed up on every side. Many of them were now trying their best to inch away from Tommy's car to prevent any damage from the flying barrels that his car continued to send into every lane of traffic. Far below them, Burt got a glimpse of docked boats on either bank of the Mississippi, bobbing peacefully on the current, oblivious to the commotion on the bridge.

And then Burt saw the big blue pickup screech out of the traffic jam and plow over the downed barrels in the median after them.

The guy in the driver's seat made Burt think of one of the big Callahan brothers at first, with his wild hair and wide shoulders. But it was just some tattooed goon in a sleeveless gray T-shirt. Burt's gaze jumped to the guy's passenger.

Burt recognized the passenger. It was the guy in the Cyclones T-shirt, fresh from the smoking remains of Lilly's apartment.

"She's right," he shouted in a voice that felt way too high to be his own. "Punch it, bro!"

More barrels went flying, and then Burt was thrown to his right, hitting the car door hard enough to crack the window. Tommy had yanked the car off the left shoulder and back onto the interstate, right past two shocked-looking construction workers holding their shovels uselessly in front of them.

"Still there," Burt called from his post at the back of the car, unable to look away from the pickup plowing through the wreckage Tommy's car left in its wake, and making some fresh wreckage of its own. The dark-haired guy in the passenger seat was pointing right at Burt and talking fast, head bobbing with each big bump the truck hit.

With a screech, Tommy forced the Grand Am onto the bridge more or less by force of will. The other cars had seen him coming and moved out of his way just enough for him to squeeze past. Burt exhaled in relief.

The pickup didn't bother with squeezing. It sent mirrors, bumpers, door handles, window glass, and other car parts flying around it in a cloud as the truck blasted after them.

Burt noticed in the dim corners of his consciousness—all of his energies were otherwise focused only on the pickup behind them—that Lilly was muttering unintelligible words from the front seat, and Corinne had gone silent next to him. The only sound other than the roar of Tommy's car was his brother's harsh breathing and his repeated question: "Are they still back there? Are they still back there?"

The blue pickup hit a garbage truck, which made the pickup spin sideways. The pickup got wedged between a bridge support and the garbage truck, and it quickly disappeared in a gray cloud of smoking coming from its spinning back tires.

"We're good, for now," Burt said, and he turned his body toward the front of the car at last.

He glanced to his left and started to reach—carefully—for Corinne, but she had clawed her way out of her car seat and was scratching madly at the door handle.

"Damn," Burt said as they roared onto the Illinois side of the bridge at last. "Glad you got childproof doors back here, bro."

"She shouldn't be able to reach the door handle from her car seat," Tommy said in a high-pitched, nearly breathless voice.

"She got out."

"What?"

"Dude, relax," Burt said. "Just drive."

He clenched his jaw and held his breath as he reached out for his furry little niece. He wished he knew how Tommy could focus the change on just part of his body, like his hands, so he could've snagged Corinne up in his clawed and muscular wolf hands. But the thought of trying to force the change now made his head hurt and his already-sore throat tighten up on him.

So he grabbed Corinne high on her pup shoulders and held on for dear life. He managed to wrap one hand around her front legs and the other around her back legs, keeping her claws at a distance. She was like a basket of snakes as she wriggled in his grip. But her struggle only last a few seconds, and then she relaxed into Burt's grip. Some of her fur started to recede. Some, but not all.

"Burt?" Tommy called. He was trying to follow the action in his rear-view mirror while swerving all over the road.

"I got her," Burt said. "She slashed through the belts holding her into her car seat. Crazy kid wanted to jump those guys in the pickup, no doubt."

Burt shivered as he spoke, knowing that Corinne would've done just that to protect her pack. He glanced up at Lilly, not sure if he wanted to see the look on her face. But she'd closed her eyes, and she appeared to be sleeping now. He wanted to reach up to her and brush the sweaty hair out of her face, but he had his hands full.

Is she really right, he wondered, *about that guy in the pickup? Or was this all some sort of weird delusion of hers?*

The car started to slow, even though they'd left the bridge and the clogged traffic behind them. It was as if Illinois had less-congested roads that started right at the border.

"Hey," Burt called out. "What's wrong? Cops?"

Tommy shook his big head back and forth, slowly.

"No. It's not that. It's just—I shouldn't be here. Running away. I should've turned around back in Iowa City and followed that guy in the pickup as soon as I saw him. I never should've given up on Dennis."

Burt rubbed Corinne behind the ears and scratched under her chin. The tension had drained out of her, and she stretched out on his lap and yawned. Two rows of tiny, white, and sharp teeth flashed at him. He caught a look of utter loss on Tommy's face from his mirror.

Burt recalled Tommy's story from earlier today. The 7 a.m. phone call, the knock on Dennis' door, the kidnapping that Tommy heard take place but could do nothing to prevent.

He'd only met Dennis a few times, and Burt had always felt compelled to run errands for him and Tommy whenever the three of them were hanging out, like getting more beers or running to the store for chips and dip. Something about Dennis made Burt feel like a third wheel. Or worse, a servant.

Plus this Dennis dude was always hanging around with the hot female student athletes from the U of I, so Burt felt more than his fair share of envy for him. Though he didn't think the dude ever deserved to get kidnapped the way Tommy had described it back in the kitchen of their rented house.

"Hey," Burt said as their speed dropped down to about 40, with cars whizzing past them on the right while they poked along in the far left lane of the interstate. "Are you trying to cause a wreck? Either punch it or get out of the fast lane, man."

"I've *been* out of the fast lane," Tommy muttered, or at least that was what Burt thought he said.

All of a sudden, Tommy was pissed off, and Burt was pretty sure it wasn't him this time, causing it. Or so he hoped.

"Pull over and let me drive," Burt said. "We've got to go to Chicago, not back to Iowa City. Not until things cool off back there. That was the plan. Plus, if we turn around now, we'll run right into those jokers in the pickup. And Lilly and I already *met* the guy riding shotgun in that truck."

Lilly snapped awake at the sound of her name with a sudden, harsh inhalation. Her eyes were wide with fear and confusion as she looked all around the car to get her bearings. Then her eyes grew tiny as slits as she squinted out through the back window at the bridge fading into the distance, all too slowly for Burt's taste.

"He wanted to kill me. Probably both of us," Lilly said in a sleepy, little-girl voice.

The car swerved again as Tommy pressed down on the accelerator and looked first at Lilly and then at Burt in his mirror.

"You knew the guy in the *passenger* seat? But that's impossible. I saw the guy *driving* the truck, back in Iowa City. This is messed up."

"Tell me about it, bro."

"We should go back there and get some answers from those two guys."

"So why you speeding up, then?"

Tommy snorted and shook his head, as if in disbelief.

"Because I just had a killer idea, that's why. Hold on tight to Corinne, bro. We're making a pit stop."

Burt sometimes wished he understood his brother better. Most days he was cool with the odd ways that Tommy sometimes acted.

Hell, I do weird shit myself, he thought. *All the time. I can't judge. Even if this time seemed a bit short on the logical side of things.*

Tommy drove them to a huge gas station with over forty pumps, just off the interstate, and backed his car into a parking spot that gave them a good view of the interstate. As soon as he shut off the car, he turned on Lilly.

"Tell me about the second guy in the pickup."

Lilly rubbed her eyes, which had grown more bloodshot as the afternoon had passed. She rubbed them with an ink-splotched hand. Burt noticed she'd dropped her pen and journal at some point, and never picked them up again. He wasn't sure if that was progress or not.

"This morning, he somehow knew I was in his head, trying to pick up his story," Lilly began in a hoarse voice. She cleared her throat. "What little details I was able to find about him reassured me that leaving town wasn't a bad idea at all."

"So he's the one that you said was a, what, a bringer of darkness?"

Lilly's only answer was a quick nod.

Tommy glanced back at Burt, just for an instant, before turning back to Lilly. Burt saw his brother's hands shaking before Tommy crossed his arms in front of his chest tightly.

"Do you know how crazy that sounds, Lilly?" Tommy asked in a soft voice.

Lilly turned her head a tiny bit, as if she was going to look back at Burt. He wanted her to, badly. He would've shown her all his support, all his burgeoning love for her. Whatever she needed, he'd give her. But she didn't turn the rest of the way toward him.

"I know," she said to Tommy. "But you have to understand. My mom was really religious. It wasn't any one particular religion. It was kind of *all* of them. She absorbed them all as she traveled, and she took the darkest aspects of each one to create her own belief system. It made for an interesting childhood for my brother and me, because we never stayed in one place long enough to put down roots."

Burt wanted to pipe up and ask about Lilly's father, but Tommy beat him to the punch with a different question.

"And you kept moving... why?"

"They were always after us."

"Okay, I thought you were gonna say that. Tell me what they were trying to do to your family. I know you said that they wanted to get you to work for them, somehow? Like they were *recruiting* you, somehow? Maybe?"

Burt watched the road connecting the oversized gas station to the interstate and fidgeted next to Corinne, who'd passed out a few minutes earlier in his arms. She was back in her car seat with its slashed restraints. She stubbornly refused to shift back into her human form.

Burt had to chuckle at that. The kid had already had a nap, and now she was crashed out again. Must've had a rough night last night.

"Yeah," Lilly said. "You could call it that. They were always really... subversive. That's the best word I can think of to describe them. Well, other than slimy. They'd get a hold of our phone numbers, even though we kept changing them every few weeks, and talking to them on the phone always made me feel like I needed a ten-minute-long shower."

"Huh," Tommy said, just as a battered blue pickup rolled off the I-80 exit half a mile ahead of them.

"Um, guys?" Burt said. "You seeing that up there?"

"Yep," Tommy said, starting up the car without a moment's hesitation. "Hang onto Corinne again."

"Whoa," Burt said. "Hold up. Are you gonna try running them off the road in your crappy Grand Am?"

Tommy flinched at that and fiddled with his keys, but didn't kill the engine.

"You want to *talk* to them?" Burt said.

"No," Lilly said.

"Yes," Tommy said.

"Then let them come to us," Burt said. "Right here, with all these witnesses around us here. No need to rush into them head-on like a defensive tackle, bro."

Tommy turned back to look Burt in the eye. Burt met his gaze, but barely. The intensity on Tommy's face scared him, but also gave him hope.

My brother is no one to mess with, he reminded himself. *In his wolf shape or not.*

A moment later, Tommy nodded and turned off the car. He glanced at Corinne and the hardness in his face softened, just a tiny bit.

"Watch over her," he said, and then pushed himself out of the car. "The rest of you stay inside, and stay alert."

"I got your back," Burt said, legs so heavy he didn't think he'd be able to get up out of the car if he'd wanted. "I'll be your wing man, um, from right here in the car."

As the pickup rumbled up to the gas station, Tommy closed his door and leaned against the car. The Grand Am's shocks squeaked from the pressure of his big, immovable body.

"This is a bad idea," Lilly whispered, rubbing her arms with blue-tinged and ink-spattered hands.

A dented chrome hubcap spun off the front tire of the banged-up pickup as the truck bounced over the curb. Its front bumper was ruined, hanging off the front at a rakish angle. The truck's engine roared suddenly, and for a bad moment Burt was convinced the truck was going to ram right into them, crushing Tommy to a pulp between the two vehicles.

But then the truck slowed, black smoke spitting out from under the hood, and it rolled to a stop a foot away from Tommy's car. The truck engine idled with a coughing sound, filling the air with the stink of burnt oil and plastic.

The bleach-blond guy with the tats rolled down his window and glared at Tommy.

"Who gave you fools permission to run off like this?" he spat in a raspy voice.

"Why are you following us?" Tommy said at the same time. "And what do you mean by *permission*, man?"

While Tommy was distracted by the driver, the guy in the passenger seat tossed a small black quarter-sized device in Tommy's direction. When it hit the closed driver's window, it stuck there like a bug.

Burt had enough time to suck in a breath before the world went completely black on him. Corinne woke and began screaming in fear and confusion next to him.

Some wing man I am, Burt thought as he tried to grab his niece in a blind panic. *Took them all of five seconds to mess us up.*

Chapter Thirteen

Tommy should've snagged the wicked little button out of the air before it ever hit the car. He should've seen this coming.

But he'd glanced at the big tattoo on the bicep of the bleach-blond guy driving the truck, and he'd let himself get distracted by it for a second too long.

Now the others in the car, he thought, *are paying for it.*

For some reason the gadget that was now stuck to his driver-side window didn't have any impact on him, but he could hear his daughter's wild screams from the back seat, along with Burt's loud, panicked pleas for her to calm down.

Those noises were more than enough to jolt Tommy into action: he scraped the black button off the window and ground it into the asphalt with the heel of his shoe.

The screams stopped immediately, though he could still hear the rattle of claws against the back door and window. He didn't dare look at Corinne at that moment, however. No more distractions.

Both guys in the pickup were trying to pull something else from their bag of tricks. Tommy reached right through the open window of the pickup. He grabbed the smaller guy by the front of his Cyclones T-shirt with his left hand, and he snagged the driver by the throat with his right. Instinctively, he'd forced the change partway into both arms, so that from the forearms down, his hands were coated in fur and tipped in claws.

"Why don't you guys come on out of there so we can *talk*?" Tommy said, his nose a few inches from the driver's face. He ended his sentence with a growl.

The sound of a car door opening made him flinch, but it was only Corinne and Burt backing him up. Corinne leapt across the dented hood of the pickup in a strawberry-blond flash, while Burt hustled around the truck so he could glare down at the passenger with his fisted hands on the door.

The inside of the truck smelled like armpits and cheap beer, which wasn't much of an improvement from the oppressive stink of gasoline from the pumps outside. Nostrils flaring, Tommy looked from his pack-mates on the other side of the truck to the wincing passenger and the fidgeting driver, and his eyes came to rest again on the bloody tattoo carved into the driver's upper arm. It was a red heart, realistically inked, pierced by two flaming arrows on either side. The tattoo looked new, and seemed to still be wet, somehow. He had to force his gaze away from it.

"Let's go," Tommy said. "Everybody out."

An awkward minute or two later, with more than a little persuasion from Tommy and Burt, the two men dragged themselves out of the cab of their truck, and then everyone gathered in a circle in the big bed of the blue pickup. Luckily there hadn't been too much broken glass and broken bits of metal and other debris to clean up after the chaos the tattooed driver had caused back at the Mississippi.

Tommy sat next to the guy with the tatts, while Burt stuck close to the dark-haired passenger who smelled bad. Corinne paced back and forth in front of both strangers, still in her wolf form. She sniffed their shoes but otherwise kept a safe distance. For now.

Neither guy seemed surprised to see a small wolf traveling with them, which made Tommy very, very suspicious.

Lilly sat in the corner of the truck bed near the driver's side, her journal held up in front of her like a protective wall. He could hear the soft, familiar scratching of her pen on the pages of her journal.

He glared at the men who'd followed them here and tried to decide where to begin. He and Burt and Corinne had experienced way too many weird occurrences and coincidences in the past day, and they needed to be explained. He thought again of Dennis and felt time slipping away from him.

While he was gathering his thoughts, Burt spoke up.

"You were in Lilly's apartment last night," he said, pointing at the passenger with the red T-shirt. "You tried to poison us both, and then you slapped a leash and a collar full of needles on me. I only have one question. Why the hell should I *not* beat you to a pulp right now?"

The guy looked up with bloodshot, light brown eyes that he focused not at Burt, but at Lilly.

"It was for your own good."

Tommy had to suppress a shudder at the sound of the guy's voice. It was completely without emotion, almost robotic. He looked closer at the guy, trying to get a better read on him—his smell was off, too, Tommy realized, almost like rotten meat, or sickness. But every time he met his eyes, Tommy's own eyes experience a weird double-vision.

What the hell, he thought, *have we gotten ourselves into?*

Burt hadn't responded to the guy's words, because he was too busy watching Lilly. She capped her pen, closed her hardcover journal, and set them down next to a broken sideview mirror that used to be attached to a red car from back at the bridge.

"For my own *good*," she repeated. "Is that what you've been telling yourself? Is that how you justify what you've been doing?"

Watching Lilly and the guy with the Cyclones T-shirt, Tommy felt something click in his head. These two knew each other, and not just from this morning. He tried to catch Burt's attention, but his big brother was just staring at Lilly, eyes wide.

"The way you were drinking, you were going to tell him everything," the guy said. This time, his words had a trace of emotion to them. Mostly anger.

Lilly sighed. "So you poisoned our wine to get me to shut up? Do I not get to have friends? Is that it?"

"Lilly," Burt said, his voice barely a whisper. "Who *is* this guy?"

Lilly looked over at Burt in surprise, as if she'd forgotten all about him until now.

"Oh," she said, catching herself as she tried to pick up her pen again. She squeezed her hands together instead. "Yeah. This is Eli. They got to him first and recruited him a few years ago. He finally caught up with me. He's my older brother."

"Whuh," was all Burt could say. It sounded like he'd been punched in the gut.

Corinne made a beeline for Burt and snuggled her furry head under his arm, as if she knew he needed comforting right then.

They, Tommy thought, feeling a sudden chill in spite of himself. *The so-called bringers of darkness.*

"You told Burt he was going to kill you both," he said to Lilly, trying to pull this conversation back around to something resembling reality. He wanted to reach out and pull his little girl close to him. "That he was in your apartment with a knife, and he could've killed you at any time last night."

"But I didn't," Eli said.

"Shut up, Eli," Tommy said without looking away from Lilly. "You burned down your apartment to get away from him. And he's your brother? Wait. You told us he was in an *institution*, Lilly. Please. *Explain.*"

She stopped wringing her hands so she could tap on her book.

"Do you really want to know?"

She was looking at Burt. He looked hurt, but Tommy could see his brother's stubbornness returning like a slow burn building heat.

"Bet your ass I want to know," Burt said.

Lilly nodded and gave him a tiny smile.

"Check out the tattoo on Eli's left shoulder," she said.

Burt made a move to reach over to Eli, but the smaller guy squirmed away from him. Corinne growled at him, just once, and Eli rolled up the sleeve of his red T-shirt to reveal a tattoo of a heart, pierced by arrows, on his shoulder. Just like the blond guy's, except Eli's was less raw-looking. He'd had this tattoo for a while.

Tommy leaned closer, still looking at the inked scar. He wanted to hold his breath to keep from inhaling Eli's earthy, almost rotten scent. Burt nearly bumped heads with him as they both leaned in over Eli.

"You see it, don't you?" Lilly said.

"What?" Tommy said, confused.

"It's bumpy underneath," Burt said, and then he snapped his fingers. "The tattoo's covering a brand like yours, Lilly."

"It's a cipher," Eli said, rolling his sleeve back down and looking at Lilly with a frown. "And the cipher is a kind of steganography. There are layers to the characters, but nobody'd notice them unless they got really close. Like microscope-close. A permanent reminder of our mom's delusions of grandeur."

"So why didn't you just *tell* me?" Burt said to Lilly. "I mean, you told me everything else—well, what I thought was everything else. The life on the run from the bad guys, the stories, the journals, all that. Did you think it'd be too much if you told me it was your *brother* we were chasing through the streets of Iowa City?"

Lilly met Burt's gaze for a few moments, and then she looked down at her hands, which for once weren't holding a writing utensil or a book.

The blond pickup driver sighed with impatience next to Tommy.

"Just wait, bud," Tommy said to him. "We're getting to you."

The guy glared at Tommy, and Tommy felt a surge of adrenaline—*Bring it, blondie.*

"Marg," Eli said. "Chill out."

"*Marg?*" Burt said, biting back a laugh. "What kind of name is that?"

"Shut it, shaggy," hissed the guy that Eli had called Marg.

"Anyway," Tommy said, feeling more pangs of impatience. "So it looks like he was protecting Lilly, I guess from herself as well as from Tommy. And when you two chased him, he ran. That makes him not trustworthy in my book. Write that down in your journal if you want, Lilly."

Lilly flinched at that, eyes widening with surprise. She'd actually been in the process of reaching for her pen again.

"What I want to know is how he's connected to my uncle," Tommy said. He pointed at Eli. "That little black button you tossed at my car. Where'd you get it?"

Eli had been inching away from this conversation for the past minute, until his back was tight against the dented bed of the truck. He looked like he was getting ready to deny everything, and then he caught Tommy's gaze and heard Corinne's low growl.

"They gave us a bag of them before we left," he said, and Marg exhaled loudly with frustration next to Tommy. Eli kept talking in his monotone. "Said we might need them to defend ourselves, and showed us how to use each kind. But that one didn't seem to bother you."

"Yeah, I noticed. So you said 'each kind.' How many different kinds are they, and who *gave* these damn things to you?"

"Five kinds. His uncle."

It took Tommy a second to figure out that Eli had answered both of his questions, and he felt a chill come over him. Eli was pointing at the guy named Marg.

Another uncle, Tommy thought. *Everyone's related. More families, more packs.*

"Where'd your uncle get those buttons?" Tommy said to Marg.

Marg crossed his arms in front of his chest.

"Forgot to ask him."

Tommy fought the urge to elbow Marg in the face. Something about him set off his aggressive side. Maybe it was the permanent sneer.

"Doesn't matter, really," Tommy said, talking mostly to Burt. "If Carl's taking orders through his website again, they could've gotten Antiwolf gear from there as easily as buying them from him in person. What I don't get is why. Why are you guys messing with *us*?"

Eli had retreated deeper into the corner of the truck bed, lips moving soundlessly as he gazed down at the floor of the cab with his odd, almost hooded eyes. Marg, on the other hand, began rocking slightly back and forth, his eyes closed tightly. His sneer had changed into a frown, which was an improvement.

"All right, Marg. Your turn. What were you doing in Iowa City this morning, driving the wrong way down the street close to where my friend Dennis lives? My friend Dennis who is now *missing*, I might add."

"What're you talking about?" the guy spat without opening his eyes. "I never been to Iowa City."

"Come on, man. Cut the crap. Were you cleaning up after your two partners when you nearly ran head-on into me?"

That got him to open his eyes, though he refused to meet Tommy's gaze.

"What partners?"

Tommy took a deep breath and let it out before he got himself covered in fur again.

"So what *were* you doing there? I know it was you—I got a perfectly clear look at your truck and your tatts, you passed that close to me."

"Tailing you," Marg muttered with an exasperated sigh. "That's my new frickin' job. Thought I lost you in those stupid one-way streets, but then I took a wrong turn, and there you were."

"Why were you following *me*?"

"They said you'd show up there, looking for your buddy. You gotta *forget* about him, man. Once they recruit someone, they're never the same."

Tommy had the guy by the arm, squeezing his bloody heart tattoo in his now furry hand.

Stay in control, he told himself, but the wolf side of him wasn't listening very well.

"Where *is* he?"

Marg was a big guy, but Tommy outweighed him by a good fifty pounds. Marg tried to break free of Tommy's grip, but Tommy held on tighter.

"Chicago!" Marg blurted out with a mix of exasperation and pain. "They're taking him to Chicago for training, okay?"

"Well hell," Burt said. "That's where we're heading anyway. We could've all carpooled there."

Tommy sniffed the air, catching a hint of something different in the gasoline-tinged air. He realized his mistake in stopping here, so close to all those gas pumps. His nose was partially blocked by the toxic fumes, preventing him from smelling every possible scent.

I'm letting myself get led, he realized, looking at his wolf daughter snuggled tight next to his pale, bearded brother. *I'm not taking the time to think this through. Too busy panicking and reacting.*

He let go of Marg's arm, barely noticing the red marks he'd made in the guy's flesh.

Letting this all get out of control.

Corinne let out a low growl that snapped Tommy out of his self-flagellation. She'd sensed something with her wolf radar. Her snout now pointed at the far end of the parking lot.

"Damn it," Tommy muttered as a dark blue Expedition with black-tinted windows rolled soundlessly into the lot. The SUV drove right up to the back bumper of Marg's truck and stopped. Its windshield was black as night.

Tommy pushed Marg up against Eli in the corner of the pickup bed until they were pressed together like sardines. He had to force himself not to crush them both with some wolf strength.

"They were just stalling until *their* backup arrived."

The engine to the Expedition revved, and then went silent. Tommy caught his brother's eye. Burt held tight to Corinne's wolf body with hands that were going thick with his own fur. Tommy kept up the pressure on Marg and Eli as both front doors of the SUV popped open.

He caught a whiff of something familiar, just for an instant, and then the wind changed and the stink of gas and oil overwhelmed him.

"*Stay*," a woman's voice said from inside the Expedition, and Tommy was unable to make another move.

Chapter Fourteen

She lied to me.

Still holding tight to his niece's wriggling body, Burt couldn't focus on any other thought or fact. Not even the sudden appearance of the Expedition and the two people who just stepped out of it.

I am such an idiot for thinking she'd be interested in me.

He stared blankly at the two newcomers—a burly, big-bellied black man in his early thirties and a thin white woman who could've been twenty-five or forty-five, with dark hair pulled back tight into a ponytail. The woman had just said something, but in his state of betrayed shock, Burt hadn't heard it.

He shifted his gaze to Lilly. She seemed tiny and defenseless from her perch in the far corner of the pickup bed. With her journal held tight to her chest, she'd backed herself up into the corner opposite of her brother.

She lied to me, he thought again. *Everything was a lie.*

Her brother. This guy Eli was her *brother*. Burt had known it was true as soon as she'd said it, just by looking at his eyes. They were the same color as Lilly's, though Burt had to focus hard to see them clearly. The guy's eyes seemed blurry, somehow.

"Burt?" Tommy whispered in a ragged voice. His brother's face was red, and he was half-way towards turning into his wolf form. But something was holding him back.

Burt waited for his brother to speak, his mind repeating the word *lies* over and over.

"Don't listen to her," Tommy said. For a second he thought his brother was talking about Lilly, then he caught Tommy's head nod in the direction of the two newcomers. "The woman from the SUV. She's a whisperer, just like Dennis and Lance back in Dyersburg. I can't frickin' *move*. Can you?"

Burt blinked and did his best to snap himself out of his Lilly-induced funk. He tried to push himself out of the truck bed, but his feet and his butt seemed to be glued to the metal floor. Even though he hadn't even *heard* the new woman's command, it kept him locked to the bed of the pickup all the same.

Marg gave a sharp laugh as he wriggled past Tommy and jumped out of the pickup bed, leaving the Roling trio behind. Corinne snapped at him on his way past her.

"Nice work, guys," he told the woman and the man. "I'll let Dad know you got here in record time."

"Yeah," the black guy said. "You do that. I was planning on staying in Chicago for another week or two instead of slumming back in dull-ass Iowa some more."

"Relax, Gerard," the woman said, without ever taking her intent gaze from the three people she'd entrapped in the truck bed. "You weren't going to be up to anything good back in Chicago. Let the trainers do their work."

"All righty," Marg said as he clapped his hands once, as if he was the world's most efficient micro-manager. "Enough talking. Let's break out the collars and leashes."

Burt heard Tommy's growl at that, and Corinne nearly slipped out of his grip. She was itching to run wild, which was her default mode lately.

And would that have been so bad? Burt thought. *Little Cory could've gotten away to safety. But knowing her, she wouldn't run, but instead she'd take a big bite out of the closest stranger.*

"When you see an opening," Burt told Tommy. "Get to your car with her. I got your back, bro."

Tommy nodded in agreement, his gaze darting to what seemed like the impossible distance between the pickup and his Grand Am.

Burt grimaced as his muscles began to stretch and fur started pushing up through his skin. And then he hit some sort of mental barrier, and the change stopped. He couldn't make himself go full wolf.

The lady that Tommy called a whisperer did this to us, he realized. *Just like one of those damn gadgets. Gotta make her take her words back. Eat those words. Yum yum.*

He didn't dare look behind him at Lilly. Even if they couldn't get out of the truck bed or finish their change, they'd make some fur fly from this spot. The whisperer couldn't hold them forever.

Tommy let out a quick, soft growl that made Burt flinch. When he looked over at his brother, Tommy was sniffing the air with his head cocked to one side.

"What?" Burt whispered, voice husky.

"I *know* them," Tommy said in a low, gravelly voice of his own. He nodded at the man and the woman talking with Marg next to the Expedition. The three of them on the ground seemed to have forgotten about the three of them stuck in the truck. "I know their scents. They were the ones who took Dennis this morning."

Corinne jumped at that, and her growl ratcheted up a notch louder.

"*Denny,*" she repeated. Her growl turned to a snarl when she bit Burt in the exact same spot where she'd bit him earlier.

"Shit!" Burt hissed.

The quick stab of pain was enough for him to lose his grip on her, and Corinne slipped out of his grasp.

In her lithe wolf's body, she jumped onto the raised tailgate of Marg's pickup. She perched there for just a split-second, and then she leaped onto the hood of the Expedition. Her paws made four sets of deep scratches in the blue paint of the hood.

Burt and Tommy leaned forward as far as they possibly could while their traitorous bodies held them captive in the truck bed. Tommy couldn't even talk; he just let out a wordless howl.

Corinne was getting ready to leap again.

"Diana!" Marg screamed as Corinne's claws screeched across the Expedition's hood. "Do something!"

"*Stop!*" the woman ordered, but Corinne didn't even hesitate. She jumped onto the woman, claws bared, yowling a battle cry.

At the same instant, Burt felt something click inside him. He was free. The power of the whisperer's voice had disappeared as soon as she'd tried to use it on Corinne.

Still leaning, he fell forward and caught himself on the tailgate of the truck an instant before cracking half his teeth on the metal.

"Let's go, bro—" he began, but Tommy had already vacated his spot in the truck.

Burt watched him bowl over Marg and then the other guy from the SUV like they were the last two pins standing in the final frame of a bowling game.

The woman named Diana was now on her back, still trying to order Corinne to stop with the little girl wolf sitting on her chest, the claws of her front paws digging into her shoulders.

Marg and the other guy were sprawled out on the asphalt and barely moving, with Tommy crouching over them. Blond fur coated every bit of his exposed skin. His face kept shifting from human to wolf like a bad special effect in a movie.

Still in the truck, Burt let out a shocked laugh at how fast all this had happened. He took a quick look around, wondering who else had witnessed this little battle. Nobody in the busy lot of the gas station had even noticed the commotion here on the far side of the lot.

"Nice work," he began, and then with a sudden jolt he remembered Lilly and her strange brother. He spun around in the now-empty bed of the pickup. Nobody there but him. He jumped out of the truck at last and checked all around— and underneath—the pickup and the Expedition.

Lilly and Eli were both gone.

* * * * *

Burt wasted no time in getting down onto the asphalt to find her scent. He didn't care about finding that crapheel Eli, but he wasn't going to let Lilly slip away from him like this. She owed him more than just a quick getaway when the time felt convenient.

She owes me an apology, Burt thought. *For breaking my stupid heart.*

The stink of gas and car exhaust pierced his sinuses like needles, but he forced himself to inhale deeply with his nose almost scraping the ground. He hated turning his back on Tommy and Corinne and their captives, but this time it was personal.

Burt sniffed in quick bursts, quickly finding the trail left by Lilly and Eli. They'd made a beeline out of the parking lot of the gas station and trampled their way through the soybean field next door. Following them was a cinch, and he let the change into his wolf body recede. For now.

Their tracks in the field led to a barbed-wire fence a hundred yards away, with a gravel road beyond that. On the other side of the road was a stand of oaks surrounded by wild undergrowth that looked like it hadn't been cut back in years. Their scents led right to the trees.

Burt leaped over the barbed wire fence, hit the ground, and then jumped over the ditch next to the gravel road. He surprised himself at his own agility, and then nearly slipped on the gravel as he slid to a stop in the middle of the road.

Their scents had *disappeared.* Just like this morning, when he was tracking Eli.

"Ah, come on," he panted. He sniffed hard, eyes closed. Nothing.

He cast a quick look behind him at the now-distant gas station, hoping Corinne and Tommy were doing all right on their own.

I'll be back there in a minute, he thought. *Maybe two.*

The thought calmed him, and he walked the rest of the way across the road with a loud crunching of gravel.

"I don't know how you *do* that," he called out. He slid down the other ditch and approached the bush-lined trees. "Dropping your scent like that. Maybe we can talk about it on our way to Chicago."

Burt held his breath and focused all of his energy on his sense of hearing. His ears tickled his scalp as they suddenly began to grow upward, coming to point somewhere above his hair.

Hope nobody sees me like this, he thought, and then he heard something move inside the trees.

He was after the sound in an instant, pushing through the wild raspberry branches and brambles that tore at his clothes and skin. He imagined his skin toughening and covered with fur, and again he was surprised when it worked. He didn't feel another scratch.

Ten steps inside the trees and undergrowth he found Lilly sitting on the ground, hugging her leather satchel. Her arms were criss-crossed with bleeding scratches, but she didn't even seem to feel them.

She looked up at Burt and whispered one word: "Sorry."

Burt couldn't help himself; he patted his ears, making sure they'd gone back to their usual jug-eared, non-pointy shape and size.

A heartbeat later, with an explosion of branches, breaking sticks, and pain-filled grunts, something big charged through the little patch of forest, heading away from Burt and Lilly.

Eli.

Burt grabbed Lilly and dragged her through the bushes back to the road. He heard her cry out multiple times as thorns caught and tore at her arms, but he forced himself to keep moving.

Thirty feet farther down the road, Eli broke through the trees at the same time and scrambled up onto the road with surprising quickness. He turned back and aimed both middle fingers at Burt, and then he took off running all-out down the gravel road away from them.

"Son of a bitch," Burt said and let the change come over him almost all the way. He felt each stretching ligament, muscle, and bone, but he wasn't going to let him get away again.

"Stay *here*," he shouted at Lilly in his guttural wolf voice, wishing it had the same commanding power that the whisperer's voice did. "I'm gonna get him and bring his ass back to the gas station."

Lilly tugged at his furry arm hard enough to knock Burt off-balance.

"Let him go," Lilly said. "He needs time by himself, to recover. He's not used to people."

She had a big scratch across her cheek from the thick bushes surrounding the stand of trees where he'd found her. She gave him a sly smile, and Burt felt a tiny piece of his iced-over heart try to thaw. He fought the feeling, even as his wolf-self retreated on him.

"He'll come around," she said.

Burt exhaled, completely human now. The change had gone away fast—faster than he'd ever remembered it happening.

"Lilly. How do you know that?"

"I know *him*. Besides," she added, still smiling, "he already got away from you once today. Save your energy."

Burt tried to ignore that jab, but when she rubbed his shoulder and then scratched the stubble on his cheek, he allowed himself a half-grin in her direction.

"You two like to run," he said, helping her across the road and through the ditch leading back to the gas station. The soybean plants had turned a sickly shade of brown from lack of rain in this region. "Makes you look guilty of something."

"I guess it's in our nature. Running, that is, not being guilty. We haven't *done* anything, Burt."

It was hard for him, but Burt kept his mouth shut until they were past the soybeans and at the edge of the parking lot to the gas station. He couldn't see Tommy or the others around the big blue SUV blocking in Marg's pickup and Tommy's car.

He took Lilly by the arm and turned her so they were facing each other.

The cut on her cheek was still bleeding, so he ran his hand gently across her face to gather up as much of it as he could. He wiped his hand on his jeans while Lilly just stared up at him. A tear slipped out of her right eye.

"You okay?" he said. "Did I hurt you?"

She just shook her head and tried to smile. He still had his hand on her arm, and he felt her body shaking.

"You're too nice to me," she said. "I don't deserve it."

Burt was at a loss. He hadn't expected that.

"No such thing as being too nice," he said, "at least not with someone you like. You know?"

Lilly wiped away her tears and shrugged, as if she didn't really know such things.

"Look," Burt said, taking both of her hands in his as they stood at the edge of the parking lot. "I want to trust you, and to believe you. You're the best thing that's happened to me in a long time. Possibly my whole life, maybe. We'll see. I mean, I've only known you for like a day. And it's been a helluva day."

He caught himself smiling at the thought, and he willed it away. He wasn't quite ready to smile.

"Just don't go running off like that. I can't protect you if you leave me." His voice wavered for a bit at that, and then he cleared his throat. "You're *safe* with me. I'm a frickin' werewolf, remember?"

"Okay," she said, moving close to kiss his bearded cheek. "I'm cool with that."

"So you didn't know those two people in the Expedition were coming?"

A flicker of anger crossed her face, and then Lilly exhaled. She shook her head, her gaze never leaving his.

"Good. For a while there I thought, well. I thought you and your brother had set us up."

"Nope," Lilly said. "I can see how it might look that way. But no. I was just hoping to get out of Iowa City before I got found again."

"Okay," he said. "Sorry. Had to ask. Think they're part of that army of darkness you were talking about?"

Lilly laughed, a bright sound that shocked Burt out of his anger. His smile snuck back onto his face.

"*Bringers* of darkness," Lilly said, shaking her head and returning his smile.

For a few seconds, Burt felt warm inside again, like last night at the bar, four or five beers in.

And then Lilly's smile disappeared.

"Yes," she said. "They're also bringers of darkness."

Ah, great, Burt thought. *Cue the Twilight Zone theme music. I just had to frickin' ask, didn't I?*

He cocked his head to one side. He thought he'd heard sharp voices near the three cars two hundred feet away from them. He let go of Lilly and rubbed the sudden gooseflesh that covered his own arms like a bad imitation of his lush brown wolf fur.

"We'd better get over there," he said. "Just in case Tommy and Corinne need an assist."

Lilly nodded without another word.

As they walked side-by-side across the bumpy asphalt of the parking lot, he stole a look at her out of the corner of his eye and felt his heart skip a beat.

This girl, he thought as all warmth left his body, replaced by the cold memory of her words. *She'd better not lie to me again. About anything.*

Chapter Fifteen

B urt!" Tommy shouted from his knees on the gas station parking lot. "Get back here!"

But he knew his brother was gone. With the stink of gas and oil—mixed with the new scents of the two newcomers—he couldn't smell him any longer.

Flaked out on me again, Tommy thought as he surveyed the weird scene spread out in front of him, caught between the three vehicles walling them in.

Corinne, still in her wolf body, had backed off just a few inches from the terrified face of the woman that Marg had called Diana. She remained perched on the woman's chest, and Diana was in the process of very slowly raising herself up on her elbows to keep a better eye on Corinne.

Diana was the whisperer, the one to watch.

The other stranger was probably just the hired muscle, and Tommy had given him a pretty hard forearm shiver when he leapt out of Marg's truck. The guy was still on his back, only now starting to regain consciousness.

Next to him, sitting and holding his head in his hands, was Marg. The blond guy rocked back and forth, not looking at Tommy, as if he was in shock or denial of all that had just happened.

"How about we *skip* breaking out the collars and leashes?" Tommy growled at Marg as he made his way over to Corinne.

Marg was smart enough to not answer. He just rocked faster.

Diana sucked in a breath as Tommy approached, and he stiffened. Corinne's growl lowered to a lethal-sounding level.

"Don't say a word," Tommy said to the woman. "It won't do you any good. Not with her at least."

Diana had pushed herself back almost to the front bumper of the Expedition, and she didn't dare remove her gaze from Corinne's teeth and claws.

Tommy reached his daughter and ran a hand down her furry, tense back.

"Easy," he said. "You did good, Corinne."

He pulled her gently away from Diana, amazed at the raw courage of his two-year-old.

Saved my ass again, he thought.

He looked from Diana to the two men, who still weren't in any hurry to join the party, and then back to her. She now met his gaze with a mixed look of fear and confusion on her face. She seemed vaguely familiar, but Tommy was sure they'd never met before. He only knew her smell.

He checked the parking lot one last time for Burt, and that was when he realized that both Lilly and her odd brother had also disappeared. That would explain Burt's absence, then. Tracking down his new lady friend.

Diana waved a hand at Tommy, though she wasn't close enough to touch him. He tensed up at the unexpected action, as did his little wolf girl.

"Don't," he warned her again, but he could tell by the look in her eyes that she meant no harm. She just wanted to say something. He nodded and said okay.

"Sorry," she said in a slightly raspy voice. "We were trying to contain the situation."

She was shaken up, in a way that made Tommy feel a touch of sympathy for her, even though she'd used her whisperer's voice on him just a minute ago. Which made him think of Dennis.

"You and this guy," he aimed his thumb at the black guy, "broke into my friend's house today and kidnapped him. Where is he?"

She shot a quick look at her buddy from the SUV, and then at Marg. She winced and leaned forward.

"Look, we didn't hurt him. Gerard led him to our Expedition peacefully, and your friend didn't put up a fight. Smart kid. He almost acted like he'd been expecting something like this."

Tommy thought about the struggling sounds from the phone call this morning and decided not to trust any of what this woman said.

"And you took him to Chicago? Why?"

"Virgil's got him," she said simply, as if that answered both questions.

Corinne growled at that. Tommy stared at the woman under his daughter, waiting for her to say more.

"That's Marg's dad. He lives in Chicago, where he runs a pile of businesses. He's a pretty important guy in the city, though you'll never read about him in the newspaper."

"Jesus, Diana," a low voice said. "That's enough already."

Tommy turned to see Marg with his head cocked in their direction, though he kept his arms wrapped tight around his knees from where he sat on the parking lot asphalt. A trickle of blood ran down his left bicep that looked like it was coming from his wet tattoo.

"You should be *proud* of him," Diana said in a cool voice. "He's done a lot for victims everywhere. And he's saved so many lives it's impossible to ever count them all."

Tommy shifted so he could see both Diana and Marg without having to bounce his gaze back and forth. He was getting sucked into this drama when he really needed to get some answers and then get back on the road.

"Oh, and also? He's a psychopath," Marg said, dabbing at his tattoo. His finger came away red and blue, as if he was bleeding ink. "A scared, controlling old bastard."

Ah, Tommy thought. *Classic Daddy issues.*

"Marg—" Diana begin.

"You really want to go into this now?" Marg said, glaring at Tommy. "With him right there? One of *them*?"

Tommy's hands clenched into fist.

"Hey, Marg, ol' buddy," he said. "You guys got my friend involved in this, and you were following *me*. I think we *do* want to go into this. Right *now*."

"Ain't saying a thing," Marg said, and he dropped his head onto his knees.

"So you claim," Tommy said, and then he tapped his daughter on her furry shoulder.

Corinne looked away from Diana, very grudgingly.

"Corinne, go keep a close eye on Mr. Marg over there for me, would you? I'll watch this one for you."

In a flash his little girl slipped off of Diana, her razor-sharp claws not leaving a single scratch in her passing. She shot over to Marg in a strawberry-blond blur. He fell over onto one side in his surprise, and when he looked up, all he probably saw was a mouthful of sharp, baby wolf teeth.

"How 'bout we talk?" Marg muttered between clenched teeth. "What do you wanna know?"

Marg helped Gerard up to his feet, and they both moved over to sit on the open tailgate of Marg's big blue pickup. Gerard had a swollen eye and a split lip, and he never once took his gaze off of Tommy. Diana was down on one knee, petting Corinne, while Tommy ran his finger over the scratches Corinne had left in the hood of the Expedition. Gerard's demeanor didn't improve when he saw him doing that.

A breeze had picked up from the west, pushing away the stench of fossil fuels and clearing Tommy's head. He knew he should feel more apprehensive about him and Corinne being outnumbered like this, but there was something defeated about the three strangers that made him lower his guard. It was like they *wanted* to talk about all this.

Marg patted his tattoo one last time, which wasn't bleeding after all, but just moist with sweat. He glanced at Corinne at his feet one last time, and then he started.

"My dad knows lots of folks in Chicago, but it was this guy running some two-bit computer operation back in Iowa City that got him really pumped up, in a way I'd never seen him before. Ol' Virgil got taken by the guy, I tell you. Sold him a bag of tricks, all to feed Dad's fear of... of *them*."

Corinne let out an odd whimper next to Diana.

"Them," Tommy said.

"You know. The wolves. The goddamn wolves. That's all Dad could ever frickin' *talk* about. Werewolves."

Tommy suddenly became aware that they were all camped out in the middle of a gas station parking lot late on a Friday afternoon. And this guy was talking about weres.

I'm not saying another word, he decided. *No way am I going to 'fess up to anything. Including who my uncle is.*

"Ever since that attack back when I was just a kid, Dad's been obsessed with keeping us all safe from the wolves. We used to go visit family up in Wisconsin and friends in Minnesota that lived way out in the sticks, but no more. He never said why, but I know now. Too risky. The wolves were thicker out where the population trickled off. Out in the boonies and forests. Frickin' nuts, I tell ya."

Tommy bit his lip and tried not to nod in agreement. He caught the look shared between Gerard and Diana, as if the big guy was worried Marg was talking too much. But Diana just shook her head and waited for Marg to continue.

"He started making connections and gathering all this info on wolves in the area, and he always said how he wished someone had a list of wolves somewhere so he could know which places were safe. He always had to keep his people and his family safe. Then he found this website that did exactly what he needed. Antiwolf dot com."

Ever since Marg had mentioned a "two-bit computer operation," Tommy had been expecting the name of that damn site to come up, and he made sure his face remained blank.

"So this guy in Iowa City starts getting some of Dad's money, but not for any computer work. Not sure how he ever found the dude, because I heard people say the guy was a drunk and a loser. But the guy had access to these special gadgets that Dad wanted."

Uncle Carl, Tommy thought, unable to hide the frown that had slipped onto his face. *Great Plains Tactical.*

He swallowed his growing sense of dread and looked back at the blond dude sitting in the back of his pickup with his legs swinging nervously. He reminded Tommy of Watts, somehow. The guy practically gave off a stink of sneakiness and deception. He wondered for a moment if Marg was a werewolf, too, but he discarded that theory. Marg would've turned earlier instead of letting Tommy nearly knock him out.

"These were tiny little black gadgets, some of them as small as a quarter. Supposed to work wonders... against *them.*"

He looked directly at Tommy, not talking for five full seconds.

Tommy met his gaze with raised eyebrows, as if he had no idea what the guy was talking about.

"They don't always work, do they?" Marg said.

Tommy scrunched up his face and cleared his throat. "What do you mean?"

"The little black switches and disks from anti-wolf dot com. Your *uncle's* website, man. Quit playing dumb and get with the program. Our buddy Eli tossed one onto your car not thirty minutes ago, and it made your daughter go nuts, but didn't so much as make you blink. Your uncle sold my dad and my uncle a bag of goods that don't work. That's why Dad cut him off earlier this year. And then your uncle just *disappears* on us. Why do you think my old man had me tailing you?"

While Marg was talking, Burt and Lilly showed up silently. Only Tommy and Corinne noticed. Lilly had a small cut on her cheek, and her eyes looked puffy from crying. Tommy could see that Burt was mad, but he was keeping it tightly under control. It was almost scary how calm Burt was.

The two of them stood listening without speaking outside the circle of Tommy, Corinne, Marg, Diana, and the now-awake but not-very-happy Gerard.

Quite the congregation we have here, Tommy thought. *All we need is Eli and we can play some four-on-four basketball.*

"To answer your question," he said at last. "No. Those anti-wolf dot com gadgets are all shit. None of 'em work. That little one Eli tossed onto my car didn't make my daughter go nuts. She was just going wild to get at you guys." He gave a sheepish smile when he realized how true that statement was. "My uncle did pull a fast one. So why don't you go find *him* and leave us the hell alone?"

"None of 'em," Marg repeated slowly, rubbing his chin. "I wonder..."

He looked away from Tommy and noticed Burt and Lilly for the first time.

"Hey. Where the hell's Eli?"

Burt just shrugged, while Lilly gazed at the ground.

"Ah man," Marg spat. "If that autistic asshat goes missing on my watch again, I'm toast. I gotta—"

"Chill," the big guy Gerard said from next to Marg. "You gotta chill. We've got more important work to do right now than chase Eli around again."

A look of panic crossed Marg's face as he took in what Gerard said, and then turned to Diana.

"What's going on here?"

Diana and Gerard both stood, one on either side of Marg.

"We're supposed to bring you back to Chicago. All of you."

Marg's face paled, then his eyes narrowed.

"Come on," he said. "We were on our way there already. No need for him to send you two—"

"Now how could he know that?" Gerard said. "For all Virgil knew, you and your buddy Eli were out road-tripping through eastern Iowa and western Illinois. Getting your kicks while the wolves went wild back in the city."

Diana cleared her throat. Tommy flinched, half-expecting her to use her voice to control things.

But all she said was, "That's enough Gerard. Marg, you and Eli ride with Gerard in the Expedition. You can leave your pickup here. I'll ride with the kids in their car, show them how to get to the office."

While Marg spluttered and complained about leaving his beloved pickup behind, Burt pushed his way past Diana and Gerard, dragging Lilly after him, until he was standing next to Tommy and Corinne.

"What if us *kids*," he said, "don't wanna go anywhere with you jokers?"

"Well—" Diana began.

"Relax," Tommy told his brother. "I'll fill you in on what you missed later. But look, Burt. We were heading to Chicago anyway."

"Yeah, and then they frickin' attacked us!"

"It was a misunderstanding. And actually, Corinne attacked *them*."

Burt jabbed a finger at Diana, who was whispering harsh words into Marg's ear.

"She used her voice on us, Tommy! How do I know you're not under her control right now?"

Tommy threw off the hand that Burt had rested on his shoulder.

"Oh really?" he said, turning on Burt, looking down at him. "Is that what you think? That I can't make up my own mind if there's a whisperer around?"

Burt shrank back, but just a bit. Tommy let out a ragged breath to calm himself.

"Burt," Tommy began, but his older brother wasn't listening.

Burt shook his head and tried to pace around. But there were too many people bunched up in his space, so he just ended up walking one step forward and two steps back. Right to Tommy's side.

"They better have a good damn story," he said, leaning against Marg's truck with a heavy sigh.

"It's actually not half bad," Tommy said. He clapped Burt on the back. "I'll tell it to you on the way to Chicago."

Tommy shrugged off the help offered by Diana as he made sure Corinne was safely secured in her car seat with its freshly re-knotted belts in the back seat. She'd finally let herself revert to her human form, and in the meantime he'd somehow managed to get a fresh diaper and some pajamas on her for the drive to Chicago without getting bit or scratched. The wind blew through the open doors of his car, carrying with it a surprising coolness after the warmth of this long afternoon.

Corinne grinned up at him, saying "Go go go. Righ' righ' *now*, Daddy!"

"We'll be going for a ride any second now," he told her, grabbing at her nose. He'd seen her in wolf form so much lately that he missed looking at her human face. Her nose, for one thing, was much smaller when he tried to grab it and pretend to steal it.

As soon as he extricated himself from the back seat, he felt his phone vibrate in his pocket. He pulled it out and checked the screen.

Attix.

"Damn," Tommy whispered as he stepped away from the car. He watched Burt slide in on one side of Corinne, while Lilly got in on the other, behind the driver seat. Diana watched Tommy with a curious look on her face from where she stood by the open shotgun door.

He tapped the Answer button on the screen of his phone after two more buzzes and prepared himself for the worst.

Attix didn't even bother with *Hello*.

"Why aren't you answering your damn phone?"

"Hey Attix," Tommy began. He'd seen the five missed calls and the five voicemails on his phone's screen before putting it to his ear. All from Attix.

"Don't *Hey Attix* me. You're in some shit, Tom. Get over to my office, now."

Tommy sucked in a quick breath. "Ah. Hmm. I'm actually not in town right now."

"You know this looks bad, right? Not just to me, after last night and then after what happened at your friend's place this morning. Why didn't you wait for my guys to show up? And now you're... where? You *never* leave town. You're always around."

As Attix spoke, Tommy's gaze wandered off into the field next to the gas station. He felt like they'd been stuck here for a day, instead of the actual hour or so that had just passed. They'd barely made it out of Iowa before trouble found them.

He watched the brown soybean plants wave in the wind, and then—speaking of trouble—he saw Eli slide down into the ditch from the road next to the bean field. He dragged his feet in the dirt, and his head was down, as if he'd been walking for miles.

Attix had gone silent on the phone. Tommy swallowed.

"We'll be back in town tomorrow," he told Attix. "The day after at the latest."

Eli raised his head at that moment and saw Tommy staring at him. He gave Tommy a half-nod, but the late-afternoon sun was at his back. Tommy couldn't see his eyes, nor could he catch the expression on the odd dude's face. Eli changed course to take a wide angle around Tommy on his way to the trio of vehicles.

"We, huh? You and your little girl just decided to take a road trip, huh? Just the two of you?"

"Yup. Visiting family back home."

Tommy had avoided ever mentioning his brother Burt to Attix, preferring to keep his trouble-seeking family off his new boss's radar.

"Dyersburg, right?"

"Uh huh," Tommy said, and then shuddered. He wished he'd never told Attix where he was from. But sometimes he couldn't help himself when it was just him and the older guy.

He found himself confessing facts about himself just to fill the silence and cut the intensity with Attix. At some point Attix was going to want to investigate him and his past. And then their working relationship would be over.

"I don't like this. I don't need people asking me too many questions. Nothing illegal about what you're doing for me, but it just won't look good if people hear about it. I really need you back here today to answer some questions in person."

Tommy looked over at his car, fighting a sudden wave of panic. Eli was leaning into Marg's pickup, where Marg had been sulking ever since Diana had announced the change in plans. He was just listening to Marg bitch, Tommy figured, before they headed back to Chicago.

We're so close to finding Dennis and clearing all this up, he thought. *I can't go back now.*

"I don't think I can get back today. It's... complicated."

"Why did I know you were gonna say that," Attix said. It wasn't a question. He let out a long, loud sigh, and Tommy had to hold the phone away from his ear for a good ten seconds.

"I *really* need to talk to you, Tom," Attix said after recovering from the sigh. His voice was lower now, softer. "Something I don't wanna discuss on the phone."

"Oh," Tommy said, just as Gerard fired up the big engine to his SUV and honked twice. "Is it, ah, something bad?"

"Maybe," Attix said. "Let's just say I have a hunch about your friend from last night, and your friend from this morning. Do *not* say their names out loud, okay?"

"Oh," Tommy said again, unable to think of anything better. Attix always made him feel like a wet-behind-the-ears kid.

"Okay, fine," Attix said in an impatient voice. "I'll handle things for today. Just get your butt back here tomorrow, as early as possible. Call me if you're gonna be running late. But yeah, we need to *talk*. Man to man, face to face."

"Right. Thanks, Attix. Sorry for the—"

But Attix had already hung up, as if he didn't have time to waste on pleasantries.

And neither do I, Tommy thought, pocketing his phone and brushing a shoulder a bit harder than necessary with Marg and he and Eli trudged toward Gerard and the Expedition. *I got a road trip to finish.*

Chapter Sixteen

Burt hadn't been to Chicago since he and two buddies had gone there for three days of Cubs games and two wild nights of bar-hopping and trouble-making after his high school graduation. He didn't remember many of the details of that trip, but he had a vague happy feeling whenever he thought of the city's skylines, taverns, and endless supply of good-looking women.

He caught himself at that and glanced over at Lilly. He'd found himself a good-looking woman of his own.

Though she didn't seem to be at her best right now. The cut on her cheek had started bleeding again, as if she'd been picking at it, and at some point she'd found one of her journals and a pen. Her curly brown hair hung down over her face, hiding those mischievous eyes of hers. She was writing fast, stopping only to glare at the woman sitting diagonally from her in the front passenger seat.

I should say something to her, he thought, the silence in the car making him edgy. *Do something to make her feel better.*

But there were all the things she'd told him today that stopped him cold. He'd pretty much come to terms with the way today started, with the needled leash and all that drama at Lilly's now-ruined apartment. That kind of crazy weirdness exhilarated Burt, made him feel truly alive. He could even deal with the facts that Eli was Lilly's so-called lost brother, and it was most likely Eli who'd slapped that leash—an antiwolf.com special, no doubt—around Burt's passed-out were self.

But the way Lilly had just run off like that had decimated the last bit of trust Burt had been holding onto for her. He wondered if she would've come back—like Eli had, reluctantly—if he hadn't gone out there to track her down. He felt proud of the way he'd found her so fast, big ears and all. But not so happy about how he felt now. Like he had to watch her all the time to keep her from running off or doing something else just as crazy.

Lilly kept scratching away at her journal, oblivious to him watching. The symbols of her scribbled code marched across the page in impossibly straight lines, despite the bumps and swerves from the road. The wind whistled in from the windows as they flew east down the interstate.

Burt didn't even notice until that moment, how he'd been hunched forward in his seat, all tensed up and waiting for someone to say something. But Tommy and Diana in the front seat were staring straight ahead like soldiers forced to put up with one another before the next big battle.

Corinne had her eyes closed next to him after the afternoon's excitement, while Lilly had her beloved journal and her cipher, most likely recording all the stories she'd snatched from thin air today since they'd left home back in Iowa City. A million miles from here.

I can't take it anymore, Burt thought, stretching. His pressed his knees into the back of the passenger seat for maximum annoyance.

"Are we *there* yet?" he called out to Tommy.

"Don't even start," Tommy said automatically, not even turning his head.

"We *dere* yet?" Corinne echoed, and Burt snickered. "We *dere* yet, Daddy?"

"Nice one," Tommy said with a groan, catching Burt's eye in the rearview. "Now we get to listen to *that* for the next two hours."

"Hush, wild child," Burt said to Corinne before he could stop himself. Tommy hated it when he called her that. "Let's just chill for a bit, okay?"

As they left the gas station miles behind them and counting, Burt finally settled back next to Corinne's car seat.

He risked reaching out to her, and she took his hand in both of hers.

"Owie," she said, patting the back of his hand with her bite marks from earlier.

He grinned at her and squeezed her fingers. Gently.

Owie. Tell me about it, kiddo.

He glanced behind them and saw Gerard's SUV twenty feet behind them, its windshield a dull black rectangle of nothingness. He wondered what they were discussing back there in the tinted darkness. Best way to skin a werewolf? Favorite gadget to keep a were from turning back to human? Silver bullets?

He made it almost ten minutes before the urge overwhelmed him again. Ten minutes without chatting had to be a personal best for him.

Corinne had let go of his hand about five miles back, and she was now snoring softly with her head turned his way. Lilly, meanwhile, hadn't let up on her coding. Tommy was grumpy, so that left only one other person.

"Diana," Burt said, eliciting another groan from Tommy. "Are you like a henchman? I mean, a hench*woman*? How's that work? You get like a salary and benefits? Healthcare? Vacation? You gotta get at least a week off, right?"

"*Burt*," Tommy said.

"It's okay," Diana said, turning halfway in her seat and craning her neck so she could see Burt in his spot directly behind her. "I'm used to this sort of thing. Long drives and all that. You don't have to make small talk to be friendly and polite."

"Aw, heck," Burt drawled. "I can't *help* but be polite, Miss Diana."

Lilly's pen paused for the tiniest fraction of a second.

"But I hate small talk," Diana said with an air of finality.

As if to say, *Shut up, wolf boy.* That just motivated Burt even more.

"You just haven't experienced *good* small talk. Allow me to demonstrate."

"Here we go," Tommy said, goosing the accelerator until their speed approached eighty-five. "We've gotta shorten this trip."

"You can jump in whenever you want," Burt said to Diana, "but only if you need to. I can do this all by myself."

He cleared his throat, rolled his neck from side to side, and made a big deal out of cracking his knuckles to finish his warm-up.

They were thirty miles from the Quad Cities now, past Davenport and Moline, and back into the flat, green and brown countryside dotted with occasional barns and farmhouses that Burt knew all too well. Rural Illinois was just as flat and dull as rural Iowa.

"So you started working for this guy Virgil a while back, maybe a couple years, probably just a year at the most, 'cause you still think he's pretty hot shit, almost heroic, right?"

As he spoke, Diana turned back to the front, but not before he caught the hint of a smile in her eyes. Like she wasn't going to try and stop him. At least not yet.

"And you never knew you had these mad skills with your voice until recently, which got you the job at Virgil's. Before that, you were just kicking around, doing odd jobs, thinking about college. Maybe drinking too much, smoking some doobie on Thursday, Friday, Saturday nights."

"This is starting to sound like someone else I know," Tommy said with a snort.

Burt ignored him. "And then you learned about weres, and your brain kinda exploded for a while. Weres like us."

Diana flinched the tiniest bit at that.

This was too easy, Burt thought, keeping his gaze on her now to catch more reactions. *Payback's a bitch, isn't it, wolf whisperer?*

"And now you work for Virgil to control any werewolves he and his cronies might dig up. The money's good, but you gotta deal with buttheads like Marg all the time. You just want people to be safe from those"—he did air quotes—"scary were-ys."

"Sherlock Holmes in my back seat," said Tommy. He glanced over at Diana, all polite and grown-up. "I'd apologize for him, but you kinda had that coming, after what you did to us in the parking lot back there."

Diana shrugged. "Like I said, small talk. And talk's cheap. *Anyone* can do it."

Burt was about to continue his analysis of the whisperer riding shotgun, but at that moment Lilly dropped her pen on the floor. He lost his train of thought. He'd forgotten about her for a few minutes, and caught himself having some fun.

"No," Lilly said. "That's not quite it." She sounded way too much like her emotionless brother Eli.

She closed her hardcover journal with a snap, but never removed her gaze from it. As if all the facts were right there on the cover. Burt's ears filled with the hum of the wheels on the highway and the whistle of the windows and Corinne's deep breathing next to him, and he couldn't say another word.

"She was dating a guy who turned out to be a wolf, like you three. He never told her until it was too late, after he'd turned and killed someone in a bar fight. It was before she knew the truth. She always wondered why he could never say no to her. It had all happened so fast she hadn't been able to say a word to prevent it. She just watched, silently, and let it all happen."

"Stop it," Diana said in a husky voice. "You're full of—"

"So Diana did some Googling about werewolves the next day, after the cops had taken him away. The others came to her the next day. They probably had computers set up to track those sort of searches, she figured. She was scared, but somehow she trusted them. So she told them all she knew, and they got real excited when she told him about her boyfriend."

"Shut *up*!" Diana shouted from the front seat. Corinne woke with a start and immediately began crying.

The car swerved, but neither Tommy nor Burt could speak. Diana's voice had silenced them.

"The rest of what he said," Lilly continued, unbothered by any of the ruckus she'd caused, "was pretty close to the truth. Except she's looking for a way out, and Tommy's friend Dennis might be it."

Burt tried to make calming sounds to Corinne, though nothing came out of his mouth. He settled for patting her cheek, the whole time studiously avoiding her teeth. She'd turned partway to wolf when Diana woke her, but as she calmed down, her fur receded, and her eyes closed again.

Lilly opened her journal and started reading the first page, as if she wanted nothing more to do with this discussion.

"You bitch," Diana muttered, glaring at Lilly sidewise across the car.

"Hey!" Burt said, elbowing Diana through the seat. He exhaled, glad to be able to talk again now that Diana had gotten distracted by Lilly. "Don't call her that."

Diana just shook her head and looked over at Tommy.

"How could she know all that? She's not a were, so... what *is* she?"

Burt bit his tongue. He'd almost said, "Good question."

Tommy didn't answer her question, either. Face flushed red, she pivoted back to the front, muttering something about small talk and psychos.

Burt reached over to Lilly, aiming for her hand. But all he ended up with was some smudged black ink on his fingers.

They rode for a good half hour in silence, everyone lost in their own thoughts, or their own codes, depending on who you were.

Watching the other cars approach and recede, Burt glanced one more time at the two women in the car. Lilly remained lost in her writing, while Diana stared straight ahead, her face tight with a frown.

He wondered how they'd ever be able to trust someone like her—someone who had the ability to control them with just a word. They'd have to keep Corinne nearby the whole time they were in Chicago, because the girl was immune to Diana's commands.

Look at it this way, he thought as he checked the knots of the seat belt keeping his little niece safe in her car seat. *At least there's one lady in my life I can completely trust. Even if she's only two.*

S o how did you guys find out about Dennis?" Tommy asked as they slowed down behind a pair of semis hogging the two left-most lanes.

Diana sighed and looked out her window without answering. Apparently she'd wasn't interested in any more chatting today.

Burt watched Tommy, watching his brother's big hands grip the steering wheel tight enough to bend it. Burt couldn't tell if it was frustration about his buddy Dennis or the growing traffic again. He'd never imagined Tommy crashing through orange construction barrels like he had earlier today. The dude was wound up tightly about all this.

Burt realized that Tommy had never said anything else about the guy he'd been tracking last night. He didn't know if he'd caught him or not. He suspected not, looking at his tensed-up younger brother now.

"Come on," Tommy said. "You were there this morning, and you know what I am. I picked up your smell, and what's-his-name's too."

"Gerard," Lilly said from the back seat, without missing a beat or stopping her pen.

"Yeah, Gerard's scent, too. You carted him off this morning, and he'd better be okay when we get there."

Silence from the front passenger seat.

Burt looked behind them, trying to find Gerard's big old SUV, without any luck.

Maybe we lost 'em, he thought. *Good riddance.*

Tommy kept up with his questions in the front seat.

"So does this Virgil guy have a directory of wolf whisperers, just like that anti-wolf website has a list of all the weres? Is that how you located Dennis three hours away in Iowa City?"

Burt had forgotten about that website. He wished he had that slip of journal paper with all the names and addresses on it from the hard drives Tommy had gotten at Carl's abandoned store. There were more and more clues, and he was having troubling holding them all in his head. He was working on way too little sleep and not near enough adrenaline. He wished he could get an adult beverage at the next convenience store they passed.

"You've got about ten more miles of this," was all Diana said in response to Tommy's questions, pointing at the growing traffic on the interstate ahead of them.

Tommy sighed.

"You couldn't get Marg to shut up earlier. And now you won't say a thing." He gave her a look of disgust, and Burt felt glad that look wasn't directed at him, for a change. "But if you're going to use Dennis as your replacement, you need to tell me what he's in for."

"Get over a couple lanes. This one ends in half a mile. Watch out for that semi."

Tommy maneuvered as ordered, and Burt saw the sheen of sweat on his brother's forehead as he checked behind them and flicked his gaze to all his mirrors in quick succession. Burt checked to make sure Corinne's seat belts were secure, and then checked his own. The joys of big-city life.

"You're good for a mile or two," Diana said, and then she turned to get a better look at Tommy.

"And it's not a bad life, if that's what your friend Dennis chooses. If he crashes and burns with the training, that's one thing. They'll send him home, no harm no foul, so long as he doesn't go whining to the cops. But he might see the good in it, and he'd be helping Virgil's people keep innocent people safe."

"From people like us," Tommy said, his voice tight with stress, and more than a little bit of anger.

"Well, *yes*. The ones who can't control it. Or be controlled."

She made an involuntary movement toward the backseat and then froze, as if catching herself about to look at Corinne. Burt stifled a growl, while Tommy snorted with disgust.

"But you had to kidnap him to get him to come along. *You* weren't kidnapped." Tommy cocked his head toward the back of the car, but didn't dare look. "She wasn't kidnapped, was she, Lilly?"

"Nope. They *recruited* her, remember?"

Tommy shot a victorious smirk at Diana.

"And we recruited *him*," Diana said.

"But how did you even hear about him? That's what I don't get."

"When we get to Virgil's office, it'll all make sense. He keeps up with these things."

Burt leaned forward to catch everything they were saying, feeling a sudden wave of heat that didn't come from the hundreds of vehicles stacked around him, engines creeping into the red as they crept forward at half the speed limit.

"Mount Vernon," Tommy said abruptly. He glanced over at Diana, looking at her a second or two longer than Burt thought was really safe, given the traffic situation. As if he was trying to place her, to remember where he might have seen her before.

Diana didn't respond.

"What did Virgil tell you about Mount Vernon?"

Tommy had turned back to the interstate and the unending streams of cars growing around them on all sides. So he didn't catch the flash of uncertainty on Diana's face. Burt looked closer at her as well, sniffing and squinting. There really *was* something familiar about her. He just couldn't figure out what.

"I haven't heard anything about Mount Vernon," Diana said after a long pause. "What did you hear?"

"A whisperer got killed there recently. Maybe as recently as last week. I ran into the guy who did the killing, and I... took care of him."

"Dude," Burt blurted out from the back seat.

Clues were being connected, at last. Or so Burt thought.

"Was that the guy from the tavern? The Fox Head? Mr. Chin Beard?"

"Hush," Tommy said, almost too softly for Burt to hear. But he caught Tommy's look in the rearview mirror.

It was the same guy. Tommy'd caught him. That's my bro.

Diana chewed her lip, thinking. Burt wondered if he should cover his ears, before she did her wolf whisperer trick on them again.

"All right," she said, as if deciding something for herself. "I may have known someone in Mount Vernon. But how reliable was this guy you ran into? And what do you mean when you say you took care of him."

"I don't think he was lying. Something the whisperer did—or *said*—to him before he killed him was driving him nuts. Said the guy had this incredible voice, like your favorite song."

Burt shuddered, feeling his wolf hairs trying to poke their way through the skin of his arms. He forced it away with all of his willpower, which took longer than he'd expected. He'd missed out on some of the conversation in the front seat he'd been eavesdropping on. Diana was talking fast now, her eyes not leaving Tommy's face.

"This was an *assassination*, for Christ's sake. I have trouble believing Jacob would let his guard down like that. The killer never said who set up the killing?"

Jacob? Burt wondered. *Must've been the guy Watts offed in Mount Vernon. Another whisperer. How many of those people were out there? Too many for my taste.*

Tommy shook his head, focusing his gaze only on the traffic now.

"He just said 'she.' Like 'she sent you after me, didn't she?'"

Burt had a feeling Tommy had been going over those words in his head ever since last night. *Dude.*

"I don't know," Diana muttered, mostly to herself. "I don't think she'd..." She stopped and took a quick breath when she realized she was talking out loud.

Burt caught the wide-eyed look Tommy gave Diana, just for a split-second before returning his attention to the interstate traffic. A car honked from off to the left, while a semi's air brakes screeched off to the right.

"What do you—" Burt began, but he was abruptly rocked forward in his seat.

Tommy had hit the brakes. Within two seconds they were at a dead stop, along with all the other cars and trucks filling the six lanes around them. The Chicago skyline opened up in front of them, appearing tantalizingly close through the windshield, but still miles ahead of them.

"It's the start of rush hour traffic," Diana said. "*Great* timing. We should get there in, oh, an hour or three."

Tommy growled and rested his head on the steering wheel for a moment, as if he would've preferred to bang his skull on it.

"Welcome to Chicago," Diana added with a grim smile.

Chapter Seventeen

Chicago looked, sounded, and smelled like hell on Earth to Tommy Roling.

Cars, trucks, and semis crowded in on all sides, with vehicles lined up in all six lanes heading into the city. Engines revving, horns honking, tires squealing. The foul taste of exhaust and burnt oil coating his nose and mouth. Stress so thick he could taste it. They crept through the five o'clock traffic ten feet at a time, Tommy's foot on the brake the whole time, with all his senses on high alert.

Hell on earth. Totally.

This was his first trip ever to Chicago. He was supposed to go there along with his senior classmates back in high school, but Mom hadn't been able to pay the fifty-five bucks for the bus and the admission to the three museums they were supposed to visit. Tommy had been fine with that, since he had an off-the-books pre-season workout with his University of Northern Iowa football teammates that day, anyway.

The only drawback had been when he heard all the stories about the city from his small-town Iowa classmates the next day at school. The small-town kids had loved the big city.

But now here he was, trying not to run into someone just outside the same city. And Tommy had thought Iowa City was big and hard to navigate. Not anymore.

Diana told him where to turn, prodded him to get over, *now*, when he needed to (he suspected she used her whisperer's voice on them in those instances, as he couldn't ignore her orders), and she helped him get past all the I-94 construction and the traffic and the suddenly appearing exits.

At last they pulled up to a gleaming blue glass skyscraper, and she told him where to park underneath it.

He'd never been more glad to kill the Grand Am's engine. He still felt the angry vibration of the highway and his own tightly-wound senses in the abrupt silence.

"*Finally*," Burt said, the first to pop out of the car. Corinne bounced out after him, and they ran in circles around the underground parking deck, laughing and whooping with childish joy.

Tommy caught himself smiling, glad to see both daughter and brother being themselves again.

As he relaxed, he felt his ears still buzzing from the traffic on the city streets, as well as the hum of his tires on the interstate.

A thought hit him then while he was tapping one of his ears. There might be something in the glovebox that could be quite handy with Diana and her boss.

I just need a chance to check, he thought, *without raising any suspicion.*

"Is anyone even going to be there?" he said to Diana. He nodded up at the building above them. He stretched and rubbed his neck, trying not to think about his glovebox for a few more seconds. He tried to act all casual as he checked the time on his phone, and he was truly shocked that they'd spent two hours creeping through traffic.

"I mean, it's after seven on a Friday night. Everyone should be heading home by now."

Diana gave him a crooked grin, the first one that looked authentic since he'd met her.

"Oh, there's *always* someone there."

Burt picked up Corinne and came back over to where Tommy and Diana stood next to the car. Tommy realized that Burt's odd little girlfriend was still inside the car, scribbling away in her journal. Maybe she didn't want to face Diana after picking the poor woman's brain like that.

That's my opening, Tommy realized. *I'll go back into the car to get her to come out, then I'll pop open the glovebox to see if they're still in there.*

"Where'd they go?" Burt said, looking from Tommy to Diana. He rapped on the car window until Lilly grudgingly got out, holding tight to her journal and her pen.

Nice one, Burt, Tommy thought.

"Who?" Diana said.

"Your buddy Gerard. We must've lost him in traffic. Nice work, Tommy."

In the madness of the rush-hour gridlock, Tommy had forgotten all about the big blue Expedition that had been behind them since close to the Iowa border.

Diana's face darkened with what just might have been worry.

"I should call him," she said. But when she pulled out her phone and noticed the time, she swore and shook her head. "Forget them. We've got to get upstairs to see Virgil. He hates waiting."

While Diana's back was to him, Tommy hurried back to his car, mumbling something about needing to make sure all the doors were locked. He dropped into the driver's seat and popped open the glovebox.

Underneath a couple years' worth of insurance and registration cards, he found them. Earplugs. Two sets, left over from his stint working on a road crew one summer, cutting pavement and running a jackhammer.

He shoved the plugs into his pants pocket, locked the doors, and hurried after the others. Diana hadn't even noticed.

Smooth, Tommy thought.

After Diana punched in a numeric code that sounded like it contained twenty digits, the elevator doors slide open. The four adults and Corinne piled into the elevator. Within seconds they were flying upwards at what felt like ten stories a second. Tommy's ears popped, and Corinne said "Owie" over and over as she jumped up and down on the smooth metal floor.

They stopped three floors from the top, on the 47th floor.

"What," Burt said, his voice cracking from nervousness despite the big grin he wore, "your buddy Virgil can't afford the top floors?"

Diana smiled to herself as she led them out of the elevator.

"Actually," she said, "he owns the whole building. And three others on this block alone."

"Oh," Burt said in a small voice, his grin gone.

They stepped out of the elevator into a thirty-foot-wide circular room with black walls and no furniture, no pictures, no signs. Not even a window looking out at the other tall buildings or Lake Michigan. Just a black chair next to a door.

In the chair a trim man sat waiting patiently with his arms crossed, gazing at the floor all lost in thought, like the next guy in line to see a doctor. His gray-white hair put him in his fifties, but his physique made Tommy think he might be a serious weightlifter. Probably Virgil's bodyguard or bouncer.

"Mr. Ericson," Diana said. "I knew you'd still be here tonight."

The older man smiled when he saw Diana, and he uncrossed his arms and stood, as if he'd been waiting for her all along. Patient as can be, in a totally abnormal way.

"Welcome back, young lady. Glad you made it back before full dark. And you brought friends."

As Diana chatted quietly with Mr. Ericson, Tommy forgot about the door and who—or what— might be waiting on the other side of it. He was intrigued by this bodyguard, just standing watch near the top of this tower, all alone, nothing to read or do but wait and protect the door.

Corinne and Burt had been walking the big circle of the black room, checking for openings or other signs of life, but now they moved in close to Tommy and Diana. Lilly was the only one hanging back, and she watched the man at the door with a distrustful look on her face.

157

"It appears the others have taken their own sweet time getting here."

Diana nodded, just once. "I think Gerard got lost in traffic. Again. That big old Expedition just can't handle actual traffic. No maneuverability."

"Don't tell Gerard that," the older man said, and they both shared a brief, soft laugh.

When she was done laughing, Diana's face returned to its usual, somber self.

"When we have a moment," she said, "we *need* to talk about Mount Vernon. You never told me about Jacob."

Tommy cleared his throat at that and stepped closer to Diana and the door man. Diana glared at Tommy as if he'd interrupted a special moment here.

"Ah," Mr. Ericson said, finally looking away from Diana. Up until that point, Tommy had felt invisible in the guy's presence, like he'd been actively willing him to disappear.

"You must be Tommy," the older man said, turning to him at last, with a sudden flick of his head.

Tommy nearly stepped back in shock when he met Mr. Ericson's eyes. They were an intense blue color that looked fake, like color contacts, and something at the edges of those eyes made Tommy's hackles stand up. Those eyes were too wide. As if he were scared, and barely holding it together.

"Yeah," was all Tommy could say with a hesitant nod.

Mr. Ericson didn't offer his hand.

"And your little one, Corinne. And that leaves your big brother, Burt. We've heard a lot about all of you."

It wasn't the same voice that he'd heard on the phone back in Carl's old computer store, but it was close.

That clinched it for Tommy. This dude was no bodyguard. He was *the* guy. The boss man. And he'd been sitting there, waiting for them, for who knew how long.

"I'd like to see my friend Dennis now," Tommy said. "If that's okay with you, Mr. Ericson. Or can I call you *Virgil*, since we're all on a first-name basis here?"

Mr. Ericson flinched when Tommy called him that, and Tommy caught Burt's wide-mouthed expression of surprise. And then the old man smiled, calm and in control again.

"Welcome," said Virgil Ericson, Marg's father, and apparently one of the most powerful men in Chicago, "to my headquarters. Second shift just started, but I don't think anyone would mind if we took a quick tour."

The door that Virgil had been guarding opened up into a honeycomb of cubicles that spread out into what looked like infinity. Unforgiving fluorescent lights filled the office with unnatural white light. The cubicles were filled with twenty-something kids with funky haircuts and trendy clothes, all of them wearing wireless headsets and staring into two, sometimes three widescreen monitors that had been attached to the beige walls of their cubes. Most of them paced around in their cubes as they spoke softly into their headsets.

Nobody so much as looked up from their code-filled monitors as Tommy, Burt, Corinne, Diana, and Lilly (a good ten feet back at all times) followed Virgil through the maze. In spite of all the people packed into the cubes as far as he could see, the place was unnaturally silent. Each worker bee was in his or her own world, the cubicle walls blocking out all sound, the monitors providing their main source of light. The weird text on all the monitors he glanced as he trotted after Virgil and Diana reminded him of what he'd seen in Lilly's journal, but he knew that it couldn't be the same code.

The *cipher*, Eli had called it. Tommy shivered suddenly as the AC kicked on above him. He kept checking on Corinne to make sure she hadn't slipped away, but Burt had been keeping close tabs on her through the narrow halls made by the cubes.

These lights and the lack of windows, Tommy decided, *would've made me nuts before I ever finished a single shift here. And I've had some crappy jobs in my time. Like digging ditches and working on a road crew.*

He patted the ear plugs in his pocket and glanced over at Burt. This was as good a chance as he was going to get, with Virgil and Diana a good ten feet ahead of them. He grabbed two plugs and pressed them into Burt's slightly sweaty hand.

"Be ready to shove these in your ears," he hissed to Burt, who gave him an uncomprehending look for a few seconds, and then his brain caught up with his hand. He grinned and nodded.

Tommy was almost out of breath by the time Virgil zigged and zagged his way to a black door that was almost hidden in the far wall of the big cube-filled room.

"That's the call center," Virgil said, nodding at the cubicles behind them. He turned the knob to the black door and pushed it open as if it weighed half a ton. "And this is the training center."

It was another black, circular room about thirty feet wide. And right in the middle of the room, sitting on what looked like the world's biggest bean bag, was Tommy's buddy Dennis.

Tommy shoved the plugs as far into both of his ears as he possibly could, and to his relief he saw Burt do the same. No way was Diana going to stop them now that he'd found Dennis again.

He charged into the room, ready to scoop Dennis up out of that ridiculous bean bag if he had to.

But he stopped just a few feet from his friend. This wasn't the same Dennis that Tommy had hung out with countless times over the past year. He was rail-thin and somewhat pale, as usual, though his long black hair had pulled loose from his ever-present ponytail. It now fell into his face, lank and loose.

But the fire had gone out of him, all in less than a day of this so-called training. He slumped in the lumpy bean bag, glaring at Tommy as if he didn't recognize him and didn't appreciate the interruption.

Then Tommy realized he wasn't glaring at *him*, but at a screen on the wall behind him.

The four-foot-wide screen showed a grainy, black-and-white video, repeating the same ten-second loop of a young woman turning from a human into a wolf. The video must've been made in the '50s or '60s, based on the style of her clothes—before they shredded off her to be replaced by thick black fur—as well as the quality of the film. It was a devastatingly real view of the were world, as the girl's plain but pretty face distorted and darkened into something monstrous, along with the rest of her body, in mere seconds.

And just like Dennis, Tommy had trouble pulling his gaze away. The transformation looked so impossible that he felt like it insulted his eyes.

With his own breath the only sound filling his ears, Tommy fought the urge to reach down and pull Dennis up from his stupor. But when Tommy moved to block the screen on the wall with its awful looping video of the were in the so-called real world, Dennis blinked and immediately shrank away from Tommy's presence.

If I reached for him right now, Tommy thought, *he'd probably shriek like a banshee.*

Instead he made sure Burt was holding tight to Corinne before he inched closer to Dennis. He hoped his friend would let them rescue him so he wouldn't have to complete Virgil's wicked training.

Diana was saying something to him, but the ear plugs were doing their job. Virgil had moved to stand in front of the door they'd come through, which appeared to be the only way in or out of the room.

We're going to have to go wolf, Tommy thought. *And bite our way out of here.*

But before he, Burt, and Corinne had time to slip into their wolf skins, Dennis popped up out of his bean bag. He swayed a bit, back and forth, as if he hadn't eaten much all day, or if getting up so fast had thrown things all out of whack.

"You let this happen to me," Dennis said. Tommy could read his lips without a hint of uncertainty. Unfortunately.

Dennis raised a shaking, bony hand toward Tommy's face, a move so unexpected Tommy couldn't react fast enough. His friend plucked the ear plug from his right ear.

"And that's why," Dennis said in a voice that Tommy could barely recognize, "we need you and the others to just *sit.*"

Tommy dropped to the floor like a sack of potatoes, unable to stop the actions of his traitorous body.

"Dennis!" he shouted, furious at his friend and at his own inability to control himself.

He turned to check on Corinne, who most certainly was not sitting. She shed her clothes on her way to wolfing it up once more, and she scampered over to him from Burt's side on all fours to lick Tommy's face. With his one functioning ear, Tommy heard Virgil's loud gasp from behind him.

Dennis had also seen Corinne's transformation from toddler to wolf, and he stumbled backwards, away from Tommy and his little wolf girl. He tripped and fell into the overstuffed bean bag again. His eyes fluttered, and then they stayed closed. He'd either fallen asleep or simply passed out.

Just like that, Tommy was able to stand up again. He felt humiliated for himself and furious at Dennis all at once.

"Some training you've given him," he spat at Virgil, who was still guarding the door and steadfastly trying to ignore them all. "He doesn't even know the limits of his skills."

"No," Virgil said in a cool voice. He stepped away from the door, but didn't get too close to Tommy or Corinne. He motioned for Diana to come closer to him, as if for protection.

Tommy scooped up Corinne and held her tightly. He didn't like the look on Virgil's face.

"But now *I* know his limits," Virgil continued. "And I know exactly what I'm going to do with them, and with *him.*"

Chapter Eighteen

Burt didn't hear Dennis use his voice on Tommy, but with his ears protected by Tommy's industrial-strength ear plugs, he watched his brother silently sit on command, and he never wanted to see something like that again. Boom. It happened that fast.

As soon as Tommy went down, Corinne shed her clothes on her way from his side to Tommy's lap, going full wolf in less than a second. Burt felt slightly lightheaded from the utter lack of sound in his head, and he took an unsteady step after Corinne.

When he saw Tommy get back to his feet again and saw but didn't hear him yell something at Virgil, he turned to check on Lilly. He caught her slipping out the door, past a white-faced Virgil. The old man was too preoccupied with the Dennis drama—along with the sight of a tiny werewolf in his office, no doubt—to try and stop Lilly from escaping.

Here we go again, Burt thought, brushing past both Virgil and Diana on his way after Lilly again. Neither of them even tried to stop him. *They didn't care about me anyway. They just want Tommy and Corinne and Dennis.*

Outside the windowless training room, rows of cubes stretched out in three directions. The ten-foot-high ceiling with its gray, sound-baffling tiles felt way too close for Burt's tastes. He hadn't ever worked in a cubicle in all of his checkered and uneven work life, and this place cinched it for him. He'd never be a cube drone.

On a hunch he turned right, sniffing the processed air for Lilly's scent of jasmine and crazy.

He checked each cubicle as he walked, left then right, then left again, and he found her in the fifth cube he checked. Once more, he hadn't smelled her at all.

She'd found an unoccupied cube with its monitors still on and its computer keyboard glowing, as if the worker bee had slipped off for a whiz or a smoke break. Burt's lips smacked unconsciously when he thought of a smoke; it had been too long. Lilly jumped at the sound of his jonesing, but she didn't look up from the keyboard she'd commandeered.

She was scrolling through lines and lines of code, a set of green text on the left monitor, a set of multi-colored symbols, numbers, and letters on the right. Her curly-haired head bounced from one screen to the next, back and forth.

"Lilly," he tried to whisper, but it only came out as a scratchy whisper inside his head.

Duh, Burt thought. He still had Tommy's ear plugs in.

He pulled them out with a popping sensation, and the dull, numbing white noise of the big office dropped onto him, along with the clatter of fingers on keys, typing at high speed.

"What're you doing?" he said. He crept closer, trying to peek at what Lilly was typing on the left screen.

She didn't acknowledge him in any way. Just kept typing.

I guess she missed her pen and journal, Burt thought.

He squinted at the green text Lilly was typing, blinking fast to see if that would help him understand what the hell she was writing. No dice. It was more of her crazy gibberish. Then she switched over to the right monitor and began adding more crazy symbols. Burt didn't even know computer keyboards could make symbols like that. They weren't the same as her cipher codes, but they were close.

"They're tracking all sorts of crazy stuff from up here," Lilly said. She still hadn't looked over at him, but Burt felt a tiny bit of relief at the sound of emotion in her voice. She didn't sound dead like Eli anymore. "Not just werewolves like you and your family, but anyone with any kind of special ability."

"How can they track—"

"I found *my* name in their database. Eli's too. And even my mom. I don't know how they found us. But this stuff can't stay here."

As she spoke, Lilly opened a browser, and then began opening tabs on the browser. Burt, who was the exact opposite of a multi-tasker when it came to computers, quickly got lost. She seemed to be hitting a bunch of websites on the right monitor, then pulling stuff over to the left monitor, somehow. It was all geek speak to Burt.

"*Hey,*" a thick voice said from behind them. "You're in my cube."

Burt turned, ear plugs at the ready. But the voice came from a tall woman in her twenties with old-fashioned black spectacles, straight black hair, and the ever-popular headset covering her ears. The headset's microphone dangled an inch from her mouth and its silver lip ring.

Burt rubbed his beard and aimed for charming.

"Oh, this is your cube? Sure is a nice one. We thought it was vacant. My bad!"

He stepped back so she could come into the cube, but she remained in the doorless doorway, staring at him with suspicious, but glazed eyes.

"Soon as my friend finishes up here, we'll be on our way. Know of another cube we could borrow? We're friends with Virgil, by the way. *Good* friends."

"Right," the girl said, shaking her head hard enough to knock her headphones off-kilter. She pointed at Lilly with a shaking finger. "She needs to get off my system, now. I'm calling Security."

The girl lifted the phone in her other hand and was about to tap on it. Instinctively, Burt snatched it from her, and then pulled her inside the cube so fast she never made a sound.

Great, he thought as he let go of the girl and moved to block her escape. *Now we got a hostage situation.*

"All done!" Lilly said at the same time. She turned off the computer and very conscientiously turned off both monitors before getting up.

Burt put a hand up to the cube owner's face, about to cover her mouth. But she didn't make a sound. She just stared and blinked fast, a confused look on her face. Burt inhaled the sharp tang of marijuana coming from her hair and her hipster clothes.

Some smoke break, he thought. *Hope they got Doritos or something in the break area.*

Lilly stood up and looked at Burt and his new friend.

"Hey," she said. She seemed almost as spaced out from her hacking as the new girl was from her doobie break. "Who's this?"

"She works here," Burt said. "That's her computer you were borrowing."

"Oh," Lilly said.

"What the hell did you *do*?" the girl said with a cough.

"You really need a better password when you lock your computer," Lilly said. "I hacked it in ten seconds. Getting the virus downloaded took just a tiny bit more time."

"No *way*," the stoned girl said.

Lilly just shrugged and smiled as she edged closer to Burt. Her eyes had a touch of mischief in them, the first time Burt had seen that since last night. He almost giggled with giddy relief at the sight.

"The virus is already running," Lilly said. "The worm I added was just an experiment to see if I could get it into the network. And I did! All your database files should be good and hosed by now, you nasty nosey bringers of darkness."

"Why?" the girl said, reaching for her phone, but Burt still had it in his hand.

They were already out in the hallway, so Burt didn't feel the urge to answer that question. He tossed the girl's phone into a wastebasket a couple cubes away, and then they were running for the elevator.

On either side of them, people talked loudly to their computers, asking "What the hell?" and other variations on that theme. Some were even standing up and looking away from their precious monitors. Lilly's virus and her worm appeared to be doing their jobs.

Burt pulled up short when the door to the round elevator room came into sight twenty cubes ahead of them.

"We need to go back and get Tommy and Corinne!" he said. "We can't just leave them back there."

"No time for that," Lilly said. "This place is going to fall apart in a minute."

She started moving again, but at a fast walk instead of a mad dash. A guy stepped out of his cube, swearing, and then backed up when he saw Burt and Lilly.

"Lilly!"

"They can catch up," she said, picking up the pace again, "when the power goes out."

"What?"

She turned so she was walking backwards as she spoke.

"I hacked 'em so the whole floor loses power. We just need to get in the elevator before that happens. I'm sure Tommy and your niece can find their way in the dark, especially when they make their little switcharoo."

Burt let out a laugh.

"You did all that in like, three minutes?"

Lilly grinned and shrugged, then turned around so they were walking side-by-side again. The bright lights overhead suddenly dimmed, filling the office with shadows and greenish glows above each cubicle. People were getting up to their feet inside their cubes now, their heads popping up like prairie dogs emerging from their holes, all of their eyes wide with confusion and fear.

This girl, Burt thought again, hurrying past dazed face after dazed face. *How can I not be crazy for her?*

Burt's good feeling lasted right up until they pushed through the door to the round room at the far end of the cubicles. They rushed over to the elevator without a word.

Lilly reached out to punch the Down button, but the elevator doors slid open before she could touch it.

Gerard, Marg, and Eli stepped out of the elevator to meet them.

Should've gone back to get Tommy and Corinne first, Burt thought, too late. *For backup.*

The lights flickered, and a red-faced Marg advanced on Burt.

"Where's my dad?" he said, reaching up like he was going to grab Burt by the neck. "What'd you do to him?"

Before Marg's hands reached him, Burt felt it come over him. His clothes ripped and his shoes burst, and a growl escaped his newly widened chest. He'd inhaled as a human, but exhaled as a wolf.

And I didn't even have to think about it, he thought as he snatched Marg's left hand with a furry paw and twisted.

He felt the bones in Marg's wrist with his clawed digits, amazed at how fragile and brittle they felt to him now. People were yelling behind them now, and with his heightened senses Burt could've sworn he heard his brother shout, and then an alarm that he didn't need his wolf senses to hear went off behind them, far off in the endless cubicled hallways.

"Let 'im go!" Gerard bellowed, reaching into his jeans pocket.

Again without thinking, Burt pivoted and kicked out with his left leg. His ruined shoe went flying as his clawed foot connected hard with Gerard's side. The big guy toppled over.

Lilly, meanwhile, had slipped around her brother with a shove that knocked Eli back a few feet, and she was now holding the elevator door open from the inside.

"You picked the wrong family to mess with," he growled into Marg's ear, and then he dragged the struggling guy farther into the hallway, away from the elevator. The lights flickered again and went dim, followed by a series of popping sounds, almost like pistol shots.

Burt let go of Marg and bared his teeth at Eli. Lilly's brother didn't flinch away, but he didn't get any closer, either. He just watched Burt pass by with a cool look on his face.

"This elevator better not lose power," he panted, his voice coming out as a growl through his wolf's mouth.

Lilly just shook her head and backed away from him into the corner of the car.

As the doors began to close with a jerky, unsteady motion, Burt couldn't help himself. He had to get one last look at the chaos that Lilly—with a tiny assist from him—had unleashed on these haters and bigots.

Through the open door of the round room leading to the cube farm, Burt saw panicked hipsters with headset cords dangling uselessly at their side, clogging the hallways that led away from the elevators. The fluorescent lights flickered even faster now, as if about to go out for good.

When the elevator doors were halfway shut, Burt caught Eli's scent just for a second. He moved closer to the slowly shrinking gap in the door just in time to see Eli raise his hand, tossing something his way. The lights on the entire floor chose that moment to go out, and Burt lost sight of whatever it was Eli threw.

Something small and black hit Burt in the forehead and stuck there. An instant later the doors closed at last.

Burt never noticed. He had shot back into what felt like his skinny and frail human body as soon as the gadget made contact, and fell backwards, right on top of Lilly. His world went as silent as it had when he'd been wearing Tommy's ear plugs. He couldn't keep his eyes open.

In Burt's new world of noiseless darkness, instead of dropping them down, the elevator lifted them up and away.

When he opened his eyes again, his new girlfriend was digging a spike out of his forehead with her bare hands. He could feel each fingertip, each fingernail, pulling at the spike. When the spike started to move, he felt it from the back of his skull all the way through to his forehead.

He was somehow able to stifle a scream at the pain, even as he fought to grab Lilly's hands to pull her away.

She's trying to kill me! he thought madly. *She's finally lost it. Gotta make the switch and knock her away.*

But his human body refused to cooperate, even as Burt felt the spike through his forehead twist and shudder in Lilly's desperate grip.

I'm a dead man. A frickin' dead man. And it's all Lilly's fault—

And then with a popping sensation, the pain suddenly receded, and Lilly fell back against the elevator wall. The spike of pain was gone.

Burt's sense of hearing returned, along with the rest of his dulled senses. The blare of an alarm stabbed at his ears, and he could hear his own panting along with Lilly's desperate gasping. He tasted coppery blood on his lips, and he smelled his own sour sweat along with the welcome return of Lilly's jasmine-and-bourbon scent.

"Lilly," he began, wincing at the unending alarm filling his ears. He felt worse than a dog for blaming her once again for his troubles.

As he called her name again, something black the size of a silver dollar fell from her right hand and dropped onto the metal floor. They were in an elevator, Burt realized.

Lilly's head slumped forward, but she kept her eyes open wide enough so she could wink at him.

He wanted to grab the gadget, but he knew better than to touch it. Instead he punched the button for the elevator alarm and exhaled at last when it stopped.

The pieces to the puzzle of what had just happened snapped together in Burt's distressed brain, and he remembered Eli tossing that nasty black thing at him right before the elevator whisked them away.

He must've had extra gadgets stuffed into his pockets, the freak, Burt thought. *And the damn elevator should've gone down, not up.*

"Thank you," he said to Lilly as he pulled her to her feet. "You saved my ass." He tried to smile and groaned. "And it's a pretty cute ass, wouldn't you say?"

"Eh," Lilly said in a tired voice. She let out a weak laugh. "I've seen better."

Burt rubbed his forehead, feeling a painful rush of blood there now that he was standing up.

That damn gadget left a dent in me, he thought, checking his hand for any blood from his forehead. Clean. *I'm gonna have a chat with Uncle Carl about this.*

Lilly bent down to grab the gadget, and Burt hissed in a sudden breath.

She picked it up, shrugged when nothing happened, and then she stuffed it into her jeans pocket.

"Just in case I need it for you, later," she said with a tiny grin.

Burt felt the words "I love you" about to bubble out of his lips, but the whispering sound of the elevator doors opening stopped him. He checked the buttons and saw that they were on the 50th floor. The top floor.

Lilly must've hit the alarm to keep the doors from opening while she pried that anti-wolf gadget off of me.

Burt looked out through the open elevator doors at one of the most surreal sights he'd seen since the tunnels underneath the unfinished houses outside his hometown of Dyersburg last year.

"Holy shit," he whispered, staring at the humming and whirring insanity that filled the top floor of Virgil's building.

Instead of cubicles and desks, row after row of black conveyor belts lined the entire length of the floor, with big machines at both ends, either spitting out black gadgets or boxing them up. Every twenty or thirty feet down each line, black robotic arms moved almost too fast for Burt's eyes to see, assembling and then tweaking lines of tiny black gadgets like the one that had just been embedded in his forehead. The spitting of tiny drills and the pop of miniature riveters filled the air along with the churning sounds of the robot arms in motion.

Everything appeared to have been automated, with just a handful of actual humans moving between the different lines, making sure the robots and other machines functioned properly. The people were too busy to notice the elevator opening, and neither Burt nor Lilly tried to stop the elevator doors from closing.

"*Virgil*," Burt whispered. He had to remind himself to blink. "Virgil, you crazy were-hating bastard."

"We've got to break this up," Lilly said. She moved toward the doors, ready to cause more damage out there on the factory floor.

"Wait," Burt said, hoping it was anger in his voice that he heard, not fear. "Hit the button for the 49th," he said. "Let's see what else is up here before we get carried away."

One of the workers had turned toward the elevator, and Burt slipped back into the corner, pulling Lilly with him. The doors closed, and they dropped down a level.

This floor was filled with pallet after pallet of boxes. On the left were a handful of people opening them and taking out the parts inside, while on the right, people at stand-up workstations typed on laptops and printed out what looked like shipping labels. A dude with ear buds and a beard down to his chest pushed a hand truck full of pallets from the left side of the floor toward a service elevator on the right.

"Filling out orders," Burt muttered, looking from right to left, "and getting more parts for upstairs."

The air on this floor was full of dust, making Burt's nose immediately clog.

"Look," Lilly said, pointing at pallet after pallet of sealed boxes in the right-hand corner. All the boxes had the words GREAT PLAINS TACTICAL printed on them like a brand.

"Damn," Burt whispered. And then he saw a black anti-wolf logo on the far wall, looking no bigger than a postage stamp from this distance.

"Damn!" Burt whispered again.

This was all Uncle Carl's fault, he realized. *He started this whole anti-wolf business last year, after Aunt Mel outed herself as a were. Tommy needed to get up here and see this.*

The place was surprisingly busy for a Friday night. Virgil's people were running at least two shifts. Possibly three.

Lilly was already pressing the Close Door button.

"Let's go," she said. "This place is insane. We gotta get out of here."

"Wait. I have to check on Tommy. Burt pulled out his phone, surprised he hadn't thought of this sooner. But Lilly had become—in just 24 hours of knowing her—a master at distraction.

As he fumbled with his phone, his vision blurring from the lingering ache in his forehead, the elevator dropped to the 48th floor. Lilly hit the button just in time to make it stop, and the elevator opened onto a floor that was completely, eerily empty. Burt rubbed at his dust-clogged nose and got a whiff of something pungent, like blood or death, emanating from this floor.

All he could see were black walls at first, but when he squinted he saw the outline of black doors almost hidden in those walls. At least two dozen doors.

And then he and Lilly heard the screams.

Burt wanted to charge out there and rip the doors from their hinges. He felt himself losing his mind from the heart-wrenching screams as he and Lilly stood there in the elevator, paralyzed. He wanted to make the change come over him and stop the screaming.

But all he could do was stand there, his body not cooperating, with the stabbing sensation returning to the middle of his skull and taking up residence there. The stink of something rotten now filled his nose.

"They're testing their gadgets," he whispered in a hoarse voice to Lilly. "On weres like me. And maybe even people like you."

Lilly nodded, her face pale and tight with rage. "This is it. The heart of the darkness."

And I don't have it in me anymore, Burt thought, hands shaking so bad he nearly dropped his phone. *I'm broken. Worthless. All because of one of those damn gadgets.*

Lilly pulled him out of the elevator at last. Burt nearly stumbled, and then he caught up to her. He had to breathe through his mouth to keep the stench away, and even that wasn't helping.

"We've already started taking them down," she said. "Can't stop now. Let's save these poor folks from being guinea pigs."

As they hurried toward the closest closed door, Burt lifted his phone at last and called Tommy. He *needed* him and Corinne up here. The phone buzzed once, twice, three times in his ear as they walked.

"Put that away," Lilly ordered.

Burt shook his head, feeling like a misbehaving three-year-old. They were halfway across the bare cement floor. A scream behind that door nearly stopped Burt in his tracks. The phone buzzed in Burt's ear for the fifth time.

"Come on," he muttered. "Answer, Tommy."

"I can hear their stories," Lilly whispered. "Everyone's stories behind these doors. It hurts me, too. We have to make it stop."

They were at the first door when Tommy finally answered.

"Burt," Tommy said. He didn't wait for a response. "Get your ass back here, now. We got a situation."

"Yeah," Burt said, barely able to speak for all the screams suddenly filling his ears and the reek of suffering in his nostrils. "I can relate to that."

"Don't do anything else stupid," Tommy said. "Was that you and Lilly messing with the lights?"

"All Lilly," Burt said. He grabbed her by the arm and gently pulled her back from the door. She let go of the doorknob.

"Get back here," Tommy said, and then he let out a sudden, shaky breath that sounded like thunder in Burt's ear. "They've got Corinne."

Chapter Nineteen

The lights flickered before Virgil could say another word about his plans for Dennis.

The older man's face darkened with irritation at the lights, even after they had gone back to their steady white brightness.

"Probably just a power hiccup," Diana said, without much confidence. She now stood next to him, like a bodyguard or a crutch.

"Check on it," Virgil said without looking at her. He was focused on Tommy's friend, who had gotten up out of his bean bag. "Now Dennis. Come here."

With a furry Corinne squirming in his arms, Tommy couldn't reach out and grab Dennis. He shouted his friend's name, trying to get his attention. But Dennis kept walking in an unsteady, herky-jerky fashion across the room toward Virgil. Like a puppet, without any strings, heading back to his master.

"Dennis!" Tommy yelled again, but his voice was drowned out by a sudden alarm out in the hallway. It rang madly for three seconds and then stopped.

"Get Security on that, too," Virgil snapped to Diana, reaching one hand behind his back as if he was having low-back pain. Diana nodded, ever loyal, and made another call on her phone, her voice a whisper.

At that moment, Tommy realized that both Burt and Lilly had slipped away, again.

Fine, he thought, exasperated. *Two less people for me to take care of.*

The lights flickered again, and this time Tommy moved. He'd had enough of waiting around for Virgil's master plan to try to take shape. With Corinne tight against his chest, he charged after Dennis and grabbed him around the skinny waist with his free left hand.

"*Dude*," Dennis slurred, trying to wriggle free. "Lemme go!"

"I got ya," Tommy said. "Don't fight. I'm getting you back home, buddy."

On his way to the door, Tommy held tight to Dennis, leading with Corinne. Her tiny, razor-sharp claws slashed at the air in front of her, accompanied by her fierce growling. Virgil flinched back, just one step, and then the lights flashed again and stayed dim, as if most of them had gone out.

That was easy, Tommy thought, reaching for the door in the weak light, his vision perfectly clear. *We could've left at any time.*

Then he froze, hand on the doorknob, when four quick popping sounds filled the air.

Pistol shots.

He turned and looked at Diana next to the door, but she looked as shocked as he felt, and she'd dropped her phone in mid-call.

It hadn't been her, but Virgil. Of course. The crazy old guy stood in the middle of the room, lowering a dull black revolver that looked like it had been left over from the Wild West days. Or a toy store discount sale.

"I have two left," Virgil said in the sudden silence of the poorly lit training room. Tommy's nostrils flared at the stink of gun smoke and fear wafting over from Virgil. "Guess who I'm saving those for?"

"Don't tell me," Tommy said, his voice barely more than a croak. He tried to hold Corinne behind him, to keep his body between her and the old man with the gun. "Silver bullets."

Corinne's claws dug into Tommy's chest and arms, and he had to let his wolf strength flow into his arms just to keep hold of her. Blond fur popped out over his bare hands and arms. He saw disgust and awe battling it out on Virgil's face.

Deal with it, old man, Tommy thought. *We are who we are.*

He had to let go of Dennis to keep from losing his handle on Corinne. Dennis drifted off until he was next to Diana. With his attention split between his daughter and Virgil, Tommy couldn't keep up with his friend. But it looked like Diana was whispering in Dennis' ear. That couldn't be good.

"They weren't easy to get made," Virgil said, all confidence and pride as he looked at the gun in his hands. "Silver's tricky to work with, they said. Have to heat it to almost a thousand degrees, if you can imagine. But I've got the resources to make it happen, and," he looked up at the ceiling, "now we've got the equipment to make them. A lot of them."

"You know that's just a myth," Tommy said.

Virgil had stepped closer to them, shaking his head angrily now.

"Don't tell me about *myths*, boy! Was it a myth that attacked my daughter, or was it one of your kin? Did a myth use its teeth and claws on her? Do you know how many stitches, how many *surgeries* she needed? All from a *myth*?"

The gun was now pointing at Tommy, and he couldn't look away from it. He kept turning to keep Corinne out of the line of fire, hoping his body would stop a bullet, silver or otherwise.

"Okay," he said. "Just let us leave here and we won't bother you. We're not like that. We've got our special, um, *skills*, under control."

Virgil laughed and kicked at Corinne's discarded clothes and shoes on the floor.

"Is that what you call under control?"

Tommy didn't care about the gun anymore. He was getting mad.

Nobody gets to talk like that about my child.

"She's a baby. She wasn't supposed to even be able to change until she was five or six, at the earliest."

"*Feral*," Virgil said. He lowered his gun and shook his head at Corinne, who was still climbing all over Tommy, trying to get free so she could get at Virgil. "I've heard about that. More and more of them lately. Wild."

Tommy fought the urge to grab Corinne's clothes from under Virgil's feet, sending him flying in the process. But they had extra clothes in the car, and it was past time for them to leave.

"We have to go," Tommy said, trying not to think about what the old man meant about *more and more of them lately*. "I just came for my friend, not to start a fight with you."

Virgil just shook his head.

Tommy was getting ready to go full wolf and charge out of here with Dennis and Corinne when the door popped open.

Gerard, Marg, and Eli trudged through the door. They all looked like they'd been through hell to get back here. Gerard was holding his side, and Marg had a fresh-looking bruise on his cheek, which made Tommy think—and hope—they'd run into Burt at some point out in the halls of cubicles.

"About time," Virgil said, glaring at Marg.

"Holy crap, Dad!" Marg shouted. "Put that thing away! Are you nuts? I *thought* I heard shots in here."

"Don't start with me, boy," Virgil said, though he did lower the revolver. "Get a leash out."

"What?" Marg said, spit flying from his mouth. "You think I carry those things in my back pocket everywhere I go? Oh, and good to see you, too, Pops."

Virgil let out a low, humorless chuckle that made the spit in Tommy's mouth dry up. Holding Corinne tight in his long, fur-covered arms, he backed up a few more steps, and then they bumped into Gerard. The guy was like a brick wall, though Tommy heard the guy grunt in discomfort at their contact.

"I can *see* the leash in your front pocket, son. Get it out and get it on that feral child," Virgil said.

Tommy growled, fur popping, limbs elongating and thickening the rest of the way into his change. He tried to stop it, knowing it was just what Virgil wanted. A reason to shoot him with the last two bullets in his gun.

To Tommy's surprise, Gerard snatched Corinne from him while he was distracted by his change and Virgil's words. Gerard held her front paws in one big hand and her back paws in another, giving Marg the two seconds he needed to slip the leash over Corinne's snapping mouth.

Tommy's clawed hand was swinging toward Gerard's neck when the black leash went around his baby's neck. He never finished the swing.

She snapped from her fur-covered wolf cub body to her pink-skinned human body in a split second.

"Daddee!" she cried out in her too-frail human voice.

Tommy grabbed her from Gerard's grip, the sight of her naked body in the hands of a stranger too sickening for words. He wrapped her in what was left of his shirt. He'd completed his change to full-on wolf at the same time she'd switched back to her human side.

"Daddee!" Corinne screamed. "Geddit off!"

Tommy reached down to pull off the collar connected to the leash, even as Virgil leveled his revolver at him again.

"Don't do it," Virgil said.

Tommy let out a roar as the leash sliced into his paws. There was something sharp embedded in the thing. He couldn't see it, but he couldn't touch it without shredding his paws. And Corinne wouldn't stop screaming.

Was it cutting her? Burning her? I'll tear my fingers off it that'll get that damn thing off my baby.

"Get it off her!" he shouted at Marg and then Gerard in his thick, gurgling wolf voice. They just stepped back, as if they'd seen this all before. "You're *killing* her!"

"She's fine," Virgil said. "The blades are all on the outside. On the inside is special technology keeping her from changing into her vile wolf form. I'm so glad to see it works on all ages of wolves."

Tommy picked up Corinne, letting the leash dangle down to the floor. Her screaming abated, and she snuggled her pink cheeks and running nose deep into the fur covering his chest.

He took two steps toward Virgil before realizing what he was doing.

"What do you *want* with us?" he panted.

"Get your brother back here," Virgil said. "And his little lady friend, too."

Tommy shook his head.

"Leave them out of this," he said. "Just let me take my little girl and my friend here back home, and we'll never bother you again. Just take this damn thing off her."

"But that's just it," Virgil said, "I don't want you to leave. I *need* your services."

Just at that moment, Tommy's phone began to buzz. He looked at his jeans, now in a pile on the floor next to the rest of his clothes and Corinne's as well.

Burt and his perfect timing, he suspected. He let it buzz.

Virgil waved his ancient gun at Tommy's buzzing pants. "You might want to answer that."

Tommy looked from Virgil to his sniffling and red-faced daughter, and then glanced behind him at Dennis and Diana, along with Marg and Gerard. He felt painfully aware of his non-human body, his elongated snout and ears. They were all staring at him, eyes wide.

Deal with it, he thought.

With Corinne balanced on one hip, he plucked the phone out of his discarded jeans and willed his clawed paw to recede into his human hand. It was indeed Burt on the phone.

"Burt," he said. "Get your ass back here, now. We got a situation."

"Yeah," Burt said, and Tommy swore he heard what sounded like screams in the background. "I can relate to that."

"Don't do anything else stupid. Was that you and Lilly messing with the lights?"

Virgil grimaced and turned to Diana. "Check on that," he ordered, "again."

"All Lilly."

"Get back here," Tommy said, and then he let out a sudden, shaky breath as he looked down at his struggling little girl. "They've got Corinne."

He hung up, hating that Virgil and the others had gotten to eavesdrop on that call.

"Well done," the old man said. "Now I'd like you to go back to your human form as well, so we can talk like civilized beings."

Tommy held tight to Corinne, careful not to poke or scratch her with his claws. He gazed defiantly back at Virgil with his wolf's eyes and waited.

"Do it!" Virgil said. The gun wavered in his hand, then went back to pointing at Tommy.

Tommy growled and watched the fear grow in Virgil's eyes.

You're gonna have to shoot me first, Tommy thought. *But you're too damn scared.*

He stared down the old man, inhaling his fear mixed with anger. Virgil put his other hand on the gun to steady it as he pointed it right at Tommy's heart. Corinne sniffled once, loudly, in his arms.

The sound of loud footsteps outside the door broke up the standoff, and a moment later, Burt stumbled into the training room with Lilly at his side.

"Gang's all here," Burt began, and then he saw the leash on Corinne. He growled. Tommy watched his brother try to make the change, but something stopped his transformation. Burt walked up to Tommy, shoulders slumped, eyes haunted.

"They broke me, bro," Burt whispered. "I don't have it in me anymore."

"Bullshit," Tommy said, the word almost unintelligible in his toothy mouth. "How? You've only been gone for fifteen minutes."

"Gadget," Burt said, holding up the remains of a nasty-looking black disk that looked bloody. He pushed up the hair falling into his eyes to show a round, red circle the same size as the disk, right in the middle of his forehead.

Damn, Tommy thought. *He's gotta be wrong about that. Because if a gadget can do that, we're all screwed.*

Virgil cleared his throat impatiently.

"Now, it's time for you all to listen."

His voice was met with three identical growls from the members of the Roling family. Virgil's mouth twitched with discomfort at that, but he quickly regained his composure.

"We need you to find your Uncle Carl for us," he said. Tommy winced at the sound of his uncle's name coming from Virgil's mouth. "I hear you're pretty good at that sort of thing."

Tommy almost asked who he'd heard that from, but caught himself. He looked over at Dennis, but he was still whispering with Diana. Dennis was leaning heavily against the wall, as if he could barely stand up.

Tommy let out a long, slow breath to calm himself. He let some of his wolf side go so he could talk easier, and he barely felt the shifting of bone and sinew in his head and face.

Virgil, meanwhile, stared at Tommy as if he were fresh roadkill under the tire of his brand-new Mercedes.

"I don't want to find Carl," Tommy said, thinking of a cold, cold night in Dyersburg when it was just him in his crappy apartment, no Corinne. She was in the back of Carl's car, heading to Iowa City and her new life. "I have *no* interest in ever seeing him again."

"Oh, we'll make it worth your while," Virgil said, giving him a grandfatherly smile.

Tommy didn't trust those words or that smile for a second.

"We've got a slight production issue upstairs," Virgil continued, all relaxed and easy now that he'd gotten this crazy situation under control. Even the lights had come back on and stayed on. "We've got twenty lines of production running up there making those special, ah, mechanisms, that your uncle showed us last year. We found we could make them faster and cheaper right here, instead of waiting for them to come to us from those horrid factories manned by children in China. But none of the gadgets we make here are reliable. Almost all of them fail these days."

"Too bad," Burt said. He seemed to have shaken himself free of the pity party he'd been throwing for himself. "Why don't you shut down your damn factory, then?"

"Not an option. Your Uncle Carl is holding out on us. He gave us bad blueprints, incorrect designs. He took my money and ran."

Virgil's voice rose with each sentence, and Tommy could tell it was the *last* detail that pissed off Virgil the most. Carl ran.

"Why," Tommy said, "would I want to help you make more gadgets that control people like me?"

Virgil laughed, as if the answer was obvious.

He stepped closer to Tommy and his daughter and brother.

"Because I know that, deep down, none of you *want* to be monsters like that. You want to be able to control your animal side. For good. To be *normal*, for the first time in your life."

Tommy gazed down at his daughter, trembling with cold at the end of Marg's leash. She'd broken one of her fingernails almost in half, probably while she was running in her wolf form. A drying line of blood ran from the jagged nail down to the first knuckle of her chubby pink finger.

He looked at Burt, who just glared at Virgil, slowly shaking his head.

And then he turned back to Virgil, whose proud smile made Tommy want to show him what feral really looked like.

You sick bastard, he thought, unable to say anything. *Someone must've messed you up big-time in the past.*

"Find Carl and bring him back here, and the leashes come off. All of them. But only if you *want* them to come off. You might find that your little one is much more, ah, manageable, with a leash on her."

"Fuck *you*," Tommy and Burt said at the same exact time.

After turning their backs on Virgil, gathering up their clothes, and grabbing Dennis once more, Tommy, Burt, and Corinne left the training room without another word.

Chapter Twenty

Burt couldn't be happier to finally get out of that high-rise office nightmare and back to the real world where things made sense. He glanced over at Lilly as the elevator doors opened onto the basement garage. Well, more or less made sense.

We got Dennis out of there, he thought. *That's the important thing. Even if Tommy let them stick a damn collar on Corinne. But we had to leave all those people up on the 48th floor. The guinea pigs.*

Burt exhaled.

This is feeling less like a victory with each passing second, damn it.

Ever since their speedy exit from Virgil's training room, he'd wanted to tell Tommy about what he'd seen, heard, and smelled on the top three floors. The pain and suffering on one floor, and the evil machinery and the clueless workers above that. But one look at his brother, and then his niece in that nasty collar, and he couldn't do it. Those poor folks up there were on their own.

"So?" he said as they headed back to the Grand Am. The shadowy lot still had cars at over half of the parking spots, and the expensive Beemers and Mercedes gave off an unfamiliar whiff of new-car scent to Burt's over-excited nose.

Virgil must pay his people well, he thought. *The bastard.*

"Are you going to try and find Carl for him? Or should we try to get this collar off her ourselves?"

"Don't," Dennis said as he dropped into the front passenger seat. "That lady Diana told me it could hurt her, bad, if we did."

"*Really*," Burt said, suddenly irritated at Dennis, feeling like a good percentage of this trouble was his fault. "She told you that, huh? What else did she tell you? Or should I say, what else did she *whisper* in your ear?"

Dennis looked like he was about to respond, but the wind went out of his sails. He sank down into his seat and fiddled with his hair. At some point he'd pulled his loose hair together and gathered it up again in its usual ponytail.

"You don't wanna know," he said, looking straight ahead at the smooth concrete wall.

Tommy fired up the engine and drove up the narrow corridor leading out of the parking deck. At the exit he stopped, leaving the car idling. Wave after wave of car headlights broke up the darkness from the busy city street. The cars rushed at them from the left at what felt like sixty miles an hour.

Friday night in the big city. Burt was glad Tommy was driving. Corinne let out a shuddering sigh next to him.

"I don't know," Tommy said in soft voice.

Burt felt a cold trickle of dread run through him. It sounded like Tommy was talking to himself, carrying on some sort of one-sided conversation as he stared straight ahead, not even seeing the traffic coming at them.

Leaning forward, Burt was about to say something when he saw that Tommy had his hands up close to his face, staring at them. Burt saw the tiny cuts covering Tommy's big fingers, over a dozen tiny horizontal scars that should've healed themselves while Tommy was in his wolf body. That's usually how it worked. But those cuts were still red and angry, and they looked like they hurt like hell.

Those damn collars, Burt thought. *Who'd* make *evil shit like that? Who could hate us like that?*

Unfortunately, he'd discovered the answers already, tonight.

With a grunt, Tommy threw the car into Park and slowly shook his head.

"You don't know what?" Burt piped up at last. Nobody else was going to respond.

Tommy sucked in a surprised breath, as if he hadn't realized anyone else was in the car. He turned back to face Burt, but his gaze locked on Corinne. She was silent in her car seat, gingerly touching her neck above and below the wicked black collar. All she wore was her daddy's ripped-up shirt.

The leash attached to the collar—it was all one seamless piece—stretched out next to her and dangled to the floor like a whip. Or a tail.

"We never should've brought her here," Tommy said, his eyes haunted. He shook his head slowly. "I don't know why we even left home."

Burt didn't answer, just pointed at Dennis in the passenger seat. He was glad to see his hand wasn't shaking when he did it.

Tommy nodded at that. "Yeah, true."

Dennis, in the meantime, was oblivious to the conversation. At some point he'd borrowed Tommy's phone, and he appeared to be busy texting someone, skinny thumbs flying around the tiny keyboard.

Probably letting his lady-friends back in Iowa City know he's safe, Burt figured. *Though who knows when—or if—he'll be coming home. Personally, I ain't got a clue.*

While they sat there idling, Tommy extracted a crumpled piece of paper from his pocket, and he squinted at it as if it was written in Chinese.

"We gotta find Uncle Carl," he said. "I know the guy could be anywhere, but we should at least start with what we got from his hard drive. *This* place made the list," he added, tapping the first address on the crumpled sheet of paper that Lilly had torn from her precious journal. "We should check out the other addresses."

Burt let out a nervous laugh. "Oh yeah. We saw a sign upstairs for Great Plains Tactical. On the other floors."

Lilly was staring at him now, along with Corinne and Tommy.

"*Other* floors?" Tommy asked.

"Yeah, Carl is *not* gonna want to see us," Burt said, doing his best to change the subject as fast as he could. "Remember the last time we saw him? He was lucky to make it out of Dyersburg alive."

Tommy rubbed his face and stifled a loud yawn that ended in a growl.

"Uncle Carl's got this coming," Tommy said in a low voice that made Burt extremely uncomfortable. But the subject was officially changed.

"Got it," Dennis said as he finished tapping on the screen of Tommy's phone. He pulled up a map of the city, with a squiggly blue line leading through the maze of streets.

"Let's get out of here first," he said, his voice gaining strength as he spoke. "I spent enough time in this place today, doing my... *training*. Look, Tom, you gotta turn right out of here, 'cause it's a one-way. Then go left in two blocks. I'll get you there. You drive, I navigate."

Burt wondered if Dennis was using his voice on Tommy right now, because Tommy immediately put the car in gear, and he found an opening in the traffic a few seconds later. With a squeal of tires that Burt approved of, they left Virgil's fifty-story headquarters. Burt watched the glass-and-concrete tower until it disappeared, creeped out by the utter darkness of the top four stories.

Maybe we imagined those screams, he thought, unable to block those memories from his head. *Maybe they were just making computer chips or cell phone batteries up there, and not were-controlling gadgets for anti-wolf dot com. Maybe. Or maybe it all really happened, and we've got to fix all this.*

He patted Corinne's hand, careful not to touch her torn fingernail. She wasn't asleep, even though it was almost ten o'clock at night. She just stared at him silently with her big blue eyes. She looked as lost and confused as the rest of them.

Even Lilly wasn't herself. She sat next to Corinne in the backseat, hand motionless on her lap, no pen, no journal. As Dennis murmured turns and tips in the front seat, Lilly caught Burt's gaze and gave him a tired smile. At least she'd been able to fry Virgil's network, and maybe throw a monkey wrench or two into his searches and spying.

Tommy's right. I don't know why we ever left Iowa City.

Burt closed his eyes.

Chicago is no fun anymore.

He heard the screams again, loud and agonized at first, and smelled death again. Then the bump of traffic and honking cars drowned out those dark memories.

He saw Lilly pressing Enter and unleashing the virus on Virgil's computer network, and then he saw her pulling that evil disk off his forehead again. Her eyes were almost black with determination, and when she turned her gaze on him, Burt nearly shouted out loud.

She looked like someone else. Someone *possessed*.

When he opened his eyes again, half an hour had passed. They weren't pulling up in front of an EconoLodge or a Days Inn like he'd been expecting, but a narrow two-story house tucked in tightly next to dozens of other narrow two-story houses.

Corinne was still awake next to him. Somehow Lilly had managed to get her out of Tommy's ruined shirt, replacing it with a fresh diaper and a nightgown, despite the car seat restraints and the collar around the little girl's neck.

He glanced over at Lilly, half afraid she'd be staring at him with those black eyes from his short-lived dream. But she was looking out at the houses with her normal, hazel eyes, most likely trying to figure out where they were.

"So *this* is how you repay me?" Tommy muttered to Dennis.

When he figured it out, Burt began to laugh softly from the back seat, careful not to let Tommy hear it.

Dennis, he thought, *you sly dog. You got in touch with the one and only person that Tommy Roling knows in Chicago.* Nina.

Tommy Roling!" Nina called as they walked up the sidewalk to her place. She stood silhouetted by the single light in the living room behind her. "You've been dragging that poor little girl through downtown Chicago this late at night? Get *in* here, all of you."

"Nina!" Corinne called as she charged away from Tommy, across the tiny front lawn, and up the three front steps into Nina's arms. "Nina Nina!"

"You've gotten so big!" Nina said, about to wrap her arms around Corinne. And then she froze. "What is *this*?"

She'd found the collar. Dennis hurried up the sidewalk after Corinne, waving at Nina with a nervous smile.

"Hey, Nina. Good to see you!" He nodded at the collar. "Don't touch it, okay? It's a long story."

"You could've told me about it when you were texting me," Nina said to Dennis.

"No," Dennis said in a guarded tone of voice. His smile went away. "Some things shouldn't ever be written down."

Lilly flinched at that, and finally Burt had to nudge both her and Tommy to get them moving toward Nina's place.

"Don' touch," Corinne said, pointing at her new collar with a solemn look on her round face. "Owies."

Nina was still holding Corinne, unable to stop looking at the collar and leash hanging down at Corinne's side. She hugged Corinne, mindful of the collar, and then she focused her attention on Tommy. Corinne slipped down her side and proceeded to run from one postage-stamp-size lawn to the next, calling out Nina's name with every step.

"Are you forgetting to *eat* back there in Iowa City?" she said, glaring down from her perch at Tommy.

Tommy fumbled for words, and then Nina laughed, a clear and happy sound that lifted Burt's spirits immediately.

"I needed to drop some pounds," Tommy said, giving her a big, sheepish grin as he walked up the steps. "It's good to see you, Nina."

Off in the distance a car honked and a siren began wailing. Corinne ran back up to Nina's side, out of breath.

Nina gave Tommy a quick, sisterly hug with a double back pat—Burt winced at that—and then she pulled him toward the house.

"Come on in," she said to Burt, Lilly, and Dennis, who were still crowded together at the bottom of the steps. "Before my neighbors calls the cops. They're a bit paranoid. Can't say I blame 'em, with a couple *weres* living in their 'hood."

She punctuated her statement with another laugh, and then they all went inside.

Nina lived in a funky, narrow house in the older part of Chicago not five miles from downtown and Lake Michigan. She shared it with her two older sisters and their kids, a little boy and a little girl. Burt was so tired he spaced their names as soon as they'd mentioned them—they were already in bed, as it was after ten p.m. already—and he was pretty sure Nina had told him her sisters' names as well, but they were lost in his tired brain as well.

Plus, the drama of seeing Tommy reuniting with Nina had demanded all of his attention. Little bro still had it bad for Nina, Burt could tell, and he couldn't blame him. Not only was she good-looking and intense in a cool way, and she'd styled her hair into an impressive new 'do since he last saw her over a year ago, but she laughed. A lot.

"At first I thought it was you texting me," Nina said, pointing first at Tommy, then at Dennis, "but it was *you*. No wonder I couldn't help but answer. I didn't know you could use your voice powers in a text."

Dennis looked surprised at that. "Neither did I. That's, um, good to know..."

Tommy wondered if Dennis had gotten a tour of Great Plains Tactical as part of his training, and if so, if he was thinking of the 48th floor. And the screaming.

"Have a seat, everyone," Nina said. They were all standing around in her living room, with Tommy blocking her TV and Corinne gazing out the picture window at the street and other houses outside. Burt and Lilly snagged the big red couch, along with Dennis, while Nina took up half of the love seat perpendicular to the couch.

Tommy did a little awkward dance move, heading a few steps toward Corinne at the window, a few steps toward Nina and the love seat, and then he ended up perching on the ledge next to Corinne at the picture window. Though Burt knew he was working hard to hide it, Tommy looked miserable.

Despite all that had happened today, Burt found himself grinning, even though he knew Tommy would crack his skull if he saw it.

"When Dennis texted me," Nina said, "he said he'd explain everything when you got here. So... let's hear it."

Tommy looked at Burt, and Burt quickly hid his grin with his hand.

"You want to start?" Tommy asked, giving Burt a look that told him he'd better say Yes.

"Sure," Burt said. "We've had an interesting 24 hours. *Very* interesting. It all started back in a funky little bar in Iowa City that had a serious stuffed fox theme. It was guys' night out. You can just imagine how fun that might be with a brother like Tommy here..."

As Burt got caught up in telling their story, he felt the weight of the past few hours drop off of him, and he reveled in the feeling of safety and friendship here. He'd missed that lately, ever since they had to move away from Aunt Mel's place. Just hanging out with family and friends, no draft beers or shots to be seen, no need to make a great impression. Just shooting the shit with the gang. The pack.

He talked for a good five minutes, feeling a buzz totally unlike the kind he got from beer.

"That's when we decided to come to Chicago and get away from it all. And we just happened to find Dennis in the process. Turns out the place we found him was hooked up with Tommy's uncle. You remember him, right?"

Nina gave a tiny nod at that, and Burt swallowed with a clicking sensation. He remembered how she looked as a wolf, and knew better than to mess with her.

"So it's needle in haystack time," he finished, wishing he had a beer or even some water. "We need to find our Uncle Carl, and then Virgil the were-hater will take off this evil collar on Corinne. But Carl could be anywhere."

Everyone was staring at him with hopeless eyes. Everyone, that is, but Nina.

"Has anyone just tried calling the guy?" she said.

Burt started at that, and then he touched the phone in his jeans pocket. He let out a laugh when he saw Tommy do the exact same thing.

"That would just be too easy," Burt said, "wouldn't it?"

Tommy beat him on the draw. He was already calling Carl's number.

"Hope he hasn't changed phones," Tommy said, holding his phone up to his ear. It looked like a kid's toy in his big hand. "But it's likely he—"

Burt got up off the couch at that. Carl had actually answered, and he needed to hear what the guy was going to say. Tommy put the call on speaker for the rest of them.

"Hello?" a familiar voice said, with the hint of a slur.

"Uncle Carl," Tommy said. "This is Tommy."

The phone was silent for so long that Burt thought they'd dropped the call. He tiptoed across the floor and sat on the other side of Corinne, so she was walled in by the two brothers. Protected.

"Damn," Carl said. "Another late-night call from my nephew. And we remember how that last call turned out last year, right?"

Tommy shook his head, face flushing red.

"I know we've had our run-ins," Tommy said, "but I really need to talk to you. Where are you?"

"No. That's not a good idea. That's a *terrible* idea. Terrible."

"Come on, Uncle Carl. Don't you want to see how big Corinne's gotten?"

"Hell no," Carl said in a voice that sounded a lot like Virgil's. Burt didn't have time to do earmuffs over his little niece's ears to protect her from the f-bomb. "I don't need to see your feral bastard child."

Tommy moved to toggle off the speaker function on his phone, but Nina touched his hand and shook her head. Burt hadn't even seen her move to Tommy's side.

"That... wasn't nice. And it sounds like you've not been up to very nice things lately, Uncle Carl. You got yourself into some fresh trouble, is what we've heard."

"Who you been talking to?"

Burt could've sworn he heard the smack of an empty shot glass hitting a table top on the other end of the line. He knew the sound well enough.

"I'll tell you all about it, in person."

"Who you been talking to, Tommy Boy?"

Tommy's face had gone hard and fierce, but his voice just got more calm.

"I'll tell you. Face to face. But first, you tell us where you're staying these days."

"Go to hell," Carl said, and killed the call.

Tommy rubbed his face with a hand shaking not with fear but rage.

"Wait'll Aunt Mel hears about this," he muttered, putting his phone away.

"That Carl never fails to impress," Nina said deadpan, and everyone looked at her for a surprised second.

Then, as if on cue, everyone cracked up laughing.

"Shh," Nina said after a few good seconds of light after the darkness of the call, and the day. "You're gonna wake the kids."

"I wonder if there's some way to trace that call, like the cops do. Can't your phone do that, with GPS?"

Tommy shook his head. "Only if you get the other person's permission. Maybe I should try that. I bet Carl would accept my request to track him via GPS, don't you think?"

He was answered by another round of cathartic laughter.

"Yeah," Burt said. "He's like an evil ring of power. He *wants* to be found."

Dennis hummed a song from *The Lord of the Rings* soundtrack, while Lilly giggled and muttered something about one uncle to rule them all.

"Okay, you guys, it's getting late," Nina said, and gave Burt a crooked look, "especially for old folks like Burt here. We've got couches and extra blankets in the basement. And I think there's an old Pack and Play for Corinne to sleep in."

Everyone stood up, eager to find somewhere to crash. Burt stayed close to Lilly, needing to get close to her and talk about the day. And maybe move in close next to her so he could sleep without any bad dreams.

They ended up on a pull-out couch in the basement, both of them so tired they barely had energy to splash some water on their faces before dropping onto the thin, lumpy mattress. Dennis was already asleep on a sleeping bag in the laundry room.

Burt lay there with his arm thrown around Lilly, spooning her still-tense body. He was amazed at how far they'd traveled today, and how much had changed in just one day.

He kissed Lilly's neck, and she relaxed against him at last.

"G'night," Burt said, already half-asleep. "Love you."

The words had slipped out before he even knew he was saying them. His eyes snapped open, wide.

Shit, he thought. *I just screwed up everything, with two little words.*

His panic lasted just two seconds, however.

"Love you too, Burt."

Burt closed his eyes, smiling, and he held Lilly tight. His sleep was deep and dreamless.

Chapter Twenty-One

Tommy finally got Corinne to sleep—collar, leash, new place and all—after an hour-long struggle. He'd wanted to use his wolf strength, or maybe a sharp knife, to cut that leash off her collar, but he was too worried something would happen. Like the collar would tighten around her tiny neck, or she'd get the leash hooked on the side of the Pack and Play. This was a whole new world now, with leashes and gadgets made to control and hurt weres like them.

So he finally just tucked the leash next to Corinne and told her to be careful with it. She'd nodded back with those solemn, almost grown-up eyes, and he felt like she understood.

He'd check on her every hour tonight, in any case.

And then, with Corinne asleep in the tiny guest bedroom down the hall and the others down in the basement, it was just him and Nina sitting on the squishy red couch in the living room.

The rest of the house was silent except for the breeze rolling in through both the front screen door and the smaller windows next to the picture window in the living room. All the lights were off except the lamp next to the red couch, where Nina was sitting.

It had been way too long since he'd seen her. He never fully realized how much he'd missed her until right now, as he stared at her slightly tired eyes and that incredible smile she would unleash on him like a sneak attack. Her hug when he'd walked in the door had been much too short for his tastes. He wanted her arms around him again.

Way too long.

Sitting next to her at last, Tommy let himself relax for what felt like the first time in months, if not years.

"That little girl of yours," Nina said, curling her legs under her and smiling. "So flipping cute! She's gotten big, too."

Tommy nodded, the proud daddy. "She's a handful, but she's still the best thing that's happened to me." He cleared his throat and reminded himself to relax and stop fidgeting. "Well, one of the best things."

Nina bumped his knee with hers, and then left it there. Her touch sent a charge through his tired body, but then somehow he found himself relaxing. Must've been that smile of hers.

"*Tommy*. Are you being all charming now?"

He shrugged, and Nina laughed again. He felt a year of loneliness and unspoken sadness drop off of him like those extra twenty-five pounds he was trying to lose.

"I thought I'd try it out. Being charming, that is. I think I'm doing pretty good so far."

Nina rolled her eyes, and then she shook her head.

"I can't believe you're here, in Chicago, sitting on my couch."

"Me neither. But I'm glad. I frickin' *missed* you, Nina."

"Well, you stopped calling and texting."

"We both did." Tommy couldn't figure out, for the life of him, why he hadn't kept in touch with this amazing woman. "I got busy, and ran out of interesting things to say. Life happened, I guess."

"Ugh," Nina said. "I hate that saying. Sounds too much like *Shit happens.*"

Tommy caught himself before saying something stupid like "Same difference."

Instead, he said, "But I'm here, now. Sorry to drop in on you like this, but here we are."

"No worries. We got the space, and we always enjoy visitors. Some crazy shit happened to you guys, that's for sure. All of you."

"Yeah," Tommy said, thinking about the other floors of that building that Burt and Lilly had visited. According to Burt, who had a lifelong knack for exaggeration, the top floors of Virgil's skyscraper sounded a mix of a high-tech factory and an evil scientist's lab, with its own shipping department. Antiwolf dot com, all over the place.

"And I brought my two-year-old along with us for it. Good thinking, huh?"

Nina grabbed his hand.

"Come on, Tommy," Nina said, pulling him closer to her. "I know how you are with Corinne. You'd never let something like this just happen. And she's... she's *different*, Tommy."

He was still processing her statement about letting this happen, and whether he needed to be pissed about that, when he heard her last sentence. A flush of guilt and shame hit him, as if Corinne's wildness was also his fault.

My ever-growing list of shortcomings, he thought. And then Nina pulled him out of his slide into self-pity.

"It's okay," she said. "Just talk to me, okay? What's going on with Corinne?"

Tommy took a deep breath, inhaling Nina's almost-forgotten scent greedily, and then he let it out.

"I'm worried," he said, "that there's something *wrong* with her."

Nina looked at him for a long five seconds without saying anything, her sharp brown eyes locked on his, as if she wasn't buying all of what he was saying.

"Well, I'm no parent, but I'm guessing that *every* mom and dad worries about that for their kids."

"It's more than that. She's wild, and getting worse. You saw how she was tonight, couldn't sit still. And that was a good night for her. Last night she ran from my aunt's house on the other side of the river, past downtown to where I was. That's got to be at least three miles. All in her wolf body."

"Damn," Nina said. "And she's only two? Some nose she's got on her. She's lucky no one saw her, or ran her over. Poor baby."

"Yeah, I can't even think about it. And that's just one example. She about clawed her cousins to death, and they both have it in them, too. If they weren't weres, she probably would've killed them."

Tommy kept stretching his legs and straightening his back, unable to get comfortable. He wasn't used to unloading his concerns on someone else like this. He was afraid of what Nina was going to think of him.

"I've heard about this, actually," she said, and then she squeezed his arm when he tried to wriggle away from her. "Just *relax*, okay? We're friends."

Tommy exhaled. He couldn't help himself—he shifted one last time so he could lean onto Nina's shoulder. He dropped his head until it touched hers.

To his relief, she stayed there instead of pulling away.

Friends, he thought. *It's a start.*

He closed his eyes, smiling in spite of himself. She smelled so good.

"What did you hear, oh wise city girl?"

He felt Nina shake her head slowly as she spoke.

"Neither of my sisters' kids have shown that they have it in them yet. But Juan's only three, and Kenya's younger than Corinne. I think they've got it—both of my sisters have it, too. It just hasn't presented itself yet."

Tommy wanted to pull himself away from Nina as he thought about that night in Iowa City. The night Corinne turned wolf for the first time, a couple months shy of her first birthday. *My poor baby.*

"But we've all been keeping an eye on them," Nina continued, her voice soft as a murmur. "And keeping our ears open with the other weres we know. That's where we heard about the *wildness*. Mostly in kids born in the past year or two."

Tommy was jealous of her insider information. He needed to work on his wolf network.

"What *is* it? What's wrong with 'em?"

"Nobody really knows what's causing it, but it sounds a lot like what you're saying about Corinne. Starting out as a were at a way younger age than we ever did. Not wanting to switch out of their wolf skin. Attacking others, not caring how big the other people are they're attacking. Can't sit still. Wild. Outta control."

"It's not just her," he thought, and ended up saying it out loud. He hated to admit it, but the overwhelming emotion he felt at that moment was *relief*. It wasn't all his fault.

He felt Nina nod. "We thought it might just be something about living in the city—something in the water, or the lack of wide open spaces to run. But if Corinne's been feeling it, too, in tiny Iowa City, then that blows away our theories. Maybe it was just something in the air two years ago." She chuckled. "Or should I say two years and nine months ago?"

Two years ago, Tommy thought. *Another lifetime. I was still with Suzanne, living in that crappy apartment back home, trying to make it all work with a new baby in my life. I didn't even know I could turn into a wolf if there wasn't a full moon. I was so dumb back then. So naive. Just two years ago.*

"We'll figure this out," he said. "We've got to fix it."

Nina smiled at him. "Had a feeling you'd say that."

Tommy tried to smile back, but talking about Iowa City and fixing things had made him remember something. Some*one*, to be exact.

"I need to call my boss," he said. "He wants me back early tomorrow, and I can tell that ain't gonna happen." He pulled out his phone and checked the time, stifling a yawn at the same time. "It's already almost one a.m."

But when he called Attix's number, he got no answer. Attix always answered his phone, even if it was after midnight on a Friday night. *Especially* when it was after midnight on a Friday night.

"This is Tommy," he said to Attix's voicemail when it finally kicked in. "Just letting you know I'm planning on getting back in town later in the day tomorrow. Wild night tonight with the family. Call me if you need me. Buh-bye."

Tommy ended the call and set his phone on the end table next to him.

"Buh-bye?" Nina said with an elbow to his side. "Really?"

"Weird," he muttered, ignoring her jabs. "Attix always picks up. I wonder what's wrong."

"You usually call your boss this late at night? This is the cop, right?"

"Yep."

"I'm sure he's fine. Probably working, like you said. I got an uncle who's a cop, and he never seems to be off work. Always tired as hell, too."

Tommy nodded, chewing at his bottom lip.

"Maybe I should try his work number—"

"*Relax.* You don't have to take care of everyone, Tommy!"

He sighed and looked at the darkness on the other side of the picture window, unable to see anything but the neighbor's spotlight and the faint glow of big city lights beyond that. He saw Nina's outline and his own reflected back at him, faceless and vague, like strangers.

When he turned back to her, she was now leaning into him, just a few inches away.

He started to say something, but Nina shushed him.

Tommy leaned closer and thought, *Why not?*

He pressed his lips to hers. She was ready for him. As if she'd been waiting for him for quite a while, actually.

Tommy let his eyes close. She tasted like red wine and cinnamon. The kiss lasted ten seconds, and he already wanted another taste.

Nina stroked his cheek and tried pulling him closer, but something stopped him.

You have responsibilities, Tommy Roling.

"I gotta go check on Corinne," Tommy said, his internal dad clock going off almost exactly an hour after he'd put his little girl to bed.

Nina caught his eye as he tiptoed down the hallway. She wasn't smiling, just shaking her head.

"Of course you do," she whispered.

Corinne was snoring softly when he peeked in at her. The leash was still tucked safely at her side, and it didn't seem to be bothering her. Poor kid was exhausted.

How many times, Tommy wondered as he closed the door almost all the way, *have I checked on this little lady, only to see her wolf snout poking up at the ceiling? So many times that looking at her pink, hairless cheeks and button nose makes me do a double-take, that's how many.*

He paused outside the door to catch his breath. His head was swimming, as if he'd had a couple glasses of Nina's wine, too. But he was dead sober.

What the hell am I doing? he wondered.

He'd just gotten up from the couch, right in the middle of their kiss. That had been his first kiss in over a year, and it had made him feel a bit crazy. He'd never met anyone in the past twelve months who'd even vaguely interested him as much as Nina, so he'd never bothered dating. As if he even had time to look.

"Nina," he said, walking back down the hall and holding his hands out in front of him like a politician about to give a speech. "I hope you don't think that I—"

"Your poor fingers," Nina said, sucking in a sudden breath at the sight of the slow-healing scars criss-crossing his digits. "You said that *collar* did this to you?"

Tommy sat down next to her again and slid his hands under his thighs. He felt each cut as he hid them.

"This Virgil guy. He's nuts. He got Uncle Carl to do some sort of crazy customizations to his gadgets. They only seem to work on weres. And Virgil had these collars and leashes made. Burt got one of them stuck on him, too, that kept him stuck in his wolf form. At least his hands healed up after that. It's like Virgil has some sort of control over our were abilities now. Even our healing powers. I don't like it, not one bit."

"He's been in the city for a long time. Him and his family."

"You've *heard* of him?"

"I grew up in Chicago, Tommy. Everyone's heard of Virgil Ericson. But my family—my pack—we always pride ourselves on knowing more. And Virgil's one bad-ass fella. My aunts did some digging on him. You guys are lucky to have gotten out of his office in one piece. All of you but poor little Corinne."

"Yeah," Tommy said, suddenly exhausted. "He really hates weres. Or actually, to be more accurate, he seems scared shitless by us."

"No surprise there. He claims his daughter was attacked by a werewolf while they were on vacation up in Wisconsin or Minnesota. That the were almost killed her, and Virgil was there to witness it all. Some people say he shot the wolf and saw it revert back to its human form when it was dying. Drove Virgil Ericson nuts, pretty much on the spot."

Tommy's mouth went dry, thinking of something like that happening to his little girl. He'd lose it, too.

"Virgil talked about that tonight," he croaked, and then swallowed. "How many stitches and surgeries his daughter needed. I can see how that might make him hate weres like us."

"*If* that's what happened. No one ever found the were's body."

"So to keep something like that from happening again, he starts making these tiny little black devices that are supposed to control us. Keep us from being deadly wolves. The way he talked, he made it sound like he was doing us a favor."

Nina sighed and fiddled with her new hair. Tommy missed the tiny dreadlocks, but he could get used to her new look. The curls made her look sexier, somehow.

"We *really* need to find your uncle."

"Yeah. Not just to get Corinne's collar off, but to find out *how* he ever figured out how to make those anti-wolf gadgets work. Maybe he can help us sabotage Virgil's factory up there." Tommy pointed out the front window, in the general direction of what he thought was the downtown area.

"Easy there, big guy," Nina said with a nervous laugh. "One step at a time."

Before Tommy could plot the next step in the downfall of Great Plains Tactical—and Uncle Carl, too—his phone buzzed on the end table next to him. He snatched it before it could buzz a second time, positive it was Attix calling him back.

But the number on the screen was from his other closest "grown-up" confidante back in Iowa City. His Aunt Melanie.

"Hey Aunt Mel," he said. "You okay?"

"Tommy," his aunt said in a soft voice. He pictured her sitting at her kitchen table, hand over the phone to keep from waking her two boys. "I'm glad you're still up. Can you talk?"

"What's wrong?"

"You've got Corinne with you, don't you?"

"Yes, she's right here. What's *wrong*?"

"Oh, good. Good. You'll never guess who was here tonight, looking for you two."

Melanie's words were a bit slurred, like they did after she'd had a couple drinks. Tommy made a pained face at Nina and put the call on speakerphone.

"Carl?" Tommy said, the name almost sticking in his throat.

Melanie sucked in a loud breath, amplified by the phone's little speaker.

"How'd you know?"

"Well, he's been a topic of conversation lately. We're actually in Chicago. You don't want to know what Carl's been up to here."

Melanie was silent for so long Tommy thought the connection had been broken.

"Did you talk to Virgil, then?"

Tommy and Nina gaped at each other.

"You know him, too?" Tommy said. "He needs Carl back here, right now. He's making us bring Carl to him, and he's..." He struggled for a way to explain the leash-and-collar situation to Mel over the phone, and quickly gave up. "He's not gonna take no for an answer."

"That's not going to work. Carl can't go to Chicago. Not any time soon."

"Let *me* talk to him," Tommy said, his face suddenly hot. He'd had enough of Carl dicking around with all of his family. "I'll get him back here."

"He's got a GPS tag on his ankle. He has to be home every night by 7 p.m. And he can't leave the state."

"*What?*"

"Some of his deals he made earlier this year caught up to him. He's a flight risk heading into trial in September. I made sure they took all the proper precautions. Including arranging to get him the worst lawyer ever to defend him."

"How do you know all this? Is he still in Iowa City?"

A long pause, long enough for Tommy to figure it out.

"Was he there at your house? I guess he can't be there now, or his GPS tag would give him away, right?"

"He just left."

"What?"

"You know Carl. He found a way to trick the GPS tag with one of his damn gadgets. But I called up two buddies on the force to escort him home, with a brand-new ankle bracelet six inches wide."

Damn, Tommy thought, impressed all over again by his defense-attorney aunt. *Don't mess with Aunt Mel.*

"Melanie, are you and the boys okay? Are you safe?"

"Yes, Tommy. I can handle myself. Just... be careful. You're on someone's radar, and it's not just Carl. It's bigger than just him now. If you come back here, don't go to your house. Come here. I know Carl or his friends have someone watching your place."

"Shit," Tommy said. "What's Carl gotten us all into now?"

"You don't want me to answer that. Drive safely, and text me when you get close. Love you, bud."

Tommy swallowed and looked at Nina, whose eyes had darkened with intensity and anger.

"I love you too. Be careful. See you tomorrow, no later than noon, at your place."

"Deal. Bye now."

"Bye."

Tommy ended the call and tucked away his phone again.

"Unbelievable," he said. "He's been in Iowa City all this time. Keeping in touch with Aunt Mel. We've gotta go back, right away."

Tommy stopped himself when he realized he was about to dig out his car keys.

"Well, not right now. In the morning. Guess I didn't need to call Attix to tell him I'd be late, after all."

Nina held out her hand, a stern look on her pretty face.

"What?" Tommy said, suddenly worried in an all new way.

"Phone. Hand it over."

"Nina, come on," Tommy said, but he pulled out his phone again and handed it to her. She made a big show about turning it off, all the way off.

"Ow," Tommy said. "That hurt."

Nina set it on the end table next to her with a dull thud, and then she flicked off the lamp. Blue-white light filtered in from the picture window, and the breeze made a swishing noise through the screen. Nina's face glowed in the soft light.

"I *believe*," she said, "before you got all distracted on me, that we were in the middle of something." She grabbed Tommy around the back of his neck and pulled him closer once more. "I'm pretty sure it was something like this."

"I need to check on Corinne—"

Nina touched her nose to his and sniffed indignantly.

"I've been listening for her all night. Her breathing hasn't hitched even once. I got your back, Iowa boy."

"Nina," Tommy exhaled. He kept looking for something, a reason, some excuse, to pull away. To not enjoy this moment.

"Shh," Nina said, and then she kissed him.

Tommy surrendered to the moment and trusted that Nina knew exactly what she was doing. In her arms, his lips against hers, the rest of his world fell away, and freedom had never felt so good.

Chapter Twenty-Two

On their early-morning drive back to Iowa City, Burt really wanted to stop by the gas station from last night and trash Marg's big blue pickup, or at least let the air out of a couple of the tires. But they flew past that stop without even slowing. He could've pulled over on his own, since he was driving Tommy's Grand Am—the thing was a real pooch compared to his Camaro—but he knew that he'd catch hell from Tommy, puttering along ahead of him in Nina's dented blue Tercel.

Burt chuckled to himself, thinking about how Tommy had tried to squeeze all of them into his car for the ride back to Iowa City. Nina had been the one to do the reality check while the rest of them stood around in the dark at six a.m.

"What if I want to get back home? I need my wheels." Tommy had looked a bit downcast at that idea, and then Nina had added, "And what'll you do when you find your uncle? You going to throw him in the trunk like I did last year?"

So Tommy had grudgingly given Burt his car keys, and he'd let Nina drive him and Dennis in her car. Burt and Lilly took Corinne in the Grand Am instead of trying to fit her car seat into the back of the tiny Tercel.

And now Corinne was sleeping fitfully in her car seat, miserable with that nasty collar still tight around her neck. Her strawberry-blond hair stood up in sweaty little spikes as she sucked hard on her thumb and dreamed.

Was it really only a day ago, Burt thought, *when I woke up with my own collar? Except that one didn't keep me human, but the opposite. Whoever's making these things is branching out, and not in a good way. Uncle Carl, we need to talk, old man.*

He yawned and pressed down on the accelerator until the Grand Am was just a few inches from the bumper of Nina's banged-up Tercel. He grinned, thinking about how his tailing would piss off his brother. And then he remembered that Nina was driving. He tapped the brakes. He had no desire to get on her bad side.

"Oops," he said with a nervous laugh. He thought about fiddling with the radio for some grunge tunes to help pass the time, but didn't do it for fear of waking Corinne. She'd be hell on wheels all the way back to Iowa City.

Instead, he looked over in the early-morning light at Lilly. Her eyes were underlined by dark circles, and she wasn't smiling as she gazed through the windshield, empty-handed. Neither of them had slept well on the pull-out bed in Nina's basement.

He recounted, for about the hundred and first time, last night's mutual "Love you" moment with Lilly.

That had really happened, right? he kept asking himself, and each time his silent answer had been, *Yeah man.*

"Burt," Lilly said in a soft voice. He caught her wiping a tear from her cheek. "I have a confession to make to you."

"Oh crap," Burt said. His grin disappeared. "That's *never* a good conversation starter."

"You're probably going to hate me when I tell you this, but I have to. I've never felt this way about someone before, especially someone I just met, for crying out loud. But you deserve to know the truth."

"No," Burt said, gripping the steering wheel tightly in both hands. "No, I don't deserve that. I can't *handle* the truth, Lilly."

Lilly ignored his half-joking, half-true pleas for ignorance.

"I've been watching you."

Burt jumped, and the wheel twitched in his hand. The Grand Am swerved to the right for a weightless instant, and then he recovered.

Corinne's in here, he scolded himself. *You're responsible for her, dummy.*

He took a breath and glanced over at Lilly. It was like she'd forgotten how to smile.

"What do you mean, watching me? At the bar?" He waggled his eyebrows, hoping he'd misunderstood her. "I was watching you too, girl."

Lilly bent down to dig into her satchel, curly brown hair in her face and hiding her eyes. He caught sight of her geometric black tattoo peeking out from under her shirt sleeve, and he remembered how the tattoo—no, it was a *brand*—felt under his fingertips.

All of this, he realized, *must've been like her worst nightmares coming true. My poor Lilly. No wonder she kept trying to run away.*

Burt watched the mostly empty interstate unfold in front of them in the growing daylight, just a half hour now from the Iowa border. Lazy lines of fog hung in the cornfields on either side of the road. Next to him, Lilly pulled out the big leatherbound book she'd saved from her doomed apartment.

"These are all the stories I've encountered since I realized what those voices in my head were."

She flipped through the first few yellowed pages, which contained row after row of Lilly's weird cipher. These symbols were larger, though, and a bit sloppier than those Burt had seen in her journal. The symbols filled the page all the way to the margin.

She skipped ahead a good two or three hundred pages to about the middle of the book. The pages were thicker now, because each one contained two smaller pages cut from one of her many journals that she'd pasted into the big book sideways. And the writing on those journal pages was tiny and precise as a computer printout.

"You got tired of copying," Burt said with a dry chuckle. He was a bit dumbfounded by all the hours of work those pages represented. *Years* of writing. Lilly kept turning pages, and she didn't seem anywhere close to the end of her work.

"I never had enough time," she said in a distracted voice, still flipping pages heavy with arcane symbols. "And a lot of the stories I started hearing when I got older weren't worth experiencing a second time. But I knew I needed to save them all, to have them all in one place."

"I'm sorry," Burt said without thinking. Her special skill was sounding more like a curse and less like a blessing. "How old were you when this all... started? Six? Seven?"

"Five. Coming up on twenty years next year. For most of my life."

"Holy crap."

Lilly finally came to the page she'd been hunting for, about three-quarters of the way through her big book of overheard stories and borrowed histories.

"Here," she said, pointing at a line of black symbols, none of which Burt recognized in the few seconds he risked taking his gaze off the interstate. "This is where I first heard your story."

Burt's skin tingled.

"At the Fox Head Tavern that night, right?"

As soon as he asked, he knew the answer was no. His breathing grew short, and felt heat coming into his face.

No more weirdness, he thought. *I've already hit my quota.*

Lilly saved her spot with one hand while flipping ahead a dozen pages to a new page of pasted journal entries later in her big book.

"*This* was from the Fox Head," she said. She didn't look up at him.

Burt blew out the breath he'd been holding, like he'd been punched in the gut.

"What, you were *following* me? Why? And don't say it was because you were too shy to say hi. Not with your special skill set. You had all sorts of, of... *material* to break the ice. "

"Try," Lilly whispered. "Try not to hate me for this. But I thought you could help me. Protect me."

"Wait. Don't tell me. From the bringers of darkness, right? *Lilly...*"

210

Burt was trying to keep from rear-ending Nina's Tercel in front of him as he got more and more worked up. He braked once more, as gently as he could to keep from waking Corinne. The morning sun had risen, angry and yellow, behind them, and it flashed in his rearview mirror like a warning beacon.

When he looked over at Lilly again, her eyes were so wide and intent upon him that they seemed to be glowing with the morning light as well.

"*Why* don't you believe me?" she whispered.

Burt didn't hesitate. "Never said I didn't."

Never said I did, either, he thought, knowing he needed to choose every word carefully right now.

"I saw how you looked at me after I told you about... about *them*. Look, my mom was too paranoid to ever send me to school, but I'm not an ignorant little girl. I've been reading since I was two, and learned more from her than I ever could've picked up in some school. It's just the stuff I learned outside of reading and writing and arithmetic is the kind of knowledge no other kids should ever have to learn. At least I hope not."

Burt realized he was barely breathing, listening to her.

This is the woman I love, he realized. *And she's messed up. Whether all this really happened or not doesn't matter. She's hurting all the same.*

"Go on," he said, his voice cracking. "I'm listening."

"I thought I would be safe, there in the middle of the country in Iowa, pretty much in the middle of nowhere. But the darker voices kept filling my head. The darkness was getting closer. I hadn't heard from Eli in months, and I started to get scared. I'd stayed in Iowa City for too long, almost three years. I *liked* it there, damn it."

They were at the bridge over the Mississippi River that carried them back into Iowa. The road crews had done a fine job of cleaning up the smashed barrels and debris that Tommy and Marg had left in the wake of their vehicles yesterday.

"Okay, Lilly," Burt said, feeling his skin fill with goosebumps against his will. Stupid skin. "I don't even know what that means. The darkness is getting closer."

She continued as if she hadn't even heard him. Like she'd been holding this story in her head too long and had to get it out or burst.

"I knew the signs, but I'd gotten slack in the past year or so. I was going out in *public* with my journal, for crap's sake. Writing my cipher right where anyone could see it. Like I wanted to get caught. Just like Eli. That's how he ended up with Marg as his best bud. Working for Virgil and Reggie, after they found out about him."

"Wait. Who's Reggie?"

And are he and Virgil the bringers of darkness? he almost asked, but caught himself before chugging the Lilly Kool-Aid.

"Reggie is Virgil's partner, and probably the most powerful man in Iowa City, if not all of eastern Iowa. At least that's what people say, though nobody's ever seen him, or run a photo of him in the newspaper. Forget the governor, we've got Reggie."

"Sounds like a good campaign slogan," Burt said with a nervous snort. He kept hearing the words echo in his head: *bringers of darkness.*

Lilly wasn't laughing.

"I kept picking more stories about violence and mayhem out of the air. At first I tried not writing those stories down, but then they'd get stuck in my head, which was much, much worse. I wrote even faster. But I couldn't get them all down. Like I told you that night we met, I had a lot of catching up to do. Still do."

Burt cleared his throat, desperate to find some stable ground for this conversation.

"Let's go back to that night we met. You were, what, stalking me? I guess I should feel honored..."

"About that," Lilly said and let out a long exhale. Burt caught a whiff of that bitter smell on her breath again, as if she still hadn't cleared all the toxins from their first night together. "I have a couple drinking holes I like to work at, and I first saw you at the Field House bar right next to campus."

Burt did some quick mental math, and he rubbed hard on his goose-bumped arms when he came to his answer. "That was back in mid-July! Three weeks ago!"

"I was intrigued by you, for a couple reasons," she added with a sly grin. "The beard is indeed a selling point."

Burt wanted to smile at that, but his stomach had turned sour.

She'd been watching me, he thought. *But never approached me. What if I'd never walked over to her the other night? Would either of us be here right now?*

"But I couldn't piece together your story. Just like I can't read your little niece. I got bits and pieces from you, most of them from just listening—you like to *talk* when you're drinking, you know. But there was a light inside of you instead of the darkness I'd been hearing. You had your secrets, including one really huge, furry one I learned about yesterday morning—holy *crap*! But you weren't bad inside."

Lilly paused and lifted a hand, as if thinking about reaching out to Burt. She held it there for a second, and then dropped it back into her lap.

"I *knew* you'd be able to protect me. And you have, so far."

Burt's eyes ached from staring so hard at the road and the bumper of the Tercel ahead of them, and he reminded himself to blink.

"So that's all I am to you?" he said at last. "I hate to break it to you, but I'm a tall, skinny dude without a ton of muscle mass. You'd be safer with my brother."

Lilly didn't respond to that. He could tell she had more to share. More to confess. She was just waiting for him to soak it all in and get up to speed.

"And?" Burt said.

"I finally ran into my brother again two weeks ago, and I told him about you. He has a way of doing that, you know? I always say too much around him. He doesn't hear stories like I do, but he *sees* things better than anyone else I know. I think that's why he can't stand being around big groups of people for too long. It's too hard to keep up with what's really *real* when you can see so deeply. If that makes sense."

Burt was thinking about yesterday morning, outside Lilly's burning apartment. How he'd looked at Eli in the crowd, and the guy's eyes had done that weird doubling. Like he had two sets of eyes, somehow.

Freaky.

"Yeah," Burt said, nodding. He was still piecing together her story, decoding it so he could write it all down in his own mental journal. "But you said Eli works for Virgil and this guy Reggie, who's the big kahuna back in Iowa City?"

Lilly took a sudden breath and rubbed her eyes, as if waking up.

"That's the part you're not going to like."

They passed a green sign reminding them that they were just thirty miles from Iowa City. The sun had risen behind them and shone down now at full force, filling the cornfields on either side of the interstate with buttery yellow light that burned away the fog and bounced off the dew.

"Oh boy," Burt said.

"I think Eli put those guys on alert. Not intentionally. It was like you and Tommy fit the description of someone who'd been on their radar for a while."

"And it probably didn't help that Tommy went snooping around our uncle's old store yesterday. Answering Carl's cell phone, for shit's sake."

Lilly nodded. "I didn't want to say anything when he was telling us about that yesterday. But yeah, not the smartest move ever."

Burt nodded, fighting an instinctive impulse to defend his little brother.

Who's to say, he thought, *that I would've been able to ignore a ringing cell phone in my hand? Especially when I was hunting for clues about my missing friend?*

He watched the three heads bobbing in the Tercel in front of them. They looked like they were talking, too, and he wondered what the topic of conversation was up there. The weather? The upcoming Iowa Hawkeye football season?

Or the end of normal life for all weres, everywhere? Or was it every *were*?

With just a few miles of interstate left before they hit Iowa City, Burt glanced back at Corinne—still zonked out, luckily—and then he looked over at Lilly. She was writing directly into her big leatherbound book this time, with one of her black pens. He wondered if she ever made a mistake, like a cipher typo.

"You said I was going to hate you for what you were telling me."

He swallowed his fear that he was saying too much, pushing too hard.

"But I'm cool with all this. You were into me, you stalked me, we hooked up. You told some dudes about my bro and me, and hey, that's kinda weird, but you were freaking out. And we ran into Virgil anyway, so it's no biggie."

"Yeah?" Lilly said, sounding only slightly surprised. "Well, good. There *is* one other thing."

"Shit," Burt said. "I *knew* there was one other thing."

"I called Eli from your house yesterday. Right after we made our plans to go to Chicago."

"What? Why?"

"I panicked. I needed to know if it was really him in my apartment that night, and if he was following orders. If he was really trying to kill you and me."

Burt caught himself nodding. It made sense, and they'd chased Eli down to the river and lost him, so she hadn't been able to ask him then.

"Go on," he said, mouth dry.

"And then I started *talking.* I told you, he knows how to do that to me. I told him all about you and Tommy, and what had happened since you and I met the night before. And..."

Burt slowed for the exit to Iowa City, and he heard Corinne shift and yawn in the back seat.

"And what?" he said.

"I told him all about Corinne."

He felt his skin prickle, but this time instead of goosebumps, he saw reddish-brown fur pop up on his arms.

"What *about* Corinne?" he growled.

"That she was a were, too, just like the two of you, and how Tommy said she was wild, almost all the time. Eli wanted to know all about that, kept asking more and more questions. *How wild? What does she do? Who does she attack?* Don't ask me why. He hates kids, usually."

Burt looked at the rearview mirror to see his niece in her car seat, one tiny hand wrapped around the ugly black leash that curled around her neck.

They were waiting for us, he thought. *With leashes in hand.*

"You set us up, Lilly," he said at last, barely able to speak through the mouthful of sharp teeth poking up in his mouth. He fought back the change, feeling his clothes and his shoes grow tight. "That leash and collar is your *fault*."

"No," Lilly said in a small voice. "I didn't mean for that to happen."

I can't tell Tommy or Aunt Mel or anyone about this, Burt realized. *They'd tear Lilly apart for betraying Corinne to her creepy brother and his powerful bosses.*

And as mad as he was with her right now, he knew he couldn't let that happen. He still loved her, though he no longer trusted her.

Corinne woke up for good just as they drove over the Iowa River next to the university campus, and by the time they pulled up to Aunt Melanie's place, she was kicking her legs and crying with impatience and frustration.

"I hear you, girl," Burt muttered. "I feel the same way."

He parked behind Nina's car in the driveway, got out, and slammed his door, not worried about making too much noise anymore. He freed Corinne from her car seat in the back of his brother's car, and she was off like a shot toward the house. Her leash flopped against her back as she ran.

Lilly remained in the car.

Burt closed the back door and paused there, hand on the cool metal doorframe.

I don't want to believe any of this, he thought. *Any of her delusions. She's the one who brought all of this on us, because she was so scared. For herself and her own well-being.*

Burt left the car without looking back at Lilly, still sitting in the shotgun seat, and walked up his Aunt Melanie's house to join Corinne and the rest of his pack.

Chapter Twenty-Three

Tommy was glad that Aunt Mel had made a fresh pot of coffee before they dropped in on her at eight a.m. that Saturday morning. He really needed a shower, and his whole body felt full of jagged edges after the awkward three-hour drive here with Nina. With Dennis curled up in the cramped back seat, snoring, Tommy had tried to talk to Nina—about anything—but his head had felt stuffed with cotton from lack of sleep and the unexpected turn of events late last night on Nina's couch. And Nina had been strangely quiet the whole drive back.

Did she regret last night? he wondered in Aunt Mel's kitchen as he handed Nina a mug of coffee with "Trust Me I'm a Lawyer" embossed on its side. *Was she seeing someone else? Was that it?*

Dennis and Mel were already in the living room, and Tommy heard Corinne burst into the house, followed by Burt calling her name softly and reminding her that her two cousins were still sleeping.

Corinne barked at everyone in her little girl's voice, a far cry from her usual throaty wolf bark. Tommy smiled with relief, though at the sight of that leash and collar his worries and fears for Corinne came rushing back hard enough to nearly take his breath away.

"You okay, big guy?" Nina said, stepping closer with her steaming mug.

"Just putting on my Dad hat again. It was nice not wearing it for a while." He blew on his coffee, and then took a big, eye-watering gulp. Aunt Mel always made the stuff extra strong, and he needed it today.

He cleared his throat. "I was actually gonna ask you the same question. You barely said a word all the way here."

Nina nodded. "I know. I was just putting all the pieces together. Trying not to stress too much about what you Roling brothers have gotten into here."

"So it's nothing to do with last night—"

"*Tommy,*" Nina interrupted. Her smile cut through her serious expression like a knife, and Tommy was so relieved to see it he nearly fell over. "Not at all. Is that what you were thinking?" She moved in fast and kissed him hard. "You don't need to worry about that. *Ever.*"

She nodded her head in the direction of the living room and said, "Come on, already."

Tommy needed a few seconds to pull himself together, all alone in the kitchen.

That girl's got my number, he thought with a grin.

He refilled his mug, took a deep breath, and walked toward the living room, which had grown suddenly quiet. Even Corinne's wild chattering and barks had stopped.

When Tommy stepped through the doorway from the kitchen, he understood why.

Sitting on a folding chair next to the couch and Melanie's favorite reading recliner was his Uncle Carl.

Tommy, don't," Aunt Mel said, right before Tommy laid into Carl with his voice and then his fists. Tommy took three more steps despite her, and then Dennis cleared his throat.

"*Relax,*" Dennis said.

Tommy dropped his cup of coffee as all the tension went out of his limbs. He instinctively thickened his skin to wolf-flesh to avoid burning himself, and the inevitable blond fur had returned as well. Nina pushed a folding chair underneath him just in time. He sat down hard and without any grace, while Burt scurried off to the kitchen and returned with a towel to soak up the spilled coffee.

"Sorry," Dennis murmured, and Tommy felt control return to his body. Dennis kept a close eye on him, just the same.

Tommy ignored the mess he'd made and glared at his uncle. Carl had lost a lot of weight, and his faded pink Hawaiian shirt hung loosely on his gaunt frame. Carl's eyes were sunken so much that he looked like he had a set of black eyes.

I can't believe he has the guts to show his face here, he thought.

Carl stared back at him, squirming only the tiniest bit.

"You know what we call you?" Tommy said when everyone else had settled back into their seats around him. He noted without a hint of emotion or curiosity that Lilly was missing again. He touched his coffee-stained shirt and growled. "Not Uncle Carl. *Druncle* Carl."

One side of Carl's mouth lifted up, not so much a grin but a smirk.

"Cute," he said in a raspy voice. "Am I supposed to feel bad about that? Like I even know you two... boys."

For a second there, Tommy had thought he was going to call them something other than boys. Something worse. Like freaks. Or werewolves.

"I can't believe you just told him that," Burt muttered to Tommy from where he sat next to Corinne and Dennis on the couch. "*Druncle*. I can think of *worse* things to call him."

"All right," Aunt Mel said. "That's enough. I didn't bring Carl here so we could all beat on him. Tempting as that might be."

Carl smirked, and when he did, Tommy got a glimpse of his yellowed teeth.

"So why *did* you bring him here," Burt asked Mel, "into your own house?"

"You guys said you needed him, so I made him come over. It's not like he hasn't been around lately. I don't think he's left town in months. He *is* supposed to be under house arrest right now, but..."

Carl leaned back in his folding chair and folded his right leg over his left knee, holding tight to his ankle. He had a smug look on his face, as if he'd just hacked his way into the bank accounts of everyone else in the room.

"I don't care about that GPS thing on your leg," Tommy said. "You need to come with us."

"*Yeah,*" Corinne added for emphasis.

She'd wriggled her way off of Burt's lap and was standing next to Tommy, hands on her hips, her nasty leash dragging on the floor and onto the towel Burt had tossed over Tommy's coffee spill.

Burt let out a snort at her outburst, while Carl just shook his head.

"Can't leave Iowa City," Carl said, patting his right ankle. "I've got a *curfew*, boys."

"Yeah, but you've got some business in Chicago you need to take care of," Tommy said. "Some faulty technology, sounds like."

Carl's face went pale, and his smirk faded.

"Is that what this is all about? You been talking to the Great Plains Tactical people?"

"The name you're looking for is Virgil," Burt said, leaning forward from his spot on the couch, unable to sit still. "He's the head honcho you screwed over with your gadgets that don't work. Well, they sometimes work, but they mostly don't." He nodded at Corinne. "This leash was *his* idea. He'll take it off when we bring you to him."

Carl's head was shaking side to side, as if his neck was full of ball bearings. He turned to Aunt Melanie, who was watching him closely, ready to spring into action if he made the wrong move.

"You didn't say this was why you made me come over here. These are not people to mess with, Melanie. Especially not with a kid in the middle of it. They'll do worse things than slap a collar and leash on all of you. They're *killers*."

"And your former employers," Tommy said. He fought the fear that grew in him with Carl's words and facial expressions. "*You're* still alive, though."

"Why do you think I got the hell out of there when Virgil thought my work was below his so-called high frickin' standards? The guy's unstable when it comes to his anti-wolf technology. I should've just let him buy me out instead of thinking we could be partners someday. I should've taken my gear and run before I ever signed his first check."

"Boo hoo," Burt muttered. "Shoulda coulda, druncle."

"Okay," Aunt Mel said. "That's enough. Carl. Tell them about Virgil's *partner*. Right here in Iowa City."

Tommy forced his face to remain expressionless, even as he heard that deep voice on Carl's old cell phone, with its strange over-emphasis on certain words: *We could* use *a fellow like you. And is your little girl at the store, too? We'd love to meet her as well.*

Virgil's partner. It had to be.

"*Wait,*" Burt said so loudly that Tommy jumped, forgetting about that creepy phone call out of the blue. "Let me guess. His name is Reggie. Am I right? Am I *right?*"

"You stupid kids," Carl spat, and Aunt Mel aimed a low growl at him. "You don't know what you're getting into here. Just step back, all of you. If you want to stay safe. And healthy."

"Now you're all concerned about our well-being," Tommy said in a low voice.

"Virgil has a real hatred for—"

Carl froze, and everyone else jumped as the front door popped open.

Lilly stepped inside, her eyes red. She nodded at Carl, not even surprised at his presence there on the hot seat.

"Why did you cross them, Carl?" she asked, still standing just inside the front door. "I can't tell. Was their money not good enough, or did you not like taking orders from Virgil?"

"Who's *this*?" Carl said, his anger replaced by sudden paranoia.

"She's with us," Burt said in a cool voice. He didn't beckon for Lilly to come sit by him on the couch, so she stood close to the door.

"She's got a good question, too," Tommy added.

As soon as he spoke, Tommy felt his phone vibrate in his pocket. He didn't dare reach for it. It buzzed four more times, and he hoped Attix would leave a voicemail and not be too pissed.

"You didn't hear the screaming," Lilly said. "Up in their lab, where they were testing the stuff you helped them make. The people were *screaming*."

Carl was flustered now, and he tried to stand up. Melanie was having none of that, though. She put him in his place with a sharp growl and a clawed hand on his arm that left red marks on his skin.

"That kind of shit," Carl said, rubbing his arm, "is why I stopped working with Virgil. He took me on a tour of his factory up in his skyscraper, which I'm sure had to be illegal. Especially those rooms at the top of his building. That's when I knew this had all gotten out of hand. But he wouldn't let me out of my contract. I thought for sure I was a dead man when I bailed on him earlier this year."

That odd, hacker-like smile came back over Carl's face. Tommy grimaced at the sight of his uncle's rotten teeth.

"But I got the last laugh when I changed the coding on the gadgets. Just by deleting a couple lines in the firmware, I made them all pretty much worthless. The old stuff was still pretty effective, but the new switches and buttons and controllers were too unreliable to sell. Not if you wanted them to do what they were designed to do."

Carl had stopped rubbing his arm where Aunt Mel had grabbed him, and he stretched in a too-casual way that Tommy thought looked fake.

Corinne had been leaning on Tommy—she'd been too wound up to sit next to Burt on the couch—and she also tensed up.

So when Carl slid his hand into the pocket of his shorts for a black disk, Corinne was ready for him.

"Here's an old reliable," Carl spat, his face red, and he threw the disk onto the floor in the middle of the room.

Everything went dark for Tommy the instant the disk struck the floor. Everyone started shouting, and Nina let out a low moan. He heard Carl's metal folding chair hit the floor, followed by panicked footsteps. He tracked his uncle's smell to the front door and leaped blindly at the scent.

While he was in mid-air, he heard a sharp crack. His vision returned to him in a flash, and he saw Carl cowering with his hand on the front door. And then Tommy slammed into him, tackling him like the scrawniest quarterback he'd ever taken down. They hit the wall, leaving a four-foot-high hole in the drywall.

"Idiot," Tommy said into his uncle's ear, and then he pulled himself off of him. The man's skin was clammy and cold, and he reeked of cigarettes and something metallic underneath.

Corinne rushed over with the pieces of the black disk that Carl had tossed at them.

"Owie," she said. "All gone, daddy!"

"Nice work, Corinne," he said, taking the pieces from her hand and fighting the urge to throw them at Carl.

"Call your friend Reggie," Tommy said, handing the remains of the gadget to Aunt Mel, who took them to the kitchen. "Tell him we need to talk."

"No," Carl said. He was taking his time getting to his feet, holding onto his back and wincing. "I can't just barge in on him. You don't get it."

Tommy pulled Carl up until the older man was standing.

"No," he said. "I do get it." He grabbed the end of Corinne's leash and held it up, careful not to pull it tight. "I get that you were in business with scumbags who hate—no, *fear*—weres like Corinne so much they put leashes like this on her to control her. Now's your chance to finally make things right, Carl."

Carl looked at Corinne, and Tommy thought he saw the man's face soften. Just for a second.

"Sure, fine, whatever," Carl said, reaching in his pocket for his phone.

Burt, Nina, and Aunt Mel all moved in close when they saw him going for his pocket again. Carl held up his phone with exaggerated helpfulness, eyes wide.

"Show us the way to Reggie's place," Burt said with sarcastic enthusiasm. "We're right behind you, Druncle Carl!"

"Screw you," Carl muttered.

Tommy turned on his uncle until his wolf snout and sharp teeth were just an inch from Carl's cringing face and rotten mouth.

"You don't get to talk to any of us like this," Tommy growled.

Carl fell back a step, then another, all of his swagger gone at the sudden appearance of Tommy's wolf face.

Tommy exhaled, hard, and felt his face go back to its human form in an instant. He hadn't even tried to go wolf on Carl. It had just happened. And it had gotten the results he wanted—Carl looked suitably cowed.

Tommy took a look around him, at his aunt and his little girl. And then at Burt and Lilly, and Dennis. Then finally Nina.

My pack, he realized. *They're all watching me.*

And he knew in that instant how this had to be done. The only way to keep everyone else safe.

"You guys stay here," he said. "Only Corinne and I need to go with Carl to this guy's house. I can't ask any of you to risk it."

Burt and Mel immediately started to argue with him and call him crazy. Nina just looked at him and shook her head.

"We'll be back in an hour or two," Tommy said. He hushed Burt's complaining with a hand to his big brother's bony chest. "Keys, please."

Burt shook his head as he pulled the keys to Tommy's Grand Am out of his jeans pocket.

"Dude, this is *crazy*," he whispered. "Carl will turn on you in a heartbeat."

Tommy laughed, thinking about his late-night hunts through Iowa City, tracking down fugitives. He always had an ace up his sleeve on those outings, and still did this morning.

"I can turn on him and his so-called friends in a way they never can," he said, and gave Burt a sharp-toothed grin. "Know what I mean?"

"At least let me be your wing man," Burt pleaded. He suddenly looked ten years old again, the sickly brother who never won a fight with a bully until Tommy came along.

Tommy held up a hand to Burt as he turned to his aunt. She stood next to Carl—but not too close—near the front door.

"Can you make sure Carl gets into my car?" he called to her. Mel gave him a grim nod and nudged her ex out the front door into the bright sunlight.

"*Follow* me," he told Burt when Mel and Carl were outside. "You and Nina and Dennis. Take Lilly too, if you want. Stay way back behind us, and come up to the house on foot if you have to. Just give me ten minutes, fifteen minutes tops, to scope out the situation. We have to let Carl and his buddies think they're in control. You know?"

Burt was nodding so hard Tommy was worried his head would come loose. Burt's big grin was infectious.

"We're gonna fix this," Burt said. "We got your back."

Tommy gave Burt a quick fist bump, and then Corinne jumped in to give him one of her own.

"See you there?" he said to Nina as he gathered up his little girl in his arms.

"Only if you promise to be careful," Nina said. "And don't try to be a hero."

Tommy leaned in and kissed her. Corinne squealed with delight.

"I promise," Tommy said, and then he walked out the door with Corinne, her leash slapping the doorframe on their way past.

Chapter Twenty-Four

Burt ran to Nina's Tercel the instant Tommy's car turned the corner towards campus, on its way to Reggie's place. He considered sliding over the hood, but thought better of it.

"Nuh-uh," Nina said from behind him. "My car. I get to drive."

"Come on! We're gonna lose them. Just toss me your keys."

Burt caught a flash in Nina's eyes that made him step aside for her.

"Nope," she said. "Passenger seat, Slim. Hurry."

Burt stomped over to the open passenger door and got in just as his seat dropped back into place. Frickin' two-doors. In the back seat he saw Dennis and, to his surprise, Lilly. She even had a pen and a journal in her hands, the sight of which made Burt feel calmer, somehow.

She looked him dead in the eyes, for just a moment. He saw the apology in her look, and he couldn't help himself. He nodded and smiled at her. Just for a second.

"Okay then," he said, slamming the door. "I'll navigate. Just don't get too close."

Nina gave him an eye roll and gunned her car's tiny engine.

They drove in a tense, awkward silence for half a minute until Burt spotted Tommy's car up ahead, making the sharp climb up past the Pentacrest, five ancient buildings on campus that included the former capitol building. The buildings were lifeless on this Saturday morning, and just a few college kids jogged through the various paths and brown grass between the buildings.

Burt squinted at a fit young lady in black tights jogging in front of the Old Capitol, wondering if he knew her, and then snapped back to attention when he heard Lilly's throat-clearing behind him. *Busted.*

He caught sight of Tommy's Grand Am four blocks ahead of them, just a few streets away from the good old Fox Head Tavern, and Lilly's old apartment beyond that. Burt rubbed his lips, thinking that a beer or some other stiff drink might be helpful right now.

He looked over at Nina.

"You ready for this? We kind of sprung all this on you last night."

In his peripheral vision he saw Dennis lean forward, listening in. The guy had been strangely quiet all morning.

"I am. I was ready the minute Tommy said he needed help last night. It's just... it's nice to be back here. I haven't been back to Iowa City in a year."

"Agreed. It's a good place, with the exception of residents like this Reggie guy and my uncle Carl." He pointed through the windshield. "See them turning up there? Looks like Reggie lives out of town."

"Got it. Thanks." Nina nodded her head off to the right. "I used to have an apartment over there. That place was a real dump."

"Brave girl," Dennis said from the back seat.

Lilly scribbled loudly in response from behind Burt. He looked over at Nina again.

"So did you feel anything when Carl threw that gadget on the floor?"

"The whole world went black for a while there. Freaked me out."

"Me too," Burt said. "Even though I saw it coming as soon as Carl pulled it out. I thought it was a grenade at first. A flat grenade. I didn't even have time to react."

"They've gotten a lot smaller since then," Dennis said. "Virgil showed me the factory, couldn't stop talking about it. Bragging. They started buying up smartphone technology to shrink the size. He said he wasn't going to stop until they made stuff too small for were eyes to see. Guy was crazy, and had to be burning through the cash like no one's business."

"All because his daughter got mauled by a bad were?" Burt scratched his beard. "Seems like an over-reaction."

"It was all over the news in Chicago," Nina said, slowing for a red light. "She nearly died. Virgil pretty much went off the radar after that."

"I wonder..." Burt began, thinking about wolf bites, but Dennis talked over him in his excitement.

"Guys, she was *there*. In his building. And guess what? She was this, well... Not a full werewolf, but like a partial one. She couldn't control how or when she turned wolf very well. It was kind of sad, actually. She was really skinny, and her fur, when she was able to turn, was gray and white, like she'd aged too fast. And she had a lot of scars, I guess from the attack."

Burt shuddered. He remembered practically begging Tommy to bite him last year to give him the werewolf gene or curse or whatever you wanted to call it.

"So it really is contagious through wolf bites?" he asked. He'd almost forgotten about Tommy and Corinne up ahead of them. The Grand Am was leaving Iowa City and crossing over I-80. Luckily, Nina was on it.

"I don't know," Dennis said. His face had grown more pale as he talked about his nightmare day yesterday. "I kind of got the feeling that Virgil hadn't wanted me to see her. He wanted me to test my skills out on some other weres that were in the building, on the—"

"48th floor?" Burt and Lilly interrupted at the same time.

Dennis let out a nervous chuckle. "Yeah. How did you know that?"

"We went exploring last night while we were there."

"In any case, she said something to me. Something I can't stop thinking about."

Burt noticed that Lilly's pen had stopped scratching code onto her journal. Nina had slowed the car down at the same time. Burt could hear his own blood, pumping loudly in his ears.

"What?" he croaked.

"Try not to listen to those who whisper."

Burt felt a chill roll through him.

"What the hell's that supposed to mean?"

Dennis shrugged, but the look on his skinny face told Burt that he'd been thinking about those words quite a bit since yesterday.

"I think she was talking about *me*," Dennis said. "And what I can do with my voice. But it felt like a warning, or something."

"Yes, that's part of it," Lilly said, her voice starting out dead and expressionless like her brother's, but gaining emotion with each word. "But there's something more. It's the whisperers. Not just Dennis, but all of them. They're being hunted down. If they don't join up, they get killed."

"Join up what?" Burt asked, but he of course already knew the answer. He hated himself for feeling embarrassed for Lilly in front of Nina and Dennis, but he couldn't help it.

"You know," Lilly said. "I have my own name for it, but let's just call it Virgil's team, for now."

Burt turned all the way back in his seat so he could look Lilly in the eye. She was smiling in a knowing way back at him, and her eyes had an enthusiasm and light in them he hadn't seen since matching drinks with her at the Fox Head.

He was starting to think he could forgive her for telling Virgil and Reggie about his wild little niece. *Maybe.*

"I hear lots of stories," she said to Dennis, "and this talk about whisperers kept coming up. I didn't understand it until I met Burt and then you yesterday. Someone wants to control the whisperers. *Recruit them or kill them*, I heard this lady say in the bar the other night. She was talking to this bad guy who was on the run. She wanted him to track down a whisperer in Iowa City that night and kill him."

"You knew this," Burt said, "and you didn't *tell* anyone? I was right there with you that night. Why didn't you say anything? Even an anonymous tip to the cops."

"Do you know how much grief I get when I try to do that? I might as well paint a bullseye on my back. Best case the cops think I'm crazy. Worst case I become a suspect and get tossed in jail."

"Guys," Nina said. "I think we've got a problem up here."

Burt turned, mind still racing with thoughts of whisperers and fugitives, and he realized he'd totally forgotten to keep up with Tommy's car like he'd promised. Luckily Nina had been able to do more than one thing at once.

They were now outside a gated community with a ten-foot-high stone wall, with a guard house the only thing breaking up the wall. The arm blocking the entrance had just dropped back down.

"What is this, Fort Knox?" Dennis said. "You'd think we were in L.A. or something."

Burt knew he needed to come up with a way to get through the front gate, but his mind had gotten tripped up by something Lilly had said.

This bad guy who was on the run.

Nina had slowed the car to a crawl, but now she picked up speed and drove past the entrance to keep the guard from getting suspicious.

"Maybe we can find a spot to jump the fence," she muttered. On the opposite side of the road stood rows of corn and a distant barn that looked too picturesque to be in use. The rich folks must've demanded a rural feel for their walled-off community outside of the city.

Tommy left the bar early that night to chase down one of his fugitives, Burt remembered. *And the guy had an odd last name. Watts. That was it. Had to be the same bad guy.*

"Lilly," he said, just as he felt something pass by them. Nina jumped as well. Burt ignored it.

"Lilly, do you know who the lady in the bar was that night? The one who wanted the wolf whisperers? And do you know who she wanted that bad guy to hunt down?"

Because Burt had a bad feeling that Watts' quarry was sitting in the back seat next to his girlfriend.

Lilly was thinking hard, eyes closed. "He never used her name, just called her 'ma'am' the whole time. But I can almost see her name. Something old-fashioned, like—"

But before she could finish her memory and her sentence, something slammed into the driver's side of the car and sent the tiny Tercel rolling onto its side, and then onto its roof.

Chapter Twenty-Five

It's come full circle, Tommy thought, glancing at Carl in the shotgun seat next to him, with Corinne in the seat behind them. *The three of us again. Just like the night he tried to take her away from me, to her new family. The pack that she'd never be a part of.*

Tommy started the car and pulled away from Aunt Mel's place. The sun had come out with a vengeance this morning, cutting through the windshield and making Tommy wish he could've scrounged up some sunglasses. They passed sleepy little ranch houses on this tree-lined street, their owners blissfully unaware of the darker things going on in this secret world that Tommy and his pack had uncovered. It was like they'd peeled at some old wallpaper in their own home and found a whole other set of rooms underneath.

This must be how those two wannabe adoptive parents felt, Tommy thought, *when they thought they were getting a new daughter in Corinne. And she turned into a wolf, right in front of their eyes.*

Carl was texting like mad next to him. Tommy noticed that Carl's phone was ancient, with a cracked screen and duct tape on the case. No surprise there.

"I hope you're not calling in the cavalry," Tommy said. "You need to tell me which way to this guy Reggie's place."

Carl never stopped tapping out words on his busted-up phone. "Turn left here."

Tommy wanted to rip the phone from Carl's hands and toss it into the Iowa River, which they were about to cross in two blocks. The University of Iowa campus loomed above them, up a steep hill that would lead them past the older buildings of the college. Tommy had never been inside any of those buildings.

Staring at the deserted campus and listening to Carl texting away next to him, Tommy realized he'd never checked his own phone to see who'd called him while Carl had been talking.

He pulled out his phone and tapped the voicemail icon.

"Careful, Daddy!" Corinne called out from the back seat in a panicked voice. Aunt Mel had hammered on him and Burt not to text and drive, and Corinne had picked up on that wholeheartedly. She warned them whenever she saw a phone in their hands while they were behind the wheel. She always got wild when Tommy had his phone out lately, it seemed.

It was Attix, just as Tommy had suspected. He spoke with a strained urgency that Tommy hadn't heard in his voice before.

"I can't wait anymore, Tom. I *really* wanted to tell you this in person, because it's pretty hard to believe, honestly. But our dead friend Watts was into something bigger. I got digging and came up with some powerful people's names. And those folks were messed up in something... *strange.* Stuff that I can't explain or even comprehend. But *you* might—never mind." Attix sighed. "Tom, I have to make myself scarce for a while. I got some friends I need to talk to. They might understand this sort of thing. Just stay out of trouble, kid. Come to think of it, if you haven't left yet, just stay outta town. Stay in Dyersburg or Chicago or wherever you are. Don't come back to Iowa City for a while."

There was a long pause, and Tommy was about to put his phone down, when he heard Attix speak again.

"Just remember," Attix added. "Try not to listen to those who whisper. And watch your ass."

The voicemail ended, and Tommy put his phone away with a shaky hand.

"Good Daddy," Corinne said.

What the hell? he thought, trying to piece together all that Attix had said. *The guy seemed drunk or stoned, almost, the way he'd been talking. Not making much sense, telling me to stay away.*

Tommy checked on Corinne. She was bouncing up in down in her car seat, still agitated from Carl's surprise attack with his disk-shaped gadget. Maybe she knew she was about to get free of her collar and leash at last. Her eyes caught the sun and glowed red, just for a disconcerting moment. Tommy quickly looked back at the road.

After a few more turns, which Carl told him about at the last possible second, they were past campus and heading through the residential part of town. Tommy caught sight of the Fox Head Tavern off to his left and had to smile despite the strange message Attix had left for him.

Try not to listen to those who whisper.

The same thing Virgil's daughter had said.

When Tommy glanced over at his passenger, Carl was staring at him with an odd look on his gaunt face. Like he wanted to ask about what Tommy had heard on his phone, but knew better.

Or possible knew *already...*

"Head toward the interstate up there," he said, and then cleared his throat.

Tommy nodded and waited for Carl to say something. But he just stared at him.

"What?"

Carl shook his head.

"You kids think I did what I did for money," he said. "And because of what happened that night, not just with your little girl, but Melanie too. That I freaked out, seeing her... *turn* like that. My wife, the wolf."

Tommy shrugged. *Whatever.*

"I know she's got my boys doing it now, too. I was pissed about that at the time, let me tell you. But you need to be able to control this. Other people do, too. Can you imagine a world full of werewolves like you? A bunch of wild-childs like Corinne?"

"What's your point, Carl?" Tommy fought to keep the growl from his voice. "You want people to see you as some sort of hero? People are being kidnapped, like my buddy Dennis, and other people are being tortured and killed, because of you and your friends."

"Collateral damage," Carl muttered under his breath, but Tommy's sensitive ears picked it up. "I'm doing the right thing, here."

"You and Virgil," Tommy said. "You think you can cure us of this. But here's a frickin' news flash, uncle. We don't want to be cured! Hell, we don't *need* to be cured!"

Tommy felt a sick pleasure at the way Carl cowered away from his as his voice rose. And then, an instant later, he just felt sick.

He made me lose control, he realized.

Carl smiled, and then shook his head again.

"I rest my case." Carl sat up and checked his phone. "And we're here. Reggie already let the guard at the gate know we were coming."

Tommy let out a long, calming breath as they rolled up to a gated community with ridiculously high stone walls surrounding it. His memory flashed back to the neighborhood with the wrought-iron fence from last year that hadn't been able to keep him out in his wolf body. He'd jumped right over it and rescued Corinne from her adoptive parents.

Or was it the other way around? He'd rescued the non-were man and his wife from Corinne in her baby werewolf body?

He saw the guard house a quarter mile away on his left and drove toward it with a humorless laugh.

"This seems like overkill," he said. "They live next to a *cornfield*, for crap's sake."

"Powerful people need their space. And their security."

"Right."

The guard at the gate wore a dark blue shirt and pants combo, and he gave Tommy's mud-spattered Grand Am a dubious look before waving them through. Tommy gave the guy a nod that wasn't returned.

"His house is at the back," Carl said, and then he gave a sniff. "You going to wear that shirt in there?"

Tommy looked down. He'd forgotten about the coffee he'd spilled all over himself earlier. His light blue shirt had taken the brunt of it. Carl was chuckling, glad to have caught Tommy off-guard.

"I've got a bag in the trunk," Tommy said, glad they hadn't unpacked at Mel's. "So there. Corinne, keep an eye on him for me."

Tommy stopped in front of a three-story, million-dollar-house with an acre-long front yard filled with impossibly green grass. He got out and was about to warn Carl about no funny stuff, but then he realized if Carl tried to run off, the guy had nowhere to go.

He popped the trunk and grabbed the cleanest shirt he could find from his bag, a black T-shirt that he considered his "dressy shirt" because it had no band names or concert dates written on it.

Before he closed the trunk again, he looked behind him for Burt and Nina. He'd seen the blue Tercel five or six times in his rear-view, always a good two blocks behind him, and its presence had kept him calm with Carl next to him. Watching for the car had also kept him from worrying too much about the upcoming encounter with Reggie.

But now he couldn't see the Tercel, and he wasn't sure how Nina was going to get through the front gate. He'd have to get Reggie to let them in, later, somehow.

Or, knowing Nina and Burt, they'll probably just find a place to scale the wall and come looking for my car.

Tommy grinned at that and closed the trunk. He saw that Carl was still in the passenger seat, to his relief.

He took one last look behind him, hoping to see the Tercel drive past the front gate, but no dice. He got in and drove them the rest of the way to Reggie's place, just the three of them once more.

* * * * *

Reggie's house was a mansion that managed to dwarf all of the other huge houses in this community, and it was the only house on the last cul de sac on the left. It was set off all by itself like a modern castle, with a three-car garages on the right-hand side of the house and a circle drive out front surrounding a fountain spraying water ten feet in the air. Tommy looked for a moat, but couldn't find it.

"Nice," he said. "A bit over the top, but I guess powerful people need their space along with their security."

Carl gave him a strange smile and told him to park on the circle, next to the fountain.

Tommy took his time getting out of the car, and twice as long to get Corinne free of her car seat. Just touching the leash made his skin crawl. He hoped Burt and Nina would be here soon.

"We're close now, baby," he told her. "We're gonna get you out of this."

"Good," Corinne whispered back. He could feel the tension in her as he pulled her out of the back seat and set her on the ground. He kept her hand tight in his. No need for any wildness at this point.

Tommy wiped sweat from his forehead and told himself to relax. He followed Carl to the front door, and his uncle just let himself in, without even knocking.

"Reggie knows it's me," he said.

Inside, the house was strangely bare. The walls were white, no pictures hanging anywhere, no rugs on the hardwood floors. The first few rooms they passed on the entrance hallway were empty altogether.

Tommy sniffed, mildew and drywall dust tickling his sensitive nose.

"Yechh," Corinne said, and then sneezed.

"Carl," Tommy began, but his uncle hushed him with a raised hand.

"Quiet. He doesn't like to be interrupted."

Attix's voice echoed in Tommy's head as they walked through the empty mansion.

Don't come back to Iowa City for a while.

They walked into the main living area at last, a big open area filled with a dozen folding tables covered in black gadgets, phones, laptops, and other bits and pieces of technology. The place smelled just like Virgil's office. Tommy reached for his uncle to stop him from going any farther into the room.

"*Carl.* What's going on here?"

"Just relax. Reggie's got to be around here somewhere. I just texted with him."

Tommy froze when he heard a low growl coming from a hallway that opened up off the living room to his left. Corinne pulled hard against his hand, almost slipping free, but Tommy still maintained his firm grip on her hand.

With his free hand, Tommy slapped at his pants pocket, not to check on his cell phone, but for his ear plugs.

Should've put them on sooner, he realized as he heard another growl. The growl was cut short abruptly, replaced by a crackling sound. Tommy heard a whimper from the hallway and a chuckle from Carl next to him, and then he had both plugs in.

Hope Corinne keeps up her streak of not needing ear plugs against the whisperers, he thought, just as a spindly wolf with gray-white fur limped out of a room in the far hallway.

Tommy picked up Corinne and moved to keep Carl between them and the wolf.

But the wolf wasn't in attack mode. He looked beaten down, and Tommy quickly saw why. He had a matching leash and collar around his thin neck. The tiny razor blades embedded in the collar caught the light, making an odd glittering.

Holding onto the leash was a tall woman with her graying black hair cropped short, but not so short that Tommy couldn't see the blaze of white at her forehead. Her eyes were a cold, pale blue, and Tommy inhaled a sickly-sweet smell of dying flowers that wafted over to him across the cluttered room. She held a small black stun gun in her other hand.

Gwen. The alpha-female were from up north. She'd come back to Iowa.

Chapter Twenty-Six

Something had happened to Burt at the instant of impact. A deeper instinct than he'd ever felt before took over him, and he shifted hard into his wolf body before the Tercel went up on its side. By the time the car flipped, he was already out of his seat belt and crouching on the roof of the car. He hadn't even felt a thing.

He reached out next to him for Nina, who'd taken the brunt of the blow. Luckily, she'd made the shift over to wolf already as well, though the impact left her unconscious. She was breathing regularly as she dangled upside-down, held up by her seat belt. Burt saw some blood in her thick black fur. The old car either didn't have air bags, or they hadn't deployed.

Lilly.

Burt left Nina for a moment and pushed his way into the tight back seat. He knew that both Lilly and Dennis had been wearing their seat belts, but Dennis' belt had failed. He was crumpled at an odd angle on the roof, one bony arm still caught in his traitorous belt.

"Holy shit," he said in a weak voice, looking up at Burt's hairy face and groaning. "What hit us?"

"I dunno," Burt growled, trying to see around Dennis to get to Lilly. "You okay?"

"I think so. My leg and neck hurt."

Burt heard a car door slam, then another. Footsteps.

Lilly moaned, and Burt leaned over the seat back and around Dennis to get to her.

Please be okay, he thought. *Please. I'll forget everything you did if you're just okay.*

The footsteps outside grew louder, along with the sound of scratching.

An angry bump stuck out from Lilly's forehead, and her face was red from dangling upside-down.

Burt slashed her seat belt with one clawed hand, catching her easily as she dropped to the roof. He kicked out the window and slid out, pulling her after him. Dennis was right behind them.

"Burt," Lilly whispered. "My head."

"It's okay," Burt said. He was shaking with relief. They'd all survived the crash in one piece. "We just need to get out of the car. And I've gotta get Nina—"

Before he could finish his sentence, a trio of oversized gray wolves clattered on top of the overturned car and dropped on them with an explosion of wild snarls.

The first wolf went down with one well-placed kick from Burt's hind leg, while the second nearly got to Lilly before Burt sank his teeth into the back of its neck and ripped the wolf away from her.

The third tackled Burt, knocking him onto his back. Black eyes rimmed with red hovered above a mouthful of sharp, white teeth. Burt snapped at the other wolf, but couldn't keep it from closing in on him.

I'm dead, he thought.

Then he heard Dennis whisper something:

"*Roll over.*"

The mangy gray wolf immediately rolled over onto its own back. Burt rolled as well, until he had all four clawed feet on the ground again. Lilly was safe, and she was already reaching into the car to free Nina.

"Thanks," he said to Dennis.

Dennis grinned and nodded back, rubbing his neck.

Burt wanted to help get Nina free—he could smell gas now, and it was getting stronger—but he'd heard footsteps again. The two-legged kind.

He risked a look around the edge of the overturned car and saw a dark Ford Expedition with a battered front bumper and two busted headlights.

"So that's what hit us," Burt muttered. "Damn. We're lucky to be alive."

He ducked back down and pried open the passenger door. Inside, Lilly struggled to free Nina, who was moving a little, but mostly moaning.

"Watch out," he said to Lilly. He cut Nina loose and gathered her up as gently as he could, despite her size and the cramped space. He got her out of the car at last. Dennis peeked over the side of the car, watching their attackers.

"That's Gerard and Diana," he said. "Virgil's people. What the hell are they doing here?"

"Really?" Burt squinted across the road. He wanted to get away from the wrecked car, but he hated to leave their precious cover. His sharp wolf eyes focused on the two people, and sure enough, it was them. The three wolves were trotting back to Diana's side, tails tucked and heads hanging low.

"Did we just get *played* this past day?" Burt said with a sinking sensation in his chest.

He looked from Dennis, whose face was tight with pain, to Nina, her fur receding as she recovered from her wounds. For a second he thought Lilly had slipped away again, but she'd reached inside the front seat to gather up the remains of both Nina and Burt's clothes. Nina would need them in a few seconds, but Burt wasn't ready to let his wolf skills drain out of him right now. He kept himself at what he thought of as half-and-half, and he hoped his wolf ears didn't look too ridiculous.

"Lilly," Burt said in his growly voice. "Can you hear their stories? Focus on Diana. I think she's the brains of the bunch."

"Here they come," Dennis said. "And they've got Tasers, it looks like. And leashes."

"Lilly? What do you hear?"

Still rubbing the bump on her head, Lilly closed her eyes.

"Too far away," she whispered.

Nina had pulled her clothes back on and returned to her human self. She seemed to have recovered from the worst of her injuries, thanks to her wolf body absorbing most of the damage.

"Hey Dennis," Nina said, hooking a thumb toward Diana, "is she a whisperer, like you?"

He nodded.

"How do we keep her from telling me and Burt here what to do?"

"Keep her distracted," Burt said, about to leap over the car and tackle Gerard and Diana head-on. Even if they did have their three wolf pets at their side again.

"No," Dennis said. He grabbed Burt with a surprisingly strong hand. "You can't do this brute-force style. Let me show you."

"Oh God," Lilly said from behind them. "Forget Diana. We've got to get to Tommy and Corinne."

Burt looked from Dennis to Lilly. He was afraid to hear what horror stories she was picking up.

He looked over at Dennis and said, "Go."

Dennis pursed his lips and let out a long, warbling whistle. Three sets of wolf ears perked up in unison. Dennis took a quick breath, and his next whistle was sharp.

Burt flinched at the sound, as did Nina, but nothing happened to them other than that involuntary twitching.

The three wolves, however, dropped onto their sides, dead asleep.

Dennis gave a sheepish grin. "Just a little something I picked up from yesterday's training."

"*Dude,*" Burt said. "Remind me not to mess with you. Ever."

"Burt," Lilly said. "I think we—"

"We're going already," he said, touching Nina's shoulder. "Come on. I think we can take them without needing to even go full wolf."

Nina nodded, and the two of them scampered away from their cover and charged at Diana and Gerard.

Gerard shot a Taser barb that Burt easily dodged, while Diana tried to command them both with a desperate "*Stay.*"

Dennis immediately overruled her with a shouted "*Go!*" just in time for Nina to tackle Diana and for Burt to take down Gerard.

"Wait!" Lilly called, just as Burt was about to swing a clawed fist at Gerard's chin. "They were just following orders! They don't know what's really going on in there."

"I don't care," Burt growled. "They could've killed us with their SUV. We need to end this and get in there to help Tommy and Corinne."

"She's right," Diana said, her voice strained from the weight of Nina on her chest. Dennis hurried to Diana's side as soon as she started talking.

"Look," Gerard said. He tried to wriggle free from Burt, to no avail. "We saw your brother go in there with Carl. Virgil called and said we had to take you out."

"*Virgil?*" Burt said. "Is *he* here? 'Cause we don't need his crazy here right now, let me tell you."

"He got a call in the middle of the night last night," Diana said. "Had to get to Iowa City right away. Because *she* was here."

"She who?" Burt said, itching with impatience. Burt looked over at Lilly, who was holding her head in both hands, eyes closed tightly.

"Hurry," she said. "They're telling the truth. I can hear their stories from the other side of the wall. They just don't know the rest of the story."

Burt grabbed the Taser and leashes from Gerard and threw them into the corn field on the other side of the road. Nina did the same with Diana's equipment.

"Try to keep up," he said to Virgil's minions. He picked up Lilly and turned all the way into his wolf body so fast that she let out a quick shout of surprise. "We're going over the wall."

Chapter Twenty-Seven

"Why are *you* here?" Tommy said, forgetting about the plugs in his ears. His voice sounded dead inside his skull with them in, so he cautiously took one out, ready to pop it back in if Gwen or Carl pulled a wolf whisperer out of thin air. Still in his arms, Corinne grabbed the ear plug from his fingers.

Gwen just smiled, and the wolf at the end of her leash started pulling, trying to get away. She held tight to the leash and showed the wolf the stun gun. It cowered behind her, though it seemed more afraid of Tommy than her weapon. Something about the wolf felt familiar.

"My partner and I have been talking," Gwen said. "And we think it's time we cut some dead weight from our business."

Partner? Tommy thought, shooting a quick glance at his uncle. Carl's face was impassive, almost impatient. As if he was ready to get this over with already.

Gwen pocketed her stun gun so she could reach behind her and slide something into the collar around the gray wolf's neck. The collar came off with a tiny clicking sound. Corinne inhaled sharply at that, touching her own collar tentatively. Tommy held onto her tightly.

Next to Gwen, the wolf shrunk in size and lost its gray fur, leaving just a shivering, naked man with gray hair. It was Virgil.

"*What?*" Tommy blurted out. "Virgil? He's got in in him, too? But he *hates* werewolves."

"Seems to be going around," Carl said with a humorless chuckle. He'd moved over next to the first table filled with gadgets, quietly resting his hands on a few while Gwen wasn't looking.

Gwen glared down at Virgil, who remained sitting on the floor, trying his best to cover himself with his arms. He looked humiliated and beaten.

"You can't deny who you are forever," she said to him in a low, almost soft voice. "I can't imagine how badly you must *despise* yourself."

Virgil shook his head.

"I have people here," he muttered. He never raised his head to meet Gwen's eyes. "I have people everywhere. You won't get away with this, this... *betrayal*."

Tommy growled, impatience filling him as fur covered his body. He didn't have time for this little power play. Not after what these jokers put him and his pack through in the past few days.

He wondered if it had been Carl on the phone yesterday, pretending to be Reggie. Disguising his voice. Sounded just like Uncle Carl's kind of thing.

We could use a fellow like you.

"You guys do whatever the hell you need to do," he said. "I did my part and brought Carl to Virgil. Doesn't matter to me if Reggie exists or not. I just need to get this damn collar off my little girl. Do that and we'll get out of your hair."

"Oh no," Gwen said. "It's not like that at all."

"I should've known," Tommy said under his breath. He caught Carl's smirk and nearly slapped him upside the head for it.

"You might not be aware of how far my pack reaches," Gwen said with pride in her voice. "We care not for state or national borders. We've pretty much taken over most of Canada and Alaska, though the warming temperatures this past century have softened our northern wolves, I fear." She shook her head at Virgil and turned her back on him, as if dismissing him. "We are not impressed by little men who think they can run just one human city. Especially when they overstep their bounds."

"So why," Tommy said, "are you here, in our little city? You looking to draft some more baby daddies?"

"Baby daddy?" Corinne asked with a giggle.

Gwen stepped forward, looking at Corinne now with an almost hungry gleam in her eye.

"How old is she now? She must be two, at least."

Tommy fought the urge to turn all the way and battle this out with tooth and claw, though he kept it under control.

For now. If he had to fight Gwen and Carl for his little girl, again, he'd do it in a heartbeat.

"What do you *want*, Gwen?"

"What's best for my pack," she answered, without hesitation. "What I've always wanted."

"At what cost to anyone else?" Tommy said, and Carl let out a quick laugh from the other side of the room.

Gwen glared for just a second at Carl, and then she turned back to Tommy. In that look, Tommy saw that this was not a partnership based on friendship, but need. *Desperate* need.

"You do not know what it cost us to work with such vile creatures as this *man*," Gwen said, pointing back at Virgil without even looking at him. Virgil still sat on the floor, naked, with his arms now crossed defiantly over his chest. His broken leash lay next to him like a dead snake.

Gwen turned her back on Virgil again, as if he no longer posed a threat. Tommy kept an eye on him, however, as well as on his uncle. This was some business deal gone bad, and none of the three partners—if that's what they all were—looked happy with the other.

"We needed to find something to control them," Gwen said, shaking her head the tiniest bit, back and forth. "They were all so *wild*..."

Tommy let out an unconscious growl when he saw that Gwen was looking right at Corinne as she spoke.

"It had been happening for years," she continued, "and most of us just didn't talk about it, didn't want to admit it. But this past year, we knew we had to act. They were nearly killing each other, and we did lose two little ones up north. It was horrible."

"She so sad," Corinne whispered in Tommy's ear. He squeezed her and forced himself to look at the vile collar and leash attached to her neck.

"Gwen," he said. "What are you talking about?"

She was just five feet away now, still looking at Corinne as if she wanted to hold her or stroke her hair.

Over my dead, furry body, Tommy thought.

"It's the babies. Our babies. They've gone wild. Some of them have even reverted to full wolf, and never return to their human bodies. It started with just a few, ten or twelve years ago. But now it's all of them. Even our new babies, with the fresh blood we've recruited from elsewhere."

Tommy grimaced, remembering how they'd tried to convince weres from his hometown to join their pack, including many against their wills.

"How about her?"

Tommy looked over at Gwen, not expecting that question.

"What *about* her?" he asked.

"Has she been wild, too? Almost... *feral?*" She said the word softly, like a curse.

Tommy shrugged, thinking, *I'm not getting into that with her right now.*

"We tried so many things to cure them. Food, meat, no meat, even herbs and medicine. Then we tried to find humans with voices to come to us, humans like Lance." Her face tightened for a moment, and then she continued. "We wanted to recruit them to help control our babies. Virgil even offered to train them for us, though we never told him why we needed them. But that became an even bigger problem, because we couldn't control those with the voices. We were foolish to even try."

Wolf whisperers, Tommy thought. *Like Dennis. And they were using freaks like Watts to recruit or kill them.*

"So we chose to eliminate those with the voices who wouldn't cooperate. Just to be safe."

Tommy let out a loud sigh, thinking of what Watts had said the other night: *It was like* music. *The best song you ever heard.*

"So you murdered innocent people, just to be safe."

Gwen couldn't be bothered by it.

"You don't understand how bad it was with our babies. We were afraid of what would happen when they got older, and bigger. Too strong for us to handle. So we made a deal with humans, like him."

Gwen pointed a long finger at Uncle Carl, who'd been busy organizing his beloved gadgets into orderly stacks and rows. He gave them a sheepish wave, smiling, but Tommy saw a darkness in Carl's bruised-looking eyes.

"I remembered him talking about his anti-wolf website, and what he was planning out next. How he wanted to do more than just list the werewolves in the world, but also to *control* them. Of course I started watching him closely after that."

From the corner of his eye, Tommy saw Carl stiffen at that. That must've been news to him, that he'd been monitored for the past year or so.

"When he started selling those mechanisms to control weres, I watched more closely. When he started working with Virgil, I pulled him aside and made him a better deal. We needed more of *those*," she waved a hand at all the tables piled high with black gadgets, "to control our babies. Even the collars, for the extreme ones. Without the razor blades, of course. We are not barbarians, like some..." she nodded her head at Virgil behind her, "... *people*."

Carl cleared his throat from the other side of one of his tables.

"Although you did hose my reputation with Virgil," he called out, "when you made me start introducing flaws into my products. See, Virgil? It wasn't my *fault*."

Here we go again, Tommy thought. *Carl's bad choices are impacting everyone—again.*

"Quiet," Gwen said.

She looked at Tommy, and then Corinne, for a long, awkward moment.

"We've finally figured it out," she said. "How to fix our babies."

"Good for you," Tommy said, backing up a step with Corinne tight in his grip. He wanted no part of any sort of fix that Gwen might have concocted in her head.

"It was a combination of things that caused it. Too much inbreeding, too much pesticides in their foods, and more than anything, too much cellular and wireless radiation in the air, polluting our babies. Affecting their brains."

Tommy had a sudden urge to turn off the phone in his pocket, or possibly just chuck it out the window altogether. Anything to help Corinne that didn't involve a leash and collar.

Then he realized that this was *Gwen* talking, the alpha female of a huge northern pack, who'd do anything to help her own family, at any cost to the rest of the world.

"Here," Gwen said, holding out a tiny metal tool the size of a paring knife. "Let me get that collar off." Her voice rose higher as she called to Corinne. "*Come*, little one."

Tommy held tight to Corinne, who was quivering with excitement from Gwen's attention. He stepped closer to Gwen, refusing to let go of his baby.

"Do *not* hurt her," he said.

He growled as Gwen reached for Corinne and slid the tool under the collar until it made a clicking sound.

"There," Gwen said. She touched Corinne's naked neck just as the leash and the now-severed collar hit the floor.

Corinne transformed into her wolf body and jumped from Tommy's arms with a squeal of delight.

An instant later, her cry of joy transformed into frantic scream of pain.

Chapter Twenty-Eight

Burt was on the sidewalk in front of the big house, just past Tommy's car, when he heard his niece's screams. He went full wolf in the instant before he hit the front door, and the door exploded inward.

That felt good, he thought, and then he was down the front hall, claws scratching up the hardwood floor as he looked for Corinne.

Unfortunately, all he had to do was follow the screaming.

Like him, Corinne and Tommy had also gone wolf there in the big living room that was missing its furniture. Tommy chased Corinne as she screamed her way around the room, knocking over the tables covered in gadgets and sending Uncle Carl scrambling into the kitchen. Corinne stopped every few wild steps to spin in a mad circle on her clawed feet, tearing up the beige carpet under her.

And she was coming Burt's way.

Burt dove into the torn-up room and wrapped up Corinne as tightly as he could in his long, well-muscled wolf arms. He had her for just a few seconds—she was all muscle and fur—before she clawed the hell out of his arms and chest.

He barely felt it. In those chaotic seconds, he saw something black on her neck. It looked like a metal tick, caught in her strawberry-blond fur.

And then Corinne broke free of his bloodied arms. But he'd bought Tommy enough time to catch up to them, and his little brother snagged Corinne in mid-leap.

"On her neck!" Burt cried out in his thick wolf's voice.

Tommy rolled with Corinne on the floor, holding her tight with three long legs while reaching for her neck with his fourth. Corinne was still screaming and howling as Tommy's hand by her neck lost it claws and furs and plucked at something in her fur.

Burt glanced around long enough to see two other people—one female and familiar, one male and naked—backing away from Corinne, and Carl all by himself under the kitchen table, surrounded by a spray of tiny black gadgets. Nina came up behind Burt silently, with Dennis and Lilly a few feet behind her.

Corinne's screaming stopped abruptly. Ears ringing, Burt looked back at Tommy and Corinne.

She'd reverted back to her human body, and Tommy now held her tight, rocking her on the floor as she sniffled and moaned. Tommy caught his eye and tossed something tiny and black to him with a white hand that was quickly turning back into furry and clawed paw.

Burt caught it without even thinking about it. He would've sworn it was a tick—it had six leg-like extensions coming out of its half-inch-wide black body—except for the fact that it was made out of metal and had a tiny red Anti-wolf logo on it.

"So it worked," the other woman in the room said. Burt recognized her scent now, though he scarcely believed it. The crazy Gwen woman, the one who tried to drive her car through the Side Entrance bar in Dyersburg. He realized with a shock that the naked man behind her was Virgil.

"Of *course* it did," Carl called from the kitchen. "Satisfied now, *partner?*"

Burt ignored them and went to Tommy's side. Nina was already there, stroking Corinne's hair.

"Is she okay?" Burt said. He could see the red welt on Corinne's neck from the metal tick, the poor girl.

"You see what we've done here, don't you?" she said, panting with excitement. "We've got the *cure.*"

Tommy growled sharply at that.

"That's no cure. That's a torture device."

"It's severe, but it serves a purpose. Our feral children will think twice about giving into their baser impulses when we have these at our disposal."

"So you're making their werewolf gene a curse, then," Tommy said.

"And you tested it out on my *niece*?" Burt said, thinking once more of the screams from Virgil's office skyscraper. "What's wrong with you, lady?"

Virgil had used the time that Tommy and Gwen spent talking to transform himself—in what looked like a very painful change—into a gray wolf.

He was one, too, Burt thought with shock, keeping a close eye on him. *He must* really *hate himself.*

Virgil the wolf crept up on Gwen while they were talking. Burt watched him the whole time, but Gwen was completely oblivious to him.

"And it *worked*," Virgil shouted, rearing up behind Gwen and raising a clawed paw. "It worked *perfectly!*"

Virgil would've taken Gwen's head off if she hadn't turned on him at the last second. His blow still sent her flying into the overturned tables where Carl's gadgets had been stacked.

"Let's get out of here," Burt whispered to Tommy as he helped his brother and niece to their feet. Tommy had gotten Corinne dressed again, but he still remained in full wolf mode.

Burt's wolf body easily receded into his human form. He glanced down at himself with relief, surprised at the ease and speed of his own change.

At least I still have what's left of my pants, he thought, *instead of walking out of the house going full commando.*

"Get her and the others to my car," Tommy said. "I'm getting Carl, and then I'll be right out."

"*Leave* him," Burt said. "Let them tear him up for supper."

"No," Tommy said. "He needs to come back and explain all this to Aunt Mel. He's not getting off that easily."

Burt winced as the Virgil screamed in pain, followed by a thud and crash as the two older wolves rolled across the floor, hissing and snapping at each other.

I guess that's what we get to look forward to in our old age, he thought.

He looked up at Tommy again. His brother looked magnificent and dangerous in his full-blown wolf body. Burt wasn't going to change his mind about Carl.

"Just be careful," Burt said with Corinne in his arms, and then he was pushing Nina, Lilly, and Dennis down the hall and out the front door.

Tommy left Gwen and Virgil snapping and clawing at each other on the floor and trotted into the kitchen to grab Carl. But his uncle had abandoned his spot under the table.

A door from the back of the house slammed, and then one of the windows in the living room burst inward. Diana and Gerard rushed in from the back, while three starved-looking wolves pushed their way in through the broken window. They converged in the living room just as Tommy found a door off the kitchen that led to the garage.

Not so fast, druncle, Tommy thought, leaving behind the chaos of the two packs fighting in the big house.

He burst through the door to the garage, leaving it hanging on one hinge, and found Carl in a cavernous garage with more tables covered in his evil black contraptions, gadgets, and machinery.

"There's a solution for all of this," Carl said, stepping out of the shadows.

He had a gun in one hand, and a handful of something else held tight in the other. He nodded his head at the house with an impatient look on his skinny face.

"They're such short-sighted idiots. But they helped me get where I needed to be." He sucked in a sudden breath, as if realizing who he was talking to. "But anyway, the solution."

He opened his fisted hand and held out seven of the tiny, tick-like gadgets to Tommy. They seemed even smaller than the one he'd pulled off of Corinne's neck. Tommy was too surprised by the sight of them to stop Carl from dropping them into his furry paw.

"This is the latest version, even better than that one Gwen had. Think of it as Were Cure 2.0."

The pride in Carl's voice for creating such twisted things made Tommy want to punch him.

"*Cure*," Tommy said. His wolf voice chewed up the word like it was bad meat.

"This one doesn't cause pain like that other one did, I swear. It's perfect. I've got enough for all of you. Even..." Carl's voice faltered, just for a moment. "Even Melanie and the boys. Just wear it under your hair or on your foot, wherever. And you don't have to worry about turning wolf ever again."

Tommy was in the process of squeezing his paw tight enough to crush the little ticks, but he stopped.

He saw Corinne's face, her *true* face, a human face without fur, blue eyes and pink skin. A normal face. A normal life.

And then he saw her growling outside the shed where he'd cornered Watts after running nearly four miles across town. He thought of that leash and collar, tight around his baby's neck.

Who am I to choose for her? he asked himself. *How do I know what's best for her?*

"We need to get out of here, Carl," Tommy said. He still held the ticks in his hand, but he was now looking at the two gas cans next to the riding lawn mower in the far corner of the garage. "Burt's waiting in the car with the others."

"No," Carl said, patting Tommy on his furry shoulder. Carl had to reach up to do it. "I've got people here. I need to go deal with them." He lifted up his gun. "Silver bullets. Virgil was actually right about those."

"Carl," Tommy said.

His uncle casually lifted the gun and pointed it at Tommy. His face was pale, but surprisingly calm. As if he'd made up his mind about this a while ago.

"I just wanted to make sure you got what you needed."

"Carl," Tommy said again, edging away from the gun. "Do *not* go back inside. You don't have to do this."

"You have them, right?" Carl said. He hadn't heard a word of what Tommy had said. "There are seven of them. Use them, Tommy. It's my life's work. Don't let 'em go to waste. It's for the best, for all of you."

And with that, Carl walked back into the house.

Tommy knew, deep down, he could've stopped him with brute force. But he got distracted by the tables piled high with black Antiwolf gadgets, and he let Carl go.

As soon as he was alone, Tommy grabbed the cans of gas and coated all of the gadgets and tables with the fuel. Carl and his so-called partners could always make more, but this would at least slow them down.

Or maybe Virgil's factory would never be able to perfect the gadgets, Tommy thought with a glimmer of hope.

Choking on the fumes, Tommy hit the button to open the garage door. He lit the first table with a lighter he'd found next to a pack of Carl's cigarettes, and he pressed the garage door button again to start closing it.

As he raced across the burning garage, Tommy couldn't help but hear the sounds of growls, howls, and desperate commands from Diana, punctuated by gunshots.

The heat was sudden and intense at his back. He made it outside just as fire covered all the tables and the garage door clanged shut.

Burt was right there with Corinne and Nina to pick him up when the garage exploded, and the rest of the house quickly caught fire.

And when he got up, he had just two of the metal ticks—Carl's cure—held tightly in his clawed hand.

Chapter Twenty-Nine

They made it back to Aunt Melanie's house at half past two that Saturday afternoon, though Tommy felt like it should be eight or nine at night. For Tommy, it was the quietest car ride ever. Even Corinne sitting on Burt's lap in the crowded back seat had been silent and still. She was almost asleep when Tommy parked the car in Melanie's driveway.

Nina grabbed Tommy by the arm before he could get out.

"Do you think anyone made it out of that house?" she said in a raspy voice. She looked just as exhausted as Tommy felt. Tommy had seen the blood on her fur from earlier, but now her skin looked whole and injury-free. He couldn't bring himself to ask about it, or her wrecked car, which they'd been forced to leave behind.

I dragged her into this, he thought, feeling cold inside. *Her and everyone else.*

"I don't know. I just needed to get rid of those gadgets. The gas cans were there, and Carl's lighter, and—"

"It's okay, bro," Burt said from the back. "I think we all would've done the same. It's just... we heard *gunshots*, dude."

Tommy nodded. "That was Carl. Said he even had silver bullets."

The car went silent again except for the ticking of the cooling engine.

Then Burt piped up. "*You* get to tell Aunt Mel about that, Tommy."

"*Thanks*," Tommy said, and almost caught himself smiling.

He turned in his seat to get a better look at the Dennis, Lilly, and Burt—holding Corinne—in the back seat, as well as

Nina next to him. "Seriously, thanks to all of you for coming along to help Corinne. I hope we stopped them from getting those gadgets into the wrong hands, but I'm worried we only just slowed them down. We need to keep our eyes open and our guard up the next few months, you know?"

"For what?" Burt said.

"For *anything*," Nina said, and then she elbowed Tommy in the side and opened her door. "Come on. Let's see if your aunt wants to celebrate Corinne's newfound freedom with us."

And with that, they piled out of Tommy's car and into Aunt Mel's house, and they spent the next hour getting Melanie up to speed on what had happened at the fake Reggie's house.

She took the news about Carl as well as she could've, Tommy thought, and then she pulled out her laptop to do some checking on her ex, his fancy house, and his so-called businesses. If Carl survived the fire and the wolves in Carl's empty mansion, his life was going to be a living hell for quite some time, thanks to Aunt Mel. Tommy loved Aunt Mel.

All afternoon, Tommy kept checking the news apps on his phone for information about a fire in the fancy neighborhood outside of Iowa City, but nothing ever came up. Not even on the TV news that evening.

I guess if you're rich and powerful enough to live there, he figured, *you're rich and powerful enough to keep curious reporters out of your business, too.*

Finally, when everyone else had wandered off to get some rest, Tommy sat on the front porch with his phone in his hand and watched the sun slowly sink toward the horizon. He had to call Attix.

It was time, he thought, *to be straight with him about who—and what—I really am. No sense trying to hide it anymore.*

"Dude probably knows already, anyway," he muttered, digging in his pocket to find those two metal ticks from Uncle Carl. He set the ticks on his knee and called his boss.

"Tom," Attix said after the second ring. "Tell me you didn't have anything to do with that fire outside Iowa City this morning."

"How'd you hear about that?"

"Damn it," Attix said. "I thought I told you to stay away."

"I couldn't," Tommy said. "It's a long story, and has to do with my uncle. You remember him, right?"

"Yup."

"But all that's done now. So are you back in Iowa City too? You said something about Watts on your voicemail yesterday. What's going on?"

Attix didn't say anything for a long time, and during that pause Tommy could hear the rumble and hum of the road in his ear. Attix was driving.

"I think I know who Watts was working for," Tommy said when Attix didn't answer. "I don't think you need to worry about them anymore."

"I wish you were right, Tom," Attix said with a loud sigh. "But nothing is as it seems with Watts and his friends. I'd tell you what they call themselves, but you'd just laugh."

"Bringers of darkness, maybe?" Tommy said, only half-jokingly.

Attix went silent again. Finally, he spoke, and Tommy swore he heard fear in the man's voice.

"Where'd you hear *that* name, Tom?"

"A friend."

"Damn it."

"Attix, it's okay—"

"No, it's not. Just lay low, now, okay? I'm on a fact-finding trip right now, and I'll be back in a week or so. That's about all the time I can afford to take off work, anyway."

"I can meet up with you, and help—"

"Sorry. I gotta do this on my own. There's a whole other world underneath the normal one you know. You don't want to get stuck in the middle of this."

Tell me about it, Tommy thought, tapping on the tiny gadgets resting on his knee.

He wanted to lay it all on the line with Attix about himself, Corinne, and the rest of his pack, not to mention Carl and Gwen and Virgil and all the other meddlers. But this wasn't the time, he realized. He needed to tell him face to face, to see how Attix reacted. On the phone it just felt crazy, like one of Lilly's overheard stories she coded into her books.

"A week or two," Tommy said at last. "Gimme a call when you're back in town."

"Mm-hmm." Attix was already distracted, moving onto his next quarry. "Just watch yourself and your family. And enjoy some time off work. Don't go tracking and catching anyone while I'm gone, okay?"

"Sure."

"And try not to listen to those who—*shit*. I gotta *go*."

"Attix? What's up?" Tommy shouted into his phone, but the call went dead. He was about to call him back, worried Attix was about to run into a tractor trailer or something, but his finger wouldn't make the call.

"Try not to listen to those who," Tommy muttered, repeating Attix's last words and finishing his sentence for him, "*whisper.*"

As much as it pained him, Tommy knew he had to let Attix go do his thing. If the guy needed him, he'd call. No sense chasing someone who didn't want his help.

The sky over Iowa City was turning purple now, and the sun fell behind the trees, lighting them up from behind. Tommy wished for a cool breeze, but the air remained calm and hot.

Inside, he could hear Corinne shouting with wild glee as she chased her older cousins around the house. It sounded like Trey was crying in pain, but Tommy could've imagined it. He *hoped* he had imagined it.

He laughed when he heard Burt scolding Corinne and ordering all three kids to go out into the back yard, "Before I kick your furry butts into the river."

No whispering going on in this *house, that's for sure,* Tommy thought.

Before he stood up, he grabbed the two metal ticks from his knee and stuffed them deep into his pocket. They poked his leg and made him want to itch.

Maybe someday I'll need those, he thought as he stretched in the warm August daylight. *But not today.*

At last, he went back inside to rejoin his pack.

About the Author

Michael Jasper loves to explore the places where the normal meets the strange. In pursuit of this fascination, he has written and published over a dozen novels, three story collections, sixty short stories, and a digital comic with artist Niki Smith.

In the past he attempted bartending, teaching junior high, painting houses, being a secret shopper, working construction, and many more jobs; he prefers fiction writing. For his day job, he works as a technical writer.

He lives with his family in North Carolina, and his website is **michaeljasper.net**.

www.ingramcontent.com/pod-product-compliance
Lightning Source LLC
Chambersburg PA
CBHW031026260626
47153CB00017B/2184